JACOB DEVLIN

BRAMBLES IN THE WISHING WELL

A NOVEL

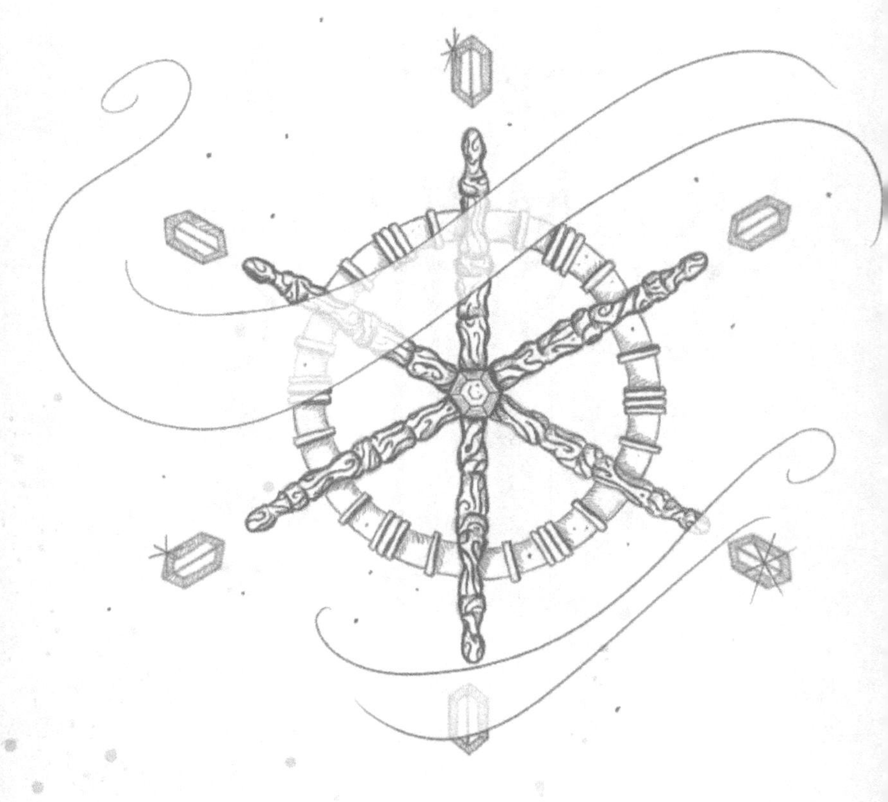

ISBN: 978-1-7342803-2-6

Cover Design
Amalia Chitulescu
Editor
Krystal Dehaba from Blaze Edits, KDehaba@blazeedits.com
Interior Formatting
Melissa Stevens, The Illustrated Author Design Services

"If there's a single lesson that life teaches us, it's that wishing doesn't make it so."

-*Lev Grossman*

DEDICATION

To anyone who's ever looked at a falling star or a coin in the fountain and asked, "But what if?"

DEAR BOOK,

HOW ARE YOU? IT'S ME, RINA ROSAS. YOU WERE A GIFT FROM ZID, AND THIS IS THE PERFECT SPACE TO WRITE ABOUT OUR ADVENTURES SINCE THE TRAIN CRASH. ONE DAY, WHEN I'M OLD, I MIGHT FORGET EVERYTHING AND EVERYONE, OR EVEN STOP BELIEVING OUR ADVENTURES WERE REAL. SO, I THOUGHT I'D START WRITING TODAY WHILE THE MEMORIES ARE FRESH. AFTER ALL, I CAN'T REMEMBER WHAT WE HAD FOR LUNCH TODAY, BUT I COULD BARELY PRONOUNCE ANY-THING ON THE MENU.

SUPER IMPORTANT PEOPLE

KARINA VIVIANA ROSAS – Yours truly. Age 12. Brave and intelligent. Arizonian. The hero.

CARLOS DANIEL MARTIN ROSAS – My annoying twin who I love. Sometimes funny.

DIEGO JOSE ROSAS JUNIOR – Our uncle. Adventurer. Nature person. TV star.

VERDORO – The dragon who kidnapped my uncle. I know it sounds super mean, but it wasn't really his fault.

LORD FALK – The evil villain who mind-controlled Verdoro into kidnapping my uncle, became a squid and ate Charlie temporarily, and who wants to steal the Wheel of Fortune. *twirls mustache* Good thing he's in Florindale Prison now and therefore we're safe. Right?

MIRABELLE – Better known as **Lady Fortune**! According to legend, she's stranded on a cloud, where she's forced to watch Lord Falk gather the pieces of her magnificent wheel.

GAVIN – Mirabelle's star-crossed lover, the court jester. Nobody knows where he is now.

ZID – Magical creature enthusiast. Dwarf with a phenomenal beard.

NIRAYA STORM – The fiercest pirate queen in all the worlds. My actual hero.

JAMES – Niraya's jaded pirate boyfriend. I *ship* the two of them. Sorry, I know that's not funny.

ENZO – King of Florindale. He's originally from our world, and he has a cool magic dagger.

ROSANA – Queen of Florindale. Has her own magic knife, but she's still learning how to use it.

IO – A lonesome werewolf from Jericho Harbor, cursed to linger there and thirst for the moon.

LADY CONSTANCE – The forest spirit in Jericho Harbor. She's the one who cursed Io and the town, and for a short while, me.

Ahem. Hi, Rina. Hi, book.

Two things. A: I'm the hero too, duh, and B: I did not give you permission to tell the world my full name. If someone finds this and publishes it, it's like, a privacy issue. I'm gonna sue. Worse, I'm telling Mom. She's gonna threaten you with La Llorona.

Wait, but if somebody does publish this, then we can be famous one day, like Tio! We'll have our own movie!

Also, I vote you change Verdoro's name to **Verdoro Rosas**, our adoptive triplet brother. #FamiliaDeLosDragones

Anyway, sorry I hijacked your book. You left this open on your bed when you were in the shower, and I saw my name, so yeah.

Love ya too, b-t-dub. Most days.

Byeeeee. – Charlie

UGH. TOLD YOU MY BROTHER WAS ANNOYING. HE HAS HIS OWN JOURNAL TO WRITE IN.

SO, I'LL START AT THE BEGINNING.

THE FERNWEH EXPRESS.

THE TRAIN THAT DOOMED OUR TRIP TO SWITZERLAND.

~~ONCE UPON A TIME~~

~~LONG AGO IN A LAND FAR AWAY~~

"HERE THERE BE DRAGONS." OUR UNCLE DECLARED IN A FORCED PIRATE VOICE . . .

PART ONE

OUR UNHAPPILY
NEVER AFTER

CHARLIE

SHORTEST VACATION EVER

If I didn't know any better, I'd swear somebody cursed my blood, and it all started with my tio.

Pop quiz: Who gets caught in a train crash and snatched up by a flying, fire-breathing death lizard in the same day? Diego Rosas does. And who does that leave to rescue him, but only after being eaten by a sea monster, spending the night in a werewolf town, and nearly being burned alive in a frozen temple infested with yetis? Me and my sister.

A shooting star sliced through the midnight sky, plummeting into the Alps. There had been three in the past ten minutes, each closer than the last. I'd been thinking about what to wish for, wondering again if there was true power to things like falling stars and birthday cakes. If kings had magic daggers and dragons were real, why not wishing stars? And why not ask for better luck?

The scent of musky denim and hotel soap filled the cold air, and a playful thump landed on my shoulder from behind. "Órálé, Charlie," Tio greeted. "Our suite has Wi-Fi and X-Box, and you're on the balcony? Outside?"

"We're in Switzerland with this view and you're playing video games?" I elbowed my tio. "You think you know a guy."

Tio zipped up his coat, rubbed his hands together, and gestured out at the mountains. "What do you think of all this?"

"It's wicked," I said. "I'm still taking it all in."

"Wicked, huh?" Tio took a seat and then propped his foot up on the wooden beams. "Good thing you're an expert at dealing with the cold now. You and your sister can handle anything after . . ." He cleared his throat. We'd made an agreement at dinner: We were never to breathe the name again for the rest of the vacation.

Falk.

"Yeah," I muttered. "After."

So many unknowns still haunted me, and I didn't exactly trust these quiet nights anymore. Not when my last cold mountain adventure was cursed with crabby snow phantoms.

How hard would it be for Lord Falk to break out of Florindale Prison, knowing my family had what he wanted?

I patted my pocket. Was a little silver pouch enough to protect two crystals with the power to control a dragon?

To fold someone through space and blast them to another world?

To grant shapeshifting abilities?

I still didn't know exactly what each crystal did, but collectively, there were seven that powered the fabled Wheel of Fortune, governing the fate of all living things. Over just a few days, my sister, my tio, and I knew we came into contact with four of them. We gave two to the king of Florindale. The others were in the flimsy drawstring in my pocket.

"I'm real proud of you, you know," Tio said. "The way you and Rina handled yourselves out there? You could be running your own show one day. Take over when I retire from the network."

"Don't hold your breath, Tio." I wagged a finger. Hopefully our adventure was a one-time thing. Not a lifestyle. "I couldn't handle all the rabid fans. Do you ever breathe your own air?"

There had already been four people in Switzerland who recognized Tio from his TV show, *Off the Beaten Path*. We all gave our restaurant server some serious side-eye when he asked if the chef should prepare a wild mountain hare when Tio had specifically ordered some potato pancake thing called *rösti*.

"That server." Tio shook his head. "He thought he was so funny, huh? If I wanted mountain hare for dinner, I'd ask *you* to cook. Apparently you're good at those now."

I wrinkled my nose. "I think you're thinking of jackalopes."

"Who wants chocolate?" Karina skipped out of the suite and onto the deck, her pink highlights bouncing on her shoulders. She clutched a thin candy bar in her hands, the foil still crisp and undisturbed. "*Swiss* chocolate. This is the real stuff."

Tio accepted the candy bar, peeled back the wrapper, and broke off a square. "Mm. Sure beats mountain hare." He passed the bar my way and asked, "Did you call your mom yet?"

"We don't have phones anymore," I reminded him. "Karina's was totaled in the train wreck, and I lost mine inside a hell squid." Just thinking about the kraken made the chocolate bar smell like fish. Without taking any of the treat for myself, I passed the candy back to Karina.

"I picked up some disposables," Tio said. "You can use those."

"Technically, Falk ate your phone," Karina reminded me. "Not a real squid."

Tio and I cringed.

"Didn't we make a deal?" Tio asked.

"Yeah, stop saying his name," I said. "Can't we just enjoy life again? Happily ever after?"

"I didn't agree to the deal," Rina said. "You know we're not done with all this. We're eventually going to face him again one day."

"No, we're not," Tio said. "We are having no more part in this Wheel of Fortune business. No Falk. No dragons. Just rest and relaxation. We've earned this. But you need to *call your ma*. No excuses."

"And what are we supposed to tell her?" I asked. "Oh, I know. How 'bout you talk to her first, and then we'll say hi."

Tio stiffened, a panicked wrinkle between his eyebrows.

Karina threw her arms up. "Well?"

"You're the ones she wants to hear from," Tio said.

"You're afraid to talk to her, huh?"

"That's not true." Tio pulled his baseball cap over his eyes and leaned his head back, taking a bite of chocolate. "Why don't we strategize? Don't talk about how a yeti nearly broke your arm, don't talk about the train—nobody's supposed to remember that anyway—don't talk about the dragon, don't talk about the pirates, and don't talk about what's in your pocket. Or the werewolves."

I snorted, my breath clouding my vision in white wisps. "That's *all* that happened to us since we last talked to her. What if she asks for a recap? I don't wanna lie."

"Wanna know a secret about her? As her younger brother, I know this: Half-truths work really well on her."

Rina and I shook our heads in protest.

"No," Karina said. "She's leveled up, Uncle D. She'll ask every question."

"Then *you* ask the questions. Ask about your stepdad or how the shop is going. Or about the weather back home."

"It's Tucson. Pretty sure it's, um, *hot.*" I calculated the odds that Mom would get suspicious about our sudden interest in her raspado business. Fortunately, little time had passed in our world—The New World, as they called it on the other side. So we didn't have much of a gap to fill with stories, even though we'd experienced a couple of weeks in Florindale. The idea was still enough to squeeze my brain like toothpaste. "Please don't make me talk."

Karina rolled her eyes. "Oh, come on. We have two whole days in Switzerland to draw from. Getting to the hotel, eating, sightseeing, Uncle D's rabid fans, looking at the mountains . . ." She jabbed a finger into Tio's shoulder. "I'll talk first. But the minute she starts asking for details I don't have, I'm putting *you* on the phone."

Tio paused mid-chew, held the chocolate in his mouth for a bit, then swallowed with an audible gulp. "That's fair. That's how it was when we were your age living with Nana and Tata."

The idea never failed to amuse me. A young Diego and Alexia Rosas, causing shenanigans at Nana's. I'd heard stories. Tio was the mischief maker. Mom was a baby angel. But then again, these were her stories. They were basically me and Karina.

Karina went inside to make the call, and I stared off into the distance, imagining where the falling stars must've landed.

"Hey, Tio," I said. "What do you think happens if more than one person wishes on a falling star? Does the first person get the wish? The truest believer? Does the star just work for everybody?"

Tio took another bite of chocolate. "Well, it's not exactly magic, Charlie. It's nature. What you're looking at are meteors entering the atmosphere and bursting into flames."

"Like my wishes?" Sure, I'd learned all this in school already, but did Tio have to be such a killjoy? "Thanks for the science documentary, Bill Nye. Now my brain hurts."

"You have one?" Tio clapped his palms to his cheeks, dropping his jaw. "Might wanna wish for one just in case."

"LOL," I deadpanned. "I'm going inside."

Diego Rosas may have been a celebrated adventurer, a Skee-Ball wizard, and a gifted close-up magician, but he was no comedian. "I'll join you in a bit," he said. "Need a minute with this beautiful view."

I slipped inside and helped myself to one of the fancy hotel waters. Our suite was ginormous. We each had a bedroom and a bathroom with a shower *and* a tub. I could hear Karina pacing around in her room, saying things like, "Why am I calling on a new number? Oh, all our phones are, uh, dead. Uncle D just picked up this little disposable phone thing for emergencies and stuff."

Half-truth detected.

"Yes. No. No. How's Jorge? Oh, *yes*, Mama, I promise Uncle Diego's feeding us. I don't know, some restaurant where I couldn't pronounce anything on the menu. Yes, it was really good . . . Yes, Mama. I miss you too."

Rina's words squeezed my heart. I missed our mom, too. Her morning hugs. Her infinite questions.

But another voice in the hotel room stopped me in my tracks.

"Are you sure you got it right? I swear, if we have to backtrack again . . ."

The voice hovered at a whisper, masking both gender and age. All I knew was the speaker was behind my bedroom door.

"*Take your grubby paws off me. Yes, I'm sure we got it right this time. This is where they went. Can't you feel it?*"

Two voices.

Did I leave the TV on? I thought.

Something thumped against the floor, the vibrations jolting my toes.

"*You bumpkin! You'd drop your own head if it weren't on your shoulders.*"

I ruled out the TV.

I pressed my face to the ground and peeked under the door. Two shadows moved around the room. *How did anyone even get in here?* The hotel was built into the mountains, my bedroom positioned over a steep slope and an icy abyss. Nobody could've come through my window unless they'd been climbing all day long.

I stood—leaving my fancy water on the ground—and put my ear to the door. "Um, housekeeping? Is that you?"

Silence.

I made a fist, ready to fight or run, when the door swung open and revealed the intruders.

To be fair, *intruders* was a harsh word. The two people standing before me weren't exactly unwelcome—just unexpected. And if anybody besides me, Karina, or Tio saw them, we'd have a lot of questions to answer about why a pirate and a queen were walking around in modern day Switzerland.

"Hello, Charlie," Queen Rosana of Florindale said. "It's nice to see you again. It's been too long."

"Uh, hi." I turned to the pirate, a hook-handed man in a long, dark-leather coat. "Not that I'm unhappy to see you or anything, but uh, what are you two doing here? And it's only been two days." I had so many other questions. Where was Niraya? Where was King Enzo? Why did Rosana and James come alone? And why were they sneaking around in my hotel bedroom?

"One full year by our calendar, lad." James extended his hand. "I trust you're well?"

"Well, yeah." I took James's hand in a rough shake. *One year? We just said goodbye to them on Friday.* "But—"

"James?" Tio walked into the room. "Your Majesty?"

Rosana curtsied. "Hello."

Tio flushed, running his hands through his hair. "How . . . What's going on?"

"Might we parley together?" James asked.

I had a feeling he didn't mean catch up over coffee and donuts. Or rösti and fancy water.

The queen took a deep breath. "There's a problem in Florindale. I insisted we shouldn't involve your family, but—"

"Niraya's missing." James reached into his pocket. When he pulled his hand back out, he held up a sheet of parchment impaled on a hook. *Lost: Captain Niraya Storm.* A beautiful woman with long wavy hair and a feathered cap stared back at me from the ink.

"Enzo, too," the queen added. "I'm doing everything I can to keep Florindale from panicking, insisting he's off on royal business, but people are starting to whisper. James and I suspect kidnapping."

My stomach contorted into knots. Captain Niraya Storm, kidnapped? *And* the King of Florindale? There was simply no way. Niraya, fierce and feisty. King Enzo, clever and well-protected. Neither of them was a force worth messing with.

"Kidnapping?" I repeated. "Who would kidnap Niraya? Or the king? They're too strong, they're too . . ."

James arched an eyebrow at me, derailing my train of thought. Here I was in a room with two strong men who had been kidnapped by a dragon. Strength had nothing to do with kidnapping.

Because there was always something stronger out there.

"You know there are people who obsess over the legend of the Wheel of Fortune. Some dedicate their lives to searching for it and will use any means necessary to gain an edge." James breathed on his hook and polished it on his jacket. "There are casual treasure hunters who see it as merely something to keep an eye out for, and then there are the full-time hunters. Legend calls them the Fortune Guard, a society of thieves solely dedicated to the search."

I swallowed a lump in my throat. "Falk's people?"

"Some," Rosana said. "But not all. Regardless of their loyalty to Falk, the Fortune Guard is very active and very dangerous. They were quiet for decades, until recently when *your family* arrived, tamed Verdoro, and put Lord Falk in prison. People have questions. They know your arrival wasn't random. Whispers are going around that one of you came into contact with at least one piece of the Wheel of Fortune. Those whispers have awakened the Fortune Guard."

"That's awful," Tio said. "Is there anything we can do?"

"We think the crystals can point the way," Queen Rosana said. "We'll gain an edge with a bit more magic at our sides. I know one thing: I'm getting Enzo back no matter what."

"We want to take them off your hands." James nodded, his gaze wandering to my pocket. "You'll be safer that way, and we can use them to save Niraya and the king. Everyone profits."

I'm not the expert on love and all that mushy goo, and I'm definitely not an expert on Queen Rosana. But when I first met her, she didn't want *any* of the gems. She and Enzo hesitated to take even two of them, wondering if they were the right people to protect them from the world. So it was strange to see Rosana come to me with such a change of heart, even if a year had passed in her time. I guessed maybe love had a way of making people do desperate things. Karina and I had been the desperate ones looking for our beloved uncle recently, so in a way, I understood.

So why was there an alarm in my body telling me not to give up the crystals? I looked down at my pocket. I hadn't even felt my fingers close over the pouch. My hand lingered there protectively, the way I used to keep it on my phone pre-kraken.

"Maybe that's for the best," Tio said to me. "I told you, Charlie. We can't be part of this. It's too dangerous."

"I don't know," I said. "Can't we help you search? Niraya helped us once. We can—"

"She wouldn't want you in the middle, mate," James said. "The winds of change are a-blowin'. Falk paces his cage like a lion. The queen and I are preparing for a storm. Better if you stay home and forget all about us and the dark waters of our world."

There was one problem with that: I didn't want to forget about Florindale. About James and Niraya, the king and queen, about Zid and the dragon? As wild as the adventure had been, I wanted to remember it forever.

Well, most of it.

Queen Rosana must've sensed what I was feeling, because she took a step forward and grasped my hand. "Charlie, this is the best way to do things. I'm sorry we didn't come to this conclusion the last time we met. But it's really for your own good. For your family, for my world, for yours, and for everybody." She squeezed my palm. "You know that, don't you?"

The queen stepped closer so our noses were inches apart, forcing me to make eye contact.

I nodded, silently marveling at how blue the queen's eyes were. Why had I not noticed this when I met her?

"Um, Rosana?" I asked. "How did you and James get here, exactly?"

Rosana took a thin, silver dagger from her jacket pocket and wiggled it in the air. "Carver magic. Enzo finally taught me how to make doors between worlds. Always wanted to learn that one."

James cleared his throat. "We probably shouldn't waste any more time, Your Majesty. We'll be taking those orbs off your hands now, lad." He clapped Tio on the shoulder and said, "It's been a pleasure seeing you again."

"Yeah," Tio said slowly. "Likewise."

Rosana smiled, and a realization hit me like a train: I'd never noticed her blue eyes before because they had always been green. Like Verdoro.

I shook Rosana's hand off my shoulder and slid back until I was at my uncle's side. "No," I said. "I'm sorry. We can't give you the stones."

Rosana clutched her chest. "Charlie, I'm hurt. After all we've been through together?"

James wrinkled his brow. "You'd be wise to think about who you're talking to. You might show us some respect."

"I don't know who you are," I said. "But you're definitely not James and Rosana."

Tio shielded me with his arm, the way my mom sometimes did when she hit the brakes too hard in the car.

"Check on your sister," he whispered, and I was so glad we were on the same page.

I turned, and Rosana blocked my path.

She dropped her hand to her pocket and withdrew two miniature spheres in her palm—both of which we'd seen before. "I don't know how you figured it out, you little twerp. But you're wrong about one thing. You will give us what we want."

And just like I saw with Falk only days before, Rosana and James concentrated and began to change. Their facades fell away and their bones contorted, their hair receded, the hook evaporated, and their skin bubbled until we were staring at two entirely different people: a blonde, bushy-browed dwarf with dragon-green eyes, and a pale slender man with pointed ears and a hook nose.

Karina entered the room, a disposable phone to her ear. "Charlie, Mom wants to talk to—"

She took a look at the strangers in our hotel room.

"Actually, Ma, we'll call you later," she said in one breath.

Karina punched the end button. When she dropped the phone, it shattered into all kinds of cheap plastic shards, kind of like my hopes that this vacation would actually go smoothly. So much for our happily ever after. This was our unhappily never after. The Swiss chocolates and postcard views couldn't last.

Maybe one day I'd meet Lady Fortune in person. I couldn't wait to ask her why her Wheel hated my family so much.

KARINA

FLIGHT OF THE BEARDED VULTURES

Seriously, trouble couldn't wait one week to find us again? Now I knew how my mom felt when Charlie and I messed up the house an hour after she cleaned it.

I'd never seen the two strangers in my hotel before, but I knew they were bad news the same way I knew puppies were cute and snakes were venomous. Sometimes, gut feelings save lives. We can thank years of evolution, or, we can thank the fact that the dwarf woman was holding a knife, the tall, pale elf guy was holding a staff, and both of them were showing their teeth—not necessarily for a Happy Meal commercial.

Uncle Diego stepped in front of Charlie, fists ready. "Who are you people?"

The elf man bowed, tipping his cane in front of him. "Friends of Falk." His voice was deep and rich. "The overlord sends his regards. He's sorry he can't greet you in person today, but he's a little *busy*, thanks to you."

Did that mean he was still locked in Florindale Prison? At least we had that much to be thankful for.

"Where are Rosana and James? The *real* ones?" Charlie asked.

"None of your blasted beeswax, twerps," the dwarf woman snarled. "Now cough up those crystals or we'll take 'em by force!"

"Better yet, Clova," the elf mused, "Lord Falk said this Diego Rosas and his younglings have a talent for finding things. If we want to please the master, we can capture these three and demand that they escort us to the Wheel itself." In a blink, he bridged the gap between himself and Uncle Diego, holding the bejeweled tip of the cane below my uncle's chin. "Imagine the reward when the master finds out we assembled the Wheel of Fortune on our own."

The dwarf narrowed her eyes and rubbed her hands together, twisting the handle of her dagger between her palms. "That's an excellent idea, Ryvendor. In fact, I'll tell the boss it was *my* idea."

"You wouldn't dare." Ryvendor the Elf Man spun on his heel and aimed the staff at Clova the Dwarf Lady's forehead. I had to wonder if he intended to bop her on the head or if there were mysterious powers imbued in the jewel. At any rate, I didn't want to find out what either of these creeps could do if we made them mad.

But if they had come for the fortune stones, there was no way we could give them what they wanted.

"So, your boss told you we're people who can find things?" I chuckled inside at the idea. We weren't treasure hunters. "I bet he left out the part that my brother is friends with a dragon. Did your master tell you Charlie tamed the Dark Dragon of the Old World with no magical powers whatsoever? And that he can summon the dragon with the snap of his fingers?"

Okay, so the finger snap was an exaggeration, but once I started spinning a tall tale . . .

Clova's knuckles whitened at her sides. "You lie."

"You'd bet on it?" I was glad Uncle Diego had caught my drift. "I doubted it before, too, and Verdoro doesn't like to be doubted. I have the cuts and scrapes to prove it."

"Cut the baloney," Clova sneered. "You can't summon a dragon from a world away. Not even if you were Merlin himself."

"Not by myself." Charlie pulled his hand out of his pocket, clutching the silver pouch we had to guard with our lives now. Seeing the pouch out in the open like that always made me sweat. We really needed to find a safer place than our pockets. As if the pouch didn't freak me out enough, Charlie had to open it up and pour the two crystals into his palm. "But if I have these . . ."

Ryvendor and Clova's mouths went flat.

So did mine.

"I could do anything right now," Charlie said.

Ryvendor slammed his staff against the ground. "I call your bluff, boy."

"Sure about that?" Charlie grinned. "I've done it before."

And now we'd backed ourselves into a corner. Either Charlie would have to use the stones, or we'd have to fight Falk's minions. If we kept this going, we'd lose. They would take the crystals.

"Take another step and I swear I'll call the dragon," Charlie said.

Clova and Ryvendor exchanged a nervous glance. The dwarf shook her head. The elf nodded.

Ryvendor took a long stride, smirking as if daring Charlie to act. "Fine. Do it. Demonstrate your power."

Charlie's shoulders sank. Did we even know how to use the stones?

Another step, and this time, Clova took one too, a sly grin creeping across her face.

Charlie closed his fist and took a step back.

"But of course." Ryvendor chuckled. "Fool. Even if you knew how to use those things, you haven't got the backbone to summon the dragon again. You got *lucky* the first time. You know if you called him to you again, he would turn on you. He's a monster with a will of his own, much like our master. And our master's will shall be done."

With that, Clova swung her arm out, coming dangerously close to snatching the fortune stones out of Charlie's hand. But Clova's arm movement was merely a distraction for what Ryvendor was doing with his staff: swinging it behind Charlie's leg to sweep him off the ground.

My brother fell on his tailbone, prompting the dwarf to lunge for the stones as they spilled out of his hand. Uncle Diego dove for them, only to be blocked by Ryvendor's staff. Luckily, I was a little bit faster than Clova and managed to catch the stones myself, but only by a fraction of a second. We were so close that I grazed her calloused fingertips. I jammed the stones in my pocket and yanked my brother to his feet.

"Let's run," I said.

"Twerps." Clova's face glowed crimson with rage. "You won't get away."

Charlie grabbed Uncle Diego's shoulders. "Tio, come on."

"You first," Uncle Diego said. "I can hold them back. Remember, I promised your mother I would protect you two."

"Seize him, Clova," Ryvendor said. "He shall be our bargaining chip! Our map to the Wheel."

Nobody was ever taking my uncle again.

I threw myself in front of him. "Charlie, take him and go get help," I said. "You creeps will have to go through me first."

"We're not leaving you, Rina," Charlie said.

Clova brandished her dagger. "Oh, so touching. It's funny how you think—"

"Shh." Ryvendor raised a hand, horror carved in his face. "Clova! Listen, you fool."

I didn't need much time to understand why the elf was so afraid. I remembered the sound all too well, more specifically the first time I'd heard it only weeks ago. How Uncle Diego had shushed us so harshly. How I asked if the *whooshing* sounds in the air were bat wings, or the wind. *Swish. Swish. Swish.*

"Rina," Charlie whispered. "Something huge is flying toward our hotel right now."

Verdoro, I thought.

We'd actually summoned a dragon somehow.

I turned around hoping to see a gold-green monster in the mountains. Instead, a flying beast made of silver and ice-blue scales soared straight for us, along with two additional men. We knew the one on the monster's back, clad in jeans and a t-shirt—one of the people we least expected to see in our own world.

The man was King Enzo riding a silver dragon.

At the beast's side, a man we'd never seen before flew entirely on his own. *Flew.* Defied gravity.

"Whoaaa," Charlie breathed. "Here, there be—"

I raced to the patio door and threw it open. "No time to gawk, Charlie. Just run." I waved my arms over my head. "Enzo!"

Enzo thrusted his blade in the air, gave me a quick salute, and returned his hands to the reins on the silver dragon.

"It's the meddlesome king," Clova said. "Shoot that creature down."

Ryvendor fired a red beam of light from the bejeweled tip of his weapon. The light reminded me of a tiny lightning bolt, and I definitely didn't want to know what would happen if we touched it. The windows disintegrated into dust as the bolt passed through and soared toward the ice dragon.

Charlie helped Uncle Diego to the door and we raced into the frosty air, the dwarf and the elf at our heels. Ryvendor kept himself occupied with the dragon, firing beams of light from his staff, while Clova hounded me for the orbs in my pocket. I struggled to fight her off as she bit my hand, slashed her dagger haphazardly through the air, and even tried to shove her hand in my pocket.

Enzo tossed a rope ladder over the dragon's side and cupped his hands to his mouth. "Get ready to jump on."

Oh snap. Our only way out of this was to board a moving dragon. And here I hoped it would land on the balcony.

"Take that monster down," Clova said.

Ryvendor slammed the base of his staff on the floor, sending a ripple of light careening from the jewel. The ice dragon veered up and dodged the ripple, and I managed to duck below it, but Charlie wasn't so lucky. The blast hit him in the back and sent him sprawling facedown. His eyes shut before he landed.

"Charlie," I cried.

Uncle Diego gritted his teeth and hoisted Charlie over his shoulders.

"Take the rope," Enzo said.

Uncle Diego seized the ladder and pulled himself up on one leg. "Come on, Rina!"

"I'm right behind you," I said.

The ladder dangled only a few yards from my face. I reached out and prepared to leap on, but as I made the jump, a cold hand closed over my ankle and ripped me backward. Ryvendor yanked me down, pulled me against his chest, and locked his forearm against my throat. His scent stung my nostrils, like mint and cinnamon. "Reach into your pocket, girl."

"She won't do it, you dummy." Clova marched to me, sweat rolling down her forehead. "Hold her still. I'll do it."

I screamed.

The Flying Man dipped low, spreading his arms apart and kicking out like he was swimming. "I've got her."

Clova jammed her finger in my pocket, poising her dagger to bust the stitches open. I squirmed with every ounce of movement I could.

"Hold still or I promise I'll be a lot less careful." Clova nicked my pocket with the tip of her blade. A single orb gleamed in the light, still begging for breath after being confined to pouches and pockets for the past week. Clova grinned. "Aha."

The next thing I saw was a booted foot coming straight for my head. I squeezed my eyes shut, and heard a sickening crunch as the Flying Man kicked the elf in the face.

Ryvendor let go of me and clutched the bridge of his nose, tears springing to his eyes. "Oh, my beautiful face!"

I rolled my eyes. The elves from *Lord of the Rings* had beautiful faces. Ryvendor kind of looked like a potato.

Free from the elf's grasp, I shoved away from Clova. She flicked her dagger at the Flying Man as if swatting a fly, but he was faster than her. In one smooth motion, he whipped to the side, swooped down, and hoisted me into the air. "Ready? Up we go."

An involuntary scream poured from my lungs. I wasn't exactly afraid of the flying dude, but then again, a hovering stranger had never lifted me in the air before. "Put me down!"

"I don't think you want me to do that." The man soared upward, dodging another swipe from the dwarf lady.

Ryvendor found his reflection in a mirror, tears filling his eyes as he clutched the bridge of his nose. "It's so unfair," he wailed.

Clova marched up to the elf and stood on her tiptoes. "Grow up, you blubbering baby." She reached up and clamped her fingertips on Ryvendor's face. A sickening crack filled the air. "You happy now? They're getting away. Give me this."

She wrenched the staff from his free hand and pointed the weapon at my head.

"Wuh-oh. Hold tight." The Flying Man rolled in the air, flipping me over his back and pulling me higher up. A fall from this height maybe wouldn't kill me, but I certainly wouldn't be okay.

A beam of golden light whizzed past my ear.

The Flying Man scowled. "That lady needs a nap or something. Hey, you're Karina, right? Hold tight, please. I gotta get you on the back of that dragon."

I looked up, too stunned to care how this stranger knew my name already. Enzo had managed to pull Uncle Diego and Charlie up on the ice dragon's back.

"Follow us, okay?" Enzo called.

With that, the ice dragon lurched and sped ahead, leaving the hotel behind in a trail of frost.

"Seriously, Snowmunch?" the stranger said. "Wait up! I'm exhausted, man. I might just drop."

A chill rolled down my back. Not the most reassuring thing to hear from a flying man.

"Who even are you?" I asked.

"I'm—" The man's stomach rumbled, radiating through his back. "Ugh. Sorry. I had a steak on the way over here, but it turns out flying burns a boat load of calories. Enzo promised we'd stop somewhere, but obviously that's not gonna happen."

"But how are you flying?"

"You got time for a colossal fairy tale the size of like three novels? Name's Pietro. I'm a friend of the king."

"Uh, hi."

A blue beam clipped past Pietro's head, and he looked down. "Oh, yeah, bad people are still after us. Hey!" He blew a raspberry, and I watched Clova's jaw drop and Ryvendor clutch his chest. "Better luck next time, punks."

Pietro turned around and pointed us toward the ice dragon, perpetually blowing snow behind its wings. "Okay, seriously though, hang on," Pietro said. "I gotta catch up to Snowmunch."

I obeyed and squeezed the Flying Man's shoulders. He doubled his speed, dropping my heart into my stomach. Despite the unpleasant winter wind whipping at my cheeks, the danger behind us, and the fear lodged in my throat, something about this was ridiculously fun.

"This is amazing!" I said.

"Don't get too comfortable," Pietro said, his voice going deep and grave. "I need you to look behind us. Are we being followed?"

I craned my neck and snuck a look behind me. No beams of light, no elves, and no dwarves trailed us, but there *were* two abnormally massive, bearded vultures—one curiously squat, and the other curiously slender with a crooked beak—soaring hot on Pietro's heels. In their talons, each of them clutched a tiny shimmering crystal.

Of course, I thought. For them to shapeshift as our friends, or a pair of birds, they must have already had part of the Wheel. I wondered if this was how Enzo found us—because Clova and Ryvendor had already come for the crystals he'd been guarding.

Braaack! The squat bird screeched.

"Yep, we're being followed." I gave Pietro's hood a light tug. "Our friends just turned into angry birds."

"Aw, man," Pietro groaned. "What can you throw at them? How 'bout those rocks in your pocket? How's your aim?"

"You mean throw the crystals?" I asked. "No! Can you hurry?"

"Can't rush me, kid. I can only keep this up for so long—"

Caw! The birds picked up speed, rose above me, and flew in a circle.

I waved my arms over my head, hoping if I stretched high enough I could swat the birds out of the sky or snag the stones from their talons.

Pietro looked up and muttered a curse under his breath. "Okay, can you grab something out of my hood?"

The squat bird dove through the air and grazed the top of my head. I flung my arm out and knocked her aside. She fluttered her wings and flapped higher.

"What do you need?" With the wind roaring in my ears, I had to scream every word to hear myself.

"See if my slingshot's in there."

"Who keeps a slingshot in their hood?"

"Just look, okay? I'm very resourceful."

I reached inside Pietro's hood. My fingers grazed a few rough objects, though none of them couldn't have been much bigger than my finger. While Pietro himself was clean enough, searching his jacket was like diving into the gritty cushions of someone's battered couch, hunting for a remote and wondering if it was all worth it. I removed a nickel and two pennies, a tiny wooden figurine, a blue paperclip—

"*Ow!*" I flinched. "One of those birds just pecked my back. Can we hurry? There's no slingshot in your jacket." I smacked the slender bird with the back of my hand, but he didn't move. He pecked me again. And again, ripping through my jacket.

"Look again," Pietro said.

I plunged my hand back into the crumby, dark depths of the Flying Man's hood, and I closed my fingers around something rough and slingshot-like in shape.

When I took my hand out, I lost my patience. "Gross! This is a T-bone!"

I chucked it over my shoulder.

Braaack! The slender bird hopped off my back. I looked up to find the fat bird wasn't circling anymore.

They were both behind and below, diving and squabbling over the greasy bone.

Birds will be birds, I guess?

With our pursuers distracted, I turned my attention back to the dragon. Enzo slowed the beast's flight, allowing us some leeway to catch up. I was relieved to see Uncle Diego strapped securely to the dragon's back. During his last dragon ride—and what I'd hoped would've been our only one—there were no straps or belts, and my uncle plummeted into the ocean below. This time, we didn't have any oceans to fall into, and an icy mountain range wouldn't break our fall as kindly.

"Get ready." Pietro pushed forward, slowly gaining speed. "I'm gonna land us on that thing's back, and once you're off *my* back, I'm taking a nap."

Pietro bridged the gap between us and the ice dragon, and I shut my eyes for the landing. In my mind, I felt like I was on a plane about to land on a *bigger* plane flying full speed. I didn't expect the transition to be so smooth, and when a warm palm touched the back of my hand and I opened my eyes to find Enzo guiding me off Pietro's back, my senses rattled.

"I got you." Enzo moved me between him and Uncle Diego, who supported my unconscious brother in front of him. "This one at least has seat belts. Strap in, okay?"

I squirmed, doing my best to settle onto Snowmunch's back. His icy, diamond scales couldn't have been more different from Verdoro's warm, leathery exterior.

Enzo winked. "And no roaming about until the captain says—"

"Uh, problem: Angry birds are back." Pietro tapped on Enzo's shoulder. "They won't stop."

The Ryvendor and Clova birds had come back with a vengeance, wings thrashing and beaks grinding at nothing in particular.

"Then we'd better get out of here." Enzo took out that famous ivory dagger I always saw him with and gave it a swipe. A tiny white light opened in the air at the tip of his blade, and with the dragon's flight, Enzo dragged the tiny pinprick into a long, horizontal stripe glowing with sunshine, just like the hole I saw him tear through a tree trunk to send us home.

He gritted his teeth, the muscles in his arms trembled, and his eyelids drooped. The birds swooped down and attempted to peck the knife out of his hand. Pietro, Uncle Diego, and I swatted them away, but they were ridiculously persistent.

"Leave us alone," I said.

The birds switched targets and descended. As we reached up to wave them away, the beast swerved, jostling us in our seat belts. The line Enzo cut beside us grew jagged and rough, like a pulse monitor.

"*Now!*" he cried.

"Hang on!" We spun in a wide, dizzying circle until we approached the bright hole Enzo had created.

The void opened up, growing and brightening until I had to shield my eyes for protection.

The world was a blur of wings, snow, wind, and light, until a faint pop sounded in my ears, warmth drenched my skin, and just like that, the world changed.

Our vacation in Switzerland was over.

CHARLIE

THE KING'S RETREAT

I wasn't surprised to wake up in Florindale. When Enzo had appeared on his dragon, I'd known what was coming. I only wished I hadn't slept through the entire flight. Dragon rides were terrifying, but they were such a rush.

I slept for the next four hours or so after the dragon landed and woke up in a place I'd never seen before. Not King Enzo's home. Not Zid's. Nowhere in Kesterfall that I recognized. Instead, I was in a high room with stained glass windows and a fountain dripping down the walls. Karina and Tio were right beside me, too.

"He's awake!" Karina sprang from a wooden chair to tap Tio on the shoulder. "I'm gonna go get Pietro." She ran from the room.

"Tio?" I moaned, my voice husky with sleep.

Tio patted my leg. "Welcome back to the living, *Bello Durmiente.* Thought you were under a curse or something." He shook his head and massaged his temples. "Thing is, that wouldn't have even been such a weird explanation."

My jaw crackled in a satisfying yawn. "What happened?"

"Well, for one thing, we flew over the Alps on an ice dragon. The place I was most excited to take you, and you slept through it. Can't take you anywhere, can I, *chiquito?*" Tio flashed a million-dollar grin.

"I missed the rest of the Alps?" I cringed. "Man."

Tio threw his head back and laughed. "That was the least of it. When we crossed into this world, we flew over a living island. I think Enzo called it Stelmorir? Crazy dangerous, he said. Quicksand, carnivorous trees, all the works. I have to check it out one day."

I rolled my eyes. "Where's the dragon now?"

"Snowmunch?" Tio said. "Enzo had only borrowed him for a while. He set him free."

Karina returned to the room, Pietro the Flying Man at her heels. "And I still have questions about why Pietro had a piece of actual beef in his hoodie," she said, pointing to Pietro. "Hey, bro."

"Where's Enzo?" I asked.

"Resting." Pietro handed me a warm mug, and when I brought it up to my lips, tendrils of cinnamon-scented steam drifted into my nose and relaxed my muscles. "He had to make a hole in the sky big enough for us to dive through on a dragon's back. Took a lot out of the poor guy. Carving something on that scale has the tendency to knock him out for a while. He'll wake up shortly and explain everything, I'm sure. For now, know you're in a secluded castle and we're retreating here until further notice. Somehow, the overlord found you, and he's sending his minions after you. You're not safe at home, so we're going to protect you."

Pietro's words were arrows to the gut. *You're not safe at home.*

I sipped from the mug. Apple cinnamon tea. Mmm. "So who exactly are you?"

"I've been a good friend of Enzo's for ages." Pietro took a seat across from me. "You ever hear of the Ivory Queen?"

I shrugged. I'd heard her mentioned a few times, but she was always a story for another day. "Sorta."

Pietro beamed. "Well, I helped Enzo defeat her. I did forty—no, like ninety percent of the work. Not to say Enzo's not a capable king, though. He's great."

I took another sip. "Okay, *Pietro*. How do I know you're really Enzo's friend and not a shape-shifting elf bird thing sent by Falk?"

Pietro leaned forward, resting his elbows on his knees. "Anyone can talk about the train wreck. About Verdoro sweeping your uncle off the ground and carrying him all the way to Kesterfall. But *I* know you befriended two wolves along the way to rescue him. You called them Oliver and Nella. They reminded you of your old family dog."

I stared at my feet.

Pietro continued. "I know Captain Storm thinks the world of you. She even sang to you while she rowed you across the Joringel Sea. I know Karina's allergic to fish and writes fantasy stories and you like to sketch your favorite superheroes in your free time." Pietro raised a brow. "Enzo listens to you. I listen to him. Should I keep going?"

I put down my mug. "Thank you," I said, "for protecting us and all that."

The Flying Man winked. "Don't mention it. I'll bill your famous uncle for it later." On the way to the kitchen, he swatted Tio's shoulder. "Just kidding, maybe."

Tio looked at me and made circles around his ears with his fingers.

Enzo woke up nearly an hour after me and shuffled out of his room with circles under his eyes and his hair a bit messier than usual. The first thing he did was grip Pietro by the shoulders. "Were we followed?"

"No evidence suggests we were." Pietro handed Enzo a mug of tea.

The answer should've given me a little comfort, but I fixed my mind on everything he *didn't* say. *Well, what if they followed us and didn't leave evidence? What if they're in this castle right now?*

"We almost trusted them," I said. "Falk's people. They made themselves look like Rosana and James."

Enzo buried his fingers in his hair, his tea untouched. "We need to be extra careful around each other. We need a password. A phrase so we can be sure we're talking to the real person."

"How 'bout *fortune?*" Karina asked.

Pietro shook his head. "Too obvious. It needs to be something only we'll know. Like T-bone."

Karina rubbed her chin. "Did we summon you all? With the nature stone, I mean? Did we call the dragon?"

"Nah," Enzo said. "We came on our own. And just in the nick of time, I'd say."

"How did you know to do that?"

Enzo rolled up his sleeve, exposing a blood-soaked bandage on his forearm. "Because Ryvendor and Clova came for us first. Pietro and I were assaulted in Grimm's Hollow last night. Once the elf and the dwarf made off with the crystals, we knew they were coming for you."

"They told us you and Niraya were missing," I said. "That's why we almost trusted them."

"No, no, as you can see, I'm alive and well and a hundred percent me." Somehow, Enzo didn't look happy to correct us. His gaze dropped to his knees. "But James and Captain Storm *are* missing, and so . . . so is Rosana."

Pietro slouched in his seat. "And Zid. It's been weeks."

My stomach lurched. All of this was worse than I thought.

"No," my sister whispered.

Enzo shut his eyes, fighting to steady his voice. "I suspect they went looking for the Wheel and that they ran into trouble somewhere."

My mind fizzed with questions. *Why would they go looking for the stones?* But ultimately, knowing them, I got it. Niraya Storm and James Hook lived dangerously. After all, they were pirates, and they weren't exactly the *lie down and drink from a coconut on the beach* kind. Leave it to them to answer the call of adventure and get in trouble.

As for Rosana, I didn't know her nearly as well, but I imagined she wasn't one to back down from a challenge, and we put her up to one when we asked her and Enzo to protect the stones. And Zid was incredibly unpredictable. He had forbidden us from going after Verdoro when we first met. In fact, Zid was terrified of Verdoro. Then at the eleventh hour, Zid met us in Kesterfall and helped us make our way to the dragon's den. Wherever he was, I could practically hear him grumbling and stamping his feet the whole way. *Harrumph.*

"That's awful," my sister said. "Are you doing okay?"

"I'm holding onto hope," the king said. "Events like this become part of the territory in Florindale. Somehow, everything works out in the end. Happily ever after, right?" He picked up a ragged red cloak hanging from a coat rack and fidgeted with the loose strings. "So far."

"I think I know how they found me," Tio said.

Quietly, I had already formed an idea of my own. "Because of your signature."

The first time we met Falk, he'd been posing as a nineteen-year-old American traveler with a fanboy crush on my uncle. *Will you sign my arm?* he'd asked. The last time we saw him, he still had that Sharpie signature sprawled on his arm. *Your signature bound you to me.*

Tio nodded. "I'll never forget what he said in that cave."

If you run, if you take that pendant from me, I vow this: I will always find you, Diego Rosas. I will hunt you and your family eternally until I have that wheel.

Tio shut his eyes and tilted his head back. "I can't be near you two anymore. It's too dangerous."

"Uncle D," Karina said.

Enzo held up a hand. "No. You must stick together. I can hide you, wave my dagger around, and hire a bunch of bodyguards, but family is the strongest protection you have. Swear to me you won't break that. Until the Wheel is secured and we figure out where the Fortune Guard is—"

"They're real? The Fortune Guard, I mean?" I asked.

"Ryvendor and Clova. They left all their own clues for you. And I'm willing to bet they are not Falk's only minions." Enzo sighed. "Swear you'll stay together. If trouble finds you, we'll fight together, but tread lightly. Don't wander off looking for trouble on your own."

Karina gave Enzo the thumbs-up. "We promise."

Enzo raised a brow. "Don't forget I was in your shoes before, always being told to stay put and let the grownups handle everything. I remember how frustrating that felt. I also remember when I didn't listen I was nearly killed."

I scoffed. "You sound just like our mom threatening us with ghost stories right now." Nothing could make me obey like the ever-looming fear of a wailing spirit throwing the screen door open and dragging me into a dry Tucson riverbed. "Chill out. Pretty sure none of us feels like dying."

That answer seemed to give Enzo some peace. At last, he picked up his tea. "Good. Then make yourselves at home. I'll work on something to eat."

And that something-to-eat was divine. While Karina and I explored the castle and poked around suits of armor and lavish study rooms, Enzo prepared a delicious spread.

There was tender pot roast, honeyed rolls, fresh salad greens, buttered potatoes, and an assortment of fruit tarts baked straight out of a fairy tale.

The problem was the limited choice of beverages, which Pietro presented as, "Red, white, or ale?"

Karina and I looked at each other, then at Tio. "Uhh—"

Enzo laughed. "Pietro, you can't give them wine. We have milk, or you two are welcome to get some water from the well outside."

"Ooo, a well?" Karina's eyes lit up. "Wait, I've never drank water from a well before. It's not dirty water, is it?"

"That well was enchanted by one of the best magicians I know, so I'd say it's the crispest, cleanest water you'll ever taste. Couldn't be safer. Go grab some, and when you come back, we'll talk about how to keep you undercover. I plan to go look for Rosana soon, and I want to make sure you're safe. We all know Florindale Prison can't hold Falk forever, and as you've seen, he has help."

We found the well behind the castle, and like Enzo's fruit tarts, somebody plucked that well straight out of a fable. The well wasn't huge, but the opening was probably as big around as the kiddie pool Karina and I used to splash in when we were tiny. There was a pulley, a seemingly infinite rope, and a simple wooden bucket resting at the top. Roses bloomed along the base, their fragrance a dizzying punch to the brain.

I could practically see the hearts in Karina's eyes. Sometimes, she was a living emoji. "O-M-G," she spelled aloud. "Charlie, we have to make a wish right now."

"Calm down, Snow White," I said. "That's drinking water. This isn't a wishing well."

"It's enchanted," Karina said. "If you're worried about contaminating it or something, it'll clean itself."

"What a waste of money," I grumbled.

Karina and I walked to the edge and peered into the depths of the well, clusters of thorns clinging to the bricks. For a second, my chest tightened. Maybe my fear of heights or deep water had kicked in, but I almost lost my balance imagining how deep and vast this well could be. I couldn't even see the bottom.

Karina whistled, the acoustics tossing the sound like a football. When the echo stopped, she reached into her pocket and grabbed a quarter Tio pulled from behind her ear earlier.

I grabbed my own quarter, and Karina and I clicked our coins together as if saying *cheers*.

I shut my eyes and squeezed the coin. "I wish for—"

"Don't say it out loud, Charlie," Karina said. "Otherwise it won't come true, remember?"

"Oh, right," I said, although I never really believed speaking a wish out loud would ruin it. I never even believed making one had any sort of power. But I listened because I decided that sometimes it's okay to have dreams that we keep only for ourselves. So I closed my eyes, concentrated, and put the coin heads-up on my thumbnail.

When I was ready, I snapped my fingers and popped the coin into the air. I opened my eyes and watched Karina drop her coin by opening her fist, and our wishes tumbled into the earth where darkness swallowed them up in seconds. I didn't even hear a splash. The coins could have poofed out of existence, for all I knew.

"The darkness just ate our wishes," I said theatrically. "This is where dreams go to die."

"Shut up, Charlie." Karina elbowed me in the gut, then plucked a flower from the base of the well and twirled the stem between her fingers. "This is where our dreams come to bloom and blossom like pretty flowers." She whacked my hand with the flower and then stuck it behind her ear.

Staring down into the abyss, I had a sudden idea, just crazy enough to bring up to my sister. I reached into my pocket and pulled out the silver pouch with the two orbs inside. Sometimes, the weight seemed like a thousand pounds. Right now, the pouch felt light as a feather. I dangled the drawstring on my finger. "Rina," I whispered. "Do you think maybe we can . . ."

I tilted my head at the pouch, then at the well.

Karina's eyes widened, and she reached out and closed my fist over the pouch. "What are you doing? Put it away, Carlos." She shook her head. "You have to."

I clutched the pouch against my chest and took a step back. "Look, I'm just saying we have an opportunity." I cocked my head toward the well. "Think about it. We've been having bad luck ever since Florindale. It's not a coincidence, and you know it. It's all because of these."

I gave the pouch a little shake then tapped the base of the well with my toe, scraping some of the dirt off the brick. And as I thought about the possibilities, my lungs worked harder, the words spilling faster from my lips. "We're not supposed to have them, Rina. And this thing could go miles underground. What if we just happen to drop these and leave? No one has to know it. Nobody would ever look, and it wouldn't be our responsibility anymore. We could say it was just an accident. We could—"

"Stop." Karina aimed a palm at me before curling it in so she was holding up her index finger. With her other hand, she reached out and plucked the silver pouch from my grasp. "These are our responsibility, Charlie. That doesn't change if we drop them down a well. If that happens and someone like Falk finds them, the whole *world* becomes our responsibility, remember?"

I lowered my head, staring into the abyss again. The way the darkness seemed to stare right back made my head spin. "I'm sorry," I said. "It just feels like too much right now. We're supposed to be on vacation. We're supposed to be enjoying our time with Tio."

"We can still do that, you know. We can still enjoy our time together." Karina pocketed the pouch and gave the well a few pats. "I know it's a lot, Charlie. One day we'll look back on all of this and we'll be proud of ourselves. But for now, let's fill our water and go back inside, okay?"

I put my arm around my sister's shoulder. "I really hate how you're always right."

"I know you do." Karina smirked and took hold of the pulley.

Come to the temple.

A cold whisper filled the air, and Karina and I both froze in our tracks.

I locked eyes with my sister and pointed a finger at her. "What did you just say?"

But the bewilderment in her eyes told me she was just as confused as I was.

Karina rubbed her elbows. I had goose bumps, and the temperature seemed to drop about ten degrees with the snap of a finger. "You heard it too?"

Come to the temple of wishes and thorns.

Either Karina had recently become a crazy good ventriloquist, or somebody was trying to talk to us. I swallowed a lump of fear in my throat, and Karina and I stood back to back, looking for the source of the mysterious voice. Dust and dried leaves swirled at our feet, the roses shaking as the weather built up some gust.

"It's just the wind," I said.

"Charlie. Karina." This time, the voice was fuller, not a breathy whisper but a full-fledged cry, distinctly female and uncannily familiar.

Karina grabbed my arm. "Did you just hear Niraya's voice?"

I didn't know how to answer. I'd thought I heard Niraya Storm calling our names, but that couldn't have been possible. The voice had to have been our imagination, or someone who sounded like her, or—

"*Help!* Down here, wildlings."

Niraya was the only person we'd ever met who called us wildlings.

I snapped my gaze in the direction the scream had come from, hardly daring to believe it.

"It's coming from inside the well." Karina leaned in. "Niraya! We can hear you. Are you down there?"

Come to the temple of wishes and thorns.

The invitation sounded again, and this time, I could see Karina's hair moving with every syllable of the whisper's wind.

"Karina, I think you should get away from there," I said.

But Karina didn't listen. She leaned in a little more, standing on her tiptoes, and shouted. "*Nirayaaa.*" The acoustics of the well swirled her voice, throwing it back at her. "*Raya, raya, aya!*"

I had a horrible feeling about all of this, a real kick in the gut. I put on the scary voice I'd learned from listening to Tio yell at Falk, and said, "Karina Rosas, you step away from the well right now, young lady."

Okay, that might have been too far. But at least I succeeded in making Karina turn away for a bit to roll her eyes. "Young lady? Really, Charlie?"

A new voice, masculine and rough, repeated the well's whispering warnings:

"*Come to the temple of wishes and thorns.*"

As if in answer, a thick red smoke rose from the well, like someone had put cherry Kool-Aid in a mist machine. Karina took a step back, and if we were feeling at all the same, her heart was probably throwing itself against her chest.

The mist formed into a large, gaseous body, reminding me an awful lot of the ghosts of Kesterfall. The ghosts we could only see when snowflakes stuck to their forms. But somehow I didn't think this new creature was a ghost. There was something more commanding about its presence. The figure seemed fully alive, from the toned muscles on its arms to the way its chest rippled with every breath. The eyes were the starkest, icy blue against its rose-red body, and the way those eyes pierced me, I decided this thing wanted nothing more than to snap me in half.

We locked eyes for no more than five seconds before the smoky red man reached out of the well, its arms like elastic and making their way toward Karina.

"Run," I yelled.

Karina was already ahead of me.

And in a few seconds, so was the smoke man's arm, stretching and extending like a rubber band until he wrapped one of his massive hands around her ankle and pulled.

"Karina!"

"Charlie." My sister skidded backward and dug her heels into the ground, struggling against the ever-growing smoke man.

I made a dash for Karina.

The smoke man yanked her a few feet, and her heels unearthed globs of mud and blades of grass.

Tears sprang to her eyes, and she shook the silver pouch in her hand. "Charlie," she said, "I think I'm about to go over. Take care of these for us, promise?"

"You're *not* going over," I insisted. "Be quiet."

As Karina's foot connected with the base of the well, she lobbed the silver pouch toward me. "Catch."

"No," I said, because Karina throwing the pouch meant she was giving up. The pouch hurtled toward me, and several things happened at once. My sister put out her newly free hand on the well's rim to catch herself and push back against the misty man, clinging to the bricks for dear life. I locked my gaze on the silver pouch in midair, calculated a jump, and made a flying leap for the tiny little bag. I extended my arms, my body almost vertical in the air.

The smoke man released Karina, changed targets, and snatched the silver pouch from the air nanoseconds before I could close my fingers around it. In fact, we touched fingers, and I was surprised that his hand felt just like anyone else's—not like wind or smoke or concentrated heat, but like rough, calloused skin.

As quickly as he'd appeared, the smoke man closed his fist, shot me a grin, and retreated into the well in a red puff of fast-dissolving mist. The ground rushed up to meet my elbows, then my knees, knocking the wind from my chest as I landed. Karina slumped against the well, and we both took a moment to catch our breath.

The silence was the stuff of nightmares. No more whispers, no more wind, no more Niraya.

I mopped dirt from my chin and spat out a drop of blood. Apparently, I'd bitten my cheek when I landed. Ouch. "What the heck was that thing?"

Karina used the well for balance as she pulled herself to her feet. The look on her face was downright terrifying. She's not scary when she tries to be, like when she gives me our mom's death stare, but in this moment when the red smoky man disappeared, Karina was livid. "I don't know. But if that thing thinks he's keeping those crystals, he's got another thing coming. I'm getting them back."

"Karina, please think for a second."

"Are you coming with me?" My sister swung her legs over the rim of the wishing well and took a deep breath.

"Don't!" I reached for her.

And she threw herself inside.

KARINA

Okay, so what I did was *stupid*—probably in the top ten stupidest things in my whole life. No one had to tell me. In fact, the second I pushed off the rim of the well and into the darkness below, a scream poured out of my lungs, and regret swept in to fill the empty space.

No matter what waited for me at the bottom, the landing was going to hurt. If I hit earth, I could break every bone in my body. If I hit water, I could still break every bone in my body, and then drown right after.

Or, you know, I could die. There was a solid chance I wouldn't even survive the fall. If only I could fly, or land on my feet without breaking a bone. But I was no

Captain Marvel. I was Karina Rosas, and I was in for a world of pain, all for a tiny silver drawstring pouch that contained the fate of the world.

It seemed like I fell for minutes, screaming and kicking and begging for a thousand feathered pillows to land in or a springy net like a trapeze artist would use, or man, even just a little pinprick of light to look at. I thought I'd seen darkness before. Nothing came close to the oppressive absence of light in the wishing well. Now I saw Charlie's point. People threw their heart's desires down here, all tumbling into infinite blackness.

If my coin was never going to reach the bottom, then I wanted it back.

And if *I* was never going to hit the bottom, falling forever would be a really terrible way to spend the rest of my life. I hadn't even brought a book with me.

But then where did that smoke thing go with the silver pouch? And was Niraya really down here? I'd stopped hearing her scream ages ago. I couldn't even hear Charlie above me anymore. Poor Charlie—my recklessness probably worried him stupid. If we ever saw each other again, he'd pinch me for being ridiculous. *I wouldn't blame him.*

I almost couldn't wait for him to have the chance. I fell for so long that when the adrenaline and fear wore off, I took an actual nap. I managed to turn on my back in midair, cross my arms over my chest, and drift off with my hair rushing over my cheeks. Who knows how long I really slept, but I know it was long enough to dream. And what's really unfair is that I was falling in my dream, too, this time from Verdoro's back and toward the Joringel Sea. Only right as I prepared to hit the surface, the water opened into a black void and made me keep falling, the darkness folding in on me once again.

"*Halt.*"

My eyes snapped open and I jerked awake, surprised to see warm torchlight all around me. I blinked and took in the light, processing the texture of the walls it revealed. I was still in the well, wet ivy and dark brambles snaking their way up the dusty brick structure, growing and stretching as if someone had sped up their life cycles.

I wasn't falling anymore, but I hadn't hit any sort of surface. I turned over in midair, so I laid on my stomach. Something kept me there about six feet from the ground, like magnets or an invisible net. Or a man made of red smoke.

Honestly, he looked a lot smaller from this angle. When he'd been climbing out of the wishing well, he seemed larger than life. But hanging above him in midair and watching him look up at me, I realized he was probably only a little taller than I was. And he was also the reason I hadn't hit the ground, which was a flat brick road paved with all kinds of glittering coins.

The smoke man stood with one arm stretched above his head and aimed toward my belly, open-palmed with his fingers sprawled out, like he was pushing against me without touching my skin. Weirdly, I felt like I was on solid ground.

When I saw the smoke man's other hand locked against his side, his fingers clutching that apocalyptic silver pouch, I lost my cool. I started writhing and kicking out like a rabid monkey, arms flailing and reaching for the pouch to no avail.

"Give that back to me. It's mine." I snarled.

The red man shook his head, his arm unwavering. "Foolish mortal. It most certainly does not belong to you. Nor does it belong to The Bramble King. You should not have followed me, you fool."

Bramble King? *Foolish mortal?* I'd never felt more insulted. But I wasn't about to let this man distract me from what I'd come here for. I stretched my arm as far as it would go, almost connecting with the tip of the red man's outstretched fingers. The feeling was like pushing against a rubber band, and I worried that the force would snap back against me. "That belongs to one person only," I said. "And it's not you. Now give it."

Then the red man did the pettiest thing I could think of: He hid his hand behind his back so I couldn't see the pouch anymore. Seriously, could he be anymore kindergarten? "No. I shall not. Foolish mortal."

Smoke could've poured from my ears. "Who even says things like that? Who are you? And where's Niraya?"

The red man scoffed, beads of sweat gathering at his forehead as though he struggled to hold me up. "Who is 'Niranha'? I'm Groff the Genie. And you're interfering with my job."

Until Groff told me he was a genie, I hadn't even realized he didn't have legs. His torso faded into a curly cue thing like the swirl on top of an ice cream cone. Groff must've seen the surprise on my face, because he laughed, a rich, deep, evil villain sort of laugh that echoed up the well.

"Well, *Groff*," I said, "I don't care what your job is. I have one, too, and you're in *my* way. So give me back that pouch, and give me back my friend."

Groff wrinkled his brow and laughed again. "There's no Niranha here, foolish mortal. I'm afraid you're out of luck. As for the pouch"—he gave it a shake—"I welcome you to take it from me. Let the game commence."

The genie drew his arm back to his side, and I dropped five feet as if all those invisible tethers had been cut away. I hit the ground with an "*Oof*," colored stars frolicking in front of me. Those same stars also laughed at my pain and pulled my hair. I must've really biffed it hard.

Upon a second glance, the stars were actually tiny little pixies as big as my thumb, like fireflies but with very human noses, disproportionately large and bulbous eyes, and tiny little teeth. I squinted at the pixies. "What the heck?"

I waved the pixies away from me then turned to look for Groff.

And oh man, how my blood boiled when he wasn't there anymore. Not a single wisp of red smoke lingered above me. I was breathing like a bull just before it charges a matador. This only made the stupid pixies laugh harder, which made me angrier, and the cycle went on.

I stood and studied my surroundings. *Where could he have gone?*

Groff could have gone anywhere. This looked more like a twisted subway system than the bottom of a well. I landed in the intersection of six pathways, each running into a dark tunnel with an arched ceiling at least ten feet high. Shiny, dark water filled in all the wedges of space between the pathways, filling my nostrils with a scent like a swimming pool. I wondered how the pail at the top of the well ever managed to retrieve any water.

Couldn't be safer? I thought. *You should rethink that, Enzo.*

There was no going back the way I came, and I stood a thin chance of catching up to Groff. He could've gone down any one of the six tunnels, and I had no way of knowing which one to follow.

Just how big was this place anyway, and what else might be hiding down here?

Come to the temple of wishes and thorns.

There was that voice again.

Groff seemed pretty bewildered that I'd followed him here. I doubted he was the person who invited me to jump on down.

So who did?

I spun around on my heel and faced the tunnel behind me, where the whispers echoed down the hall. I didn't know which way Groff went, but right now, one tunnel was as good as any other, and the whispers were coming from only one direction. If I didn't find Groff right away, at least I'd find the "temple of wishes and thorns," for better or worse.

I took my first step toward the whispers before stopping at the sound of screams above me. I looked up to see my brother falling down the well.

"Charlie." I could've hugged him. I could've strangled him.

He tumbled in wild midair somersaults, arms and legs flailing in the dark, until the swarm of colorful pixies rushed up to catch him by his hair. For little creatures that seemed no bigger than bumblebees, they must've been incredibly strong. There were only six of them, each clutching a lock of Charlie's hair while he kicked out and panicked over the fall. By the way they were snickering and plucking at his hair like guitar strings, I don't think the pixies caught him to save him. I think they saw him as a toy.

And I could've made him my personal punching bag.

"Charlie." I grabbed him by the ankles and gave him a good tug. "What the H-E-double toothpicks were you thinking? Why did you follow me here?"

"Are you kidding me? What were *you* thinking? *Ow!*" Charlie waved his hands over his head, trying to grab the pixies. I was in a pretty good game of tug-o-war with them, which couldn't have been much fun for my brother. And yet when he looked at the ground, a huge grin spread across his face. "Oh, hey, look at all this money. We're rich!"

I picked up a coin and flicked it in Charlie's direction, aiming for one of the pixies. "Put my brother down."

The pixies obeyed, dropping Charlie in a heap and buzzing away in six different directions, giggling all the while.

"Oh, Charlie," I said. He looked so sad when he hit the ground, like the frown was permanently chiseled onto his face. I grabbed his elbow and helped him up, but he kept his gaze on his feet. "Come here. Now again, why?"

Charlie's arms hung limp at his sides while I hugged him. "Well, you didn't expect me to stand there while you were falling, did you?"

"If you were smart, you would've asked Uncle Diego for help. Now we're both stuck."

"If *you* were smart, you wouldn't have jumped in the first place, duh." Charlie looked up. "Tio's gonna lose it. You know that, right?"

I frowned. Poor Uncle Diego. In all fairness though, we'd recently spent a lot of time agonizing that he'd become possible dragon food. Maybe it was his turn to worry. "We'll make it up to him when we get back up, but it's not time to stress about that yet. That thing that came out of the well is a genie named Groff, and he got away with the Wheel of Fortune's stones. We're not looking for a way up until we take them back."

Charlie blew a raspberry. "Of course we're not. And of course he is. I guess we can't just wish our way back to the top, huh?" He gestured to the six paths around us. "So which way do we go, then?"

I bit my lip and spun in a circle. Six paths. One hub.

"I don't know," I said. "But are you noticing the same thing I am?"

Charlie studied the ceiling. The ground. The hallways. "What? No exit signs? No arrows? How observant of you."

"Look how this is laid out." I counted the paths out loud, slowly and deliberately. Then I pointed to the ground at our feet. "Six paths, and we're right in the middle of them all. This can't be a coincidence, right?"

My brother wrinkled his brow. "I don't get it."

"Charlie," I said, "It looks like the Wheel of Fortune. And we're standing at the center."

DIEGO

MY HIATUS

Pop quiz.

Your niece and nephew went to fetch some water from an enchanted well and didn't come back. You were supposed to be taking care of them, and you can already think of about ninety-nine ways you failed before you got to Switzerland. You were never supposed to let them out of your sight, and Diego Rosas, you did it again. You're Tio of the Year. What do you do?

I would've jumped into the wishing well for them, where my gut told me they were. My time in the wild gave me this funny intuition, the same way animals flee from their homes hours before a natural disaster strikes.

Only in my case, a tsunami had already hit, and I didn't see it coming. I only saw what it washed away.

Enzo, Pietro, and I spent some time searching the grounds, and the wishing well wasn't there.

Well, maybe it was, but it was impossible to tell based on the growing network of thorns that covered the hills, taunting us. The branches were like the arms of a sea monster, writhing and coiling in on themselves. Enzo described them as a magic far beyond his own. He'd never be able to clear them.

I kicked things for a while, cursing myself. And when I was finished venting, I had an idea.

"Take me to him," I told Enzo, my fists at my sides.

The king didn't have to ask who I meant. He also didn't love my plan, but I didn't either.

"Keep an eye on things here," he instructed Pietro. "If you find the twins, keep them safe. We'll be back."

Pietro did a little salute. "You got it."

After hours of travel, Enzo and I stared up at a tower that reminded me of something out of a dark fairy tale. Vines the color of charcoal clung to beige, rounded cinder blocks. Armored guards circled the perimeter with spears and staves. Some sat mounted on horses that easily could've kicked me into next Friday.

Enzo handed his horse's reins to one of the guards, who guided the steed away from us and secured him to a metal post. "I did keep my word to you and your family. We doubled the guards. We thickened the walls. We strengthened the chains. Nothing gets in—or out—of Florindale Prison without me knowing about it."

Florindale Prison.

A chill scuttled down my spine. Falk sat less than a hundred yards in front of us, sealed away by little more than a brick wall.

"Must be a popular place for birthday parties," I said. "Something tells me you don't throw the bread thieves in here."

"This place isn't for the petty criminal," Enzo said. "It's for the dark sorcerers, illegal dragon breeders, pirates . . ."

I raised a brow. "So people like Zid and that Captain Storm?"

"Zid never tried to breed a behemoth under the city. Ever see the *Godzilla* movies?" Enzo asked with a wink. "And Niraya hasn't sailed halfway across the ocean with my dagger, or anything that belongs to the people of Florindale. Captain Storm wouldn't pocket a grain of sand off our beaches. She may be wanted in other lands, but that's her own business."

I rubbed my chin. "Godzilla dragons and theft from the king. Did both of those things actually happen?"

"Stuff happens every single day here." Enzo drew a sleepy breath. "You sound far too intrigued by the dragon."

"Curious, I guess. It's kind of on brand for me now."

Enzo smirked. "Well, one day, I must take you to the Archive of Mysterious Beasts. Right now we're here to visit our old friend."

He greeted the guards with a nod. All six promptly stepped aside, clicked their staves against the ground, and then took a knee. The gate went up with an eerie screech, revealing the cold, dark maw of Florindale Prison.

"My king," one of the guards said. "Shall we escort you?"

Enzo tapped the guard on the shoulder. "No, thank you." He put on his best game face, the one I used when I was starting a dangerous climb up a formidable mountain. Eyes narrowed. Jaw tight. "I know the way."

The king stepped inside and pried a flaming torch from the grip of a white hand-shaped fixture in the wall. When the hand let go, it melted into the brick and disappeared. Hot orange light warmed the path in front of us, revealing a labyrinth much wider and longer than the tower looked from the outside.

"Stay close," Enzo said. The smell of soggy earth filled my lungs, and tiny little bumps rose on my arms as the temperature dropped beyond the doorway.

Suits of armor bowed as Enzo walked past them. The way the metal screeched and echoed, I could've sworn at least a few of them were empty. I wanted to remove one of their helmets and find out for sure.

I willed myself not to make eye contact with anyone in the cells, remembering that these weren't common bread thieves. Some complained that they were bored and asked if it was tomorrow yet. Others? I swore another was muttering "Rosas . . . Rosas . . ." under their breath, and I picked up my pace.

Magic is terrifying, I thought.

"We're going down seven levels," Enzo said. "Falk is in the lowest level. Alone." He approached a door to a spiral staircase leading us deeper into the earth. My shoulders tightened. Cramped spaces never bothered me. But I had asked Enzo to lead me into a dangerous situation.

We passed several guards, doors, and bowing suits of armor on the way down. Blood rushed in my ears, nearly drowning out my own footsteps.

"Don't worry," Enzo said. "Falk can't hurt you where he is. There's every precaution imaginable down there." He stopped in front of a large door engraved with a fire sign and locked by a series of intricate dials.

Enzo pressed his hand to the fire symbol, and it glowed. The dials whirred, some going clockwise and others going counter, each clicking and stopping at a different time until the door swung open.

I followed Enzo into a narrow space manned by two guards, who opened a second door only after the first closed behind us.

"Your Majesty," one of the guards greeted.

The second entrance concealed a large, round chamber, like a bubble. The room smelled of mildew and was divided in half by a series of bars. On our side of the bars, two more suits of armor stood stone still with spears in hand. If these bowed or greeted the king, I didn't see it happen. I was too focused on the other side of the bars, where Lord Falk sat cross-legged on the ground with his head in his hands and his elbows resting on his thighs.

My attention went straight to his forearm, my hasty signature smudged in black ink. The one that bound me to him. After a year, the lines still hadn't faded away.

"Every day they try to scrub it off him," Enzo said as if he'd read my mind. "To cover it up. But it won't give. It's like the ink is seared into him. Like a shadow stuck to his toes."

"And now he's my shadow."

Falk's gaze remained fixed on the ground. His side of the room had a bucket. Piles of straw and rocks. An empty wall of stone. If I squinted, I noticed little wrinkles in the air between the bars that contained him, like a thin haze.

Enzo crossed his arms. "There's an enchantment in this room. He can't see or hear anything we're discussing right now. He may assume we're in here at any point, but he has no way of knowing for sure."

Metal, stone, and spellwork. Was it really enough? I'd known snakes to charm their way out of some pretty tight cages.

"I wanna talk to him," I said.

Enzo gave me a stern look. "On one condition. Don't provoke."

I said nothing.

Enzo muttered something to the guards. One waved a hand, and the air rippled in front of Falk's cage. I thought of a curtain falling from a window. As soon as the ripples disappeared, Falk looked up, an air of recognition in his eyes.

"Diego Rosas." He grinned then turned to Enzo. "Your Majesty."

My neck prickled at the venom in his voice.

I cleared my throat. "You know something, Falk," I said. "You told me you would always find me. You sent two of your people after me and my family. Next thing I know, my niece and nephew are missing."

"Missing?" Falk frowned. "My, what tragic news. You must be so heartbroken."

"As a matter of fact, I'm furious." I took a step forward, nose to the bars. "What did you do?"

Falk clutched his chest. "What do you mean? This whole time, I've been all on my own, wasting away in this tiny little cage and thinking about how much I miss our games. How could you accuse me of kidnapping those sweet young cubs? A dreadful accusation." He raised his right hand, suddenly much less animated. "On my honor, Mr. Rosas, I had nothing to do with your family's current whereabouts. Ask these guards. And it's too bad. Few have played the game of fortune better than you and your kin. I thirst for one final round."

I rolled my shoulders. That couldn't have been it. He had to know more.

Enzo nudged me. "Remember, gentle."

"I know you're up to something," I said. "And you should know we're all much stronger now. We're stronger as a family, and we know who you are now. We're ready for you."

Falk flashed a creepy half-smile that only used the lower half of his face. His eyes were all predator. "I think you'll find that I'm much stronger, too, Diego Rosas. And I promise you'll learn this much sooner than you think. This humble prison will hardly contain me forever. Are you sure I'm not exactly where I want to be right now?"

Enzo clapped a hand on my shoulder. "We won't accomplish anything more here today. I think we should leave."

Falk picked up a rock and tossed it up and down. "Goodbye, gentlemen. I'll see you soon."

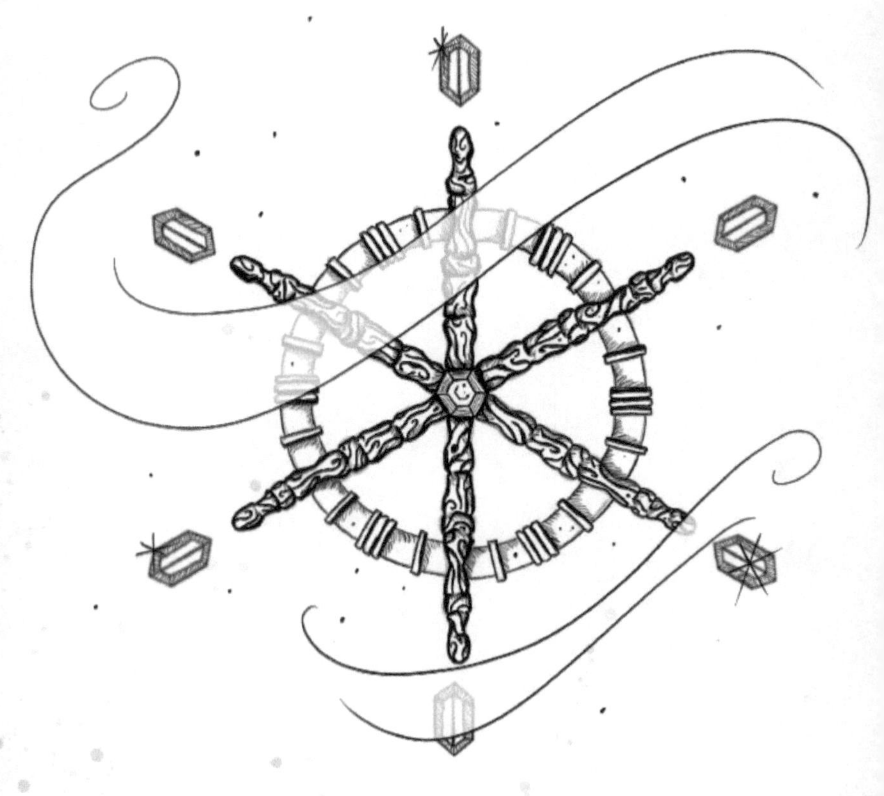

PART TWO

THE BRAMBLE KING

CHARLIE

MONSTER IN A MAZE

It was official: Fortune hated us. The Wheel of Fortune taunted us everywhere we went. All throughout Florindale, we had seen it painted on walls, etched into floors, and I was willing to bet that wasn't all. Now we were literally thousands of feet under the earth, tracing an outline of the wheel in a dark, musty well.

Karina and I had chosen a path at random. I wanted to think there was a correct way for us to go somewhere in the wishing well, a path that Karina and I were "supposed" to follow. But it wasn't long after we started following that tunnel that it forked into three other paths, and I realized it never would've mattered which one we chose. This wasn't any ordinary wishing well. This was a straight-up labyrinth, where wishes came to get lost—and we did too.

Torchlight guided our way, spreading a warm glow along the brick walls and damp ground, where coins and moneys of different nations and cultures glittered at our feet. There were American quarters, silver dollars, euros, gold medallions, and multicolored coins I'd never seen before. I wondered how they all got here. Did they really all manage to roll this far from the opening in the well? Were there other openings back to the surface? How much money was down here?

I picked up a shiny disk of Martian-red metal, on which a shaggy willow dripping with leaves had been engraved on both sides. I wiped the moisture on my shirt and flipped the coin between my fingers. "Hey, Rina, where do you think this came from?"

"We shouldn't touch any of those," Karina answered. "Those are people's wishes, you know."

"You really think touching them erases them or something?"

Karina shrugged. "It's not like I know the magic behind it. But, like, would you want somebody touching your wish?"

"I don't really care."

My sister raised an eyebrow.

"I'm serious," I said. "Okay, so what happens to all the coins we throw in the fountain outside the Tucson Mall? They don't stay there. Somebody collects them and then they go to, like, the bank or the janitor or something. I don't know." I tossed the red coin over my shoulder and listened to it *tink* on the wet brick behind me.

"Or something," Karina repeated. "You don't actually know because you don't see anyone take them out. What if they all just disappear overnight and go somewhere else? Wherever wishes go? What if they all come here?"

I swear I rolled my eyes so hard I almost saw my brain. "Or what if Santa Claus collects them?"

Karina scoffed. "You're so boring. *Zero* imagination whatsoever." She stuck her tongue out at me, complete with the humming noise and everything. "Hater."

The word *hater* signaled that my sister was in a petty mood, one where it was more important for her to win than it was to be the bigger person. So I didn't argue back, and in my mind that meant *I* won. So ha.

"I'm worried about Niraya. And James. And Rosana. And Zid," I said.

"They're strong," Karina said. "They're strong, and so are we. We can handle anything life throws at us, remember?"

"That's just it, Rina. Something feels wrong about all of this. Remember when we learned about the big underground maze? The skating rink, I think it was called?"

"Daedalus's Labyrinth," Rina said. "I remember. Well, the labyrinth wasn't a wishing well, so that's not where we are right now."

"But doesn't it feel wrong? Any time you watch a movie about a maze, there's always some sort of monster hiding in it. Ten times out of ten. I promise you there's going to be a giant spider or the little ghost girl from *The Ring* or like a flying, three-horned, child-eating—"

"Okay, Charlie." Karina clapped her palm over my mouth, sealing the words inside. "You can be done now. You made your point."

I licked Karina's hand, and she jerked it away and wiped it on her pants, a note of sheer horror on her face. "Oh no, I need poison control."

"I'm just saying," I said. "Mazes are never a good thing, and we should be ready in case we see any clowns or anything."

"*Clowns?*" Karina threw her hands up. "Really?"

"Rina, it's not like we know for sure."

She gave me the side-eye and kept walking. "This is a wishing well, Charlie. There are only happy thoughts down here." She skipped, and I could tell she was working really hard to distract herself. "Puppies and duckies and all the ice cream we can dream about. What's your happy place?"

Come to the temple of wishes and thorns.

I froze. "Did you hear it again?"

Karina rubbed her elbows. "It's getting closer."

A lot closer. "Or maybe we are."

"Do we turn back?" Karina's voice was like tissue paper, brittle and feather light.

I swallowed, lowering my voice to match hers. "I won't turn back if you won't."

In the silence between us, I noticed another sound canceling out the quiet all around us, in the walls, on the ground, over our heads. The sound reminded me of tree branches crackling on a dry afternoon. Like skeleton fingers dragging along the brick walls. Like rattlesnakes winding through the desert grounds. And it was coming toward us from the path ahead. Karina and I looked at each other, and I became aware of my heart smacking against my rib cage. Maybe that was a cue for Rina and me to run, too.

"Charlie," Karina whispered, her eyes narrowed. "You jinxed us."

"Oh, man, if it's clowns . . ."

Thick coils of brambles snaked out of the darkness, clinging to every inch of the walls and unspooling from the water. Even the ones that should've been wet looked bone dry. Brown as dirt. Sharp as needles. The ones at our feet slithered and stretched toward us, pushing coins out of the way and creating an eerie jingle through the halls. Some of the branches had become as thick as Tío's torso, and I definitely didn't want to touch the thorns.

I felt like I might've planted roots in the ground, my legs holding all the weight of my fear. Still, my heart told me we needed to see what was ahead. Maybe the thorns were part of a monster that was blocking our path. Karina and I had defeated monsters before, and we could do it again.

Despite what my heart told me, my body pressured me to run the other way before the thorns surrounded us entirely. When one of the branches curled around my ankle like a snake, I kicked and struggled in its hold. "This is not a good thing."

Karina stomped on the branch, the wood letting out a snake-like hiss. As if to take revenge, the vine tightened its grip on me, a single thorn biting through my pant leg and grazing my shin.

Karina stomped on it two more times, finally breaking it with a satisfying *crack*. The part that had my ankle loosened its hold, but it twitched the way a lizard's tail freaks out when it gets detached from the rest of its body. When the vine loosened up enough for me to grab it, unwind it, and chuck it behind me, the most surprising part was that the branch hit a dead end.

A brick wall that definitely wasn't there before, covered in more vines.

"Rina," I said. "The path behind us is blocked."

My sister rubbed her hand along the bricks, tapping them at random. "Where did it come from?"

I yanked a torch out of the wall, ready to burn any vines that came for my ankles again. With my free hand, I checked my leg and was relieved that the thorns hadn't drawn blood. "Something doesn't want us to turn back. Which is stupid. We don't even know where we're going in the first place." I kicked the barrier and shouted into the darkness. "You hear me? We don't even know where we're going."

"I can assure you," a gravelly voice answered, "that you are going in precisely the right direction."

My heart dropped into my stomach. The voice was much closer and louder than I was comfortable with.

When a pair of amber slits glowed in front of us, I shielded Karina and raised my torch.

Here's our monster.

Karina gently brushed me aside and took a step forward.

"Rina," I whispered.

My sister cleared her throat and straightened her back. "Show yourself, please."

She sounded like a legit grown-up.

The thorns and vines wriggled a bit, and the amber slits moved closer. Instead of footsteps, the only sound of movement was distinctly plant-like, reminding me of branches being dragged on dry ground.

Karina and I stood side by side and watched as a full face manifested under the amber eyes. First there was a large, bulbous, gnarled nose. Then a pair of pointy, twisted ears. Everything appeared to be scarred or incredibly wrinkled, but when the figure got closer to the light of my torch, I realized the stranger was made of tree bark. Instead of eyebrows, dry grass clung to his face. Strings of ivy protruded from the top of the stranger's head and under the nose, creating the illusion of hair and a beard.

Below the face, everything was a tangle of branches and thorns. He had clear arms and legs, but he didn't actually walk or seem to use them at all. He just kind of . . . grew . . . crept . . . always being pulled along by the vines and roots attached to the rest of him.

Had I seen this stranger *before* the days when I was introduced to dragons, werewolves, and sea monsters, I probably would've found him terrifying. Rina and I had seen scarier things. Still, I couldn't look away, even though my mom reminded me every single day that staring was rude.

The stranger looked us up and down.

Maybe it's not a monster, I thought. A man made entirely of dry plant life wouldn't want to fight somebody with a flaming torch, right?

Besides, I could tell a lot by looking at somebody's face, and even though this stranger didn't have any human features, I had a pretty good idea he wasn't here to hurt us. He looked more curious. Pained. Sad.

I mean, if *I* were a tree, I'd probably be sad, too. But that's just me.

The plant man took a bow, nearly scraping his gnarled nose on the ground. "I'm pleased you accepted my invitation."

CHARLIE

THE PLIGHT OF THE BRAMBLE KING

The whispers echoed in my memory: *Come to the temple of wishes and thorns.*

"That was you?" I asked. "You invited us to the temple of wishes and thorns?"

The man nodded, a sad grin spreading across his rough, ashen cheeks. "Yes. It was I. Call me Thorne," he said. "The Bramble King."

I squirmed in my shoes. "Uh, nice to meet you."

Karina seemed to be choosing her next words carefully, speaking slowly and deliberately. "Well, we thank you, O King Thorne, for inviting us to your temple." She looked around the tunnel, studying the dried, pointed walls that squirmed all around us. "It's really lovely. You have a beautiful home."

"Thank you, dear one. And now, tell me, noble roses." Thorne wove his hands together, his fingers creeping around each other like vines. "Where is the third one of you? He with the tall, slender bones?"

Oh man. Tio.

Karina elbowed me. "Where's Uncle Diego?" she whispered.

A pang of guilt trickled up my chest, weaving a knot in my throat. Tio was probably back up on the ground, freaking out about not being able to find us . . . having to explain to our mom that he didn't know where we went . . . most likely blaming himself every minute until we got back to him. The poor dude didn't need any more stress in his life without me and Karina disappearing on his watch.

Unless he did something stupid like come down to look for us.

I shook my head. "It's not like I know," I mumbled back to my sister. "I jumped in right after you. Tio wasn't outside with us."

Thorne raised a pointed eyebrow. "You did not bring the tall one with you?"

My heart sped up a few notches, like an alarm. Why was this Thorne guy so interested in Tio?

Karina and I exchanged glances. I really wished she would've been the one to talk, but her eyes were pleading with me to start.

"Our Uncle Diego didn't come down here with us," I said simply. I didn't feel like I owed Thorne an explanation.

Thorne frowned, looking a bit like a dry, splintered puppet—the kind some creepy ventriloquist would use on one of those talent search shows. I could almost hear the wood creaking when he narrowed his eyes. "So I see," he mused. "Perhaps he will accept the invitation at a later time. Wouldn't that be nice?"

"Oh, *so* nice." I elbowed Karina and added, "He sure would love that, wouldn't he, Ka—"

"Why did you invite us here?"

Never in my life have I shut my mouth so quickly. Karina might as well have dropped a grenade for the look I gave her. Thorne made me uncomfortable, but at least I was trying to get along with him. Why did my sister have to go and make it awkward? The silence that followed was thick enough to jump up and down on. I lowered my gaze and pretended to be interested in my shoes, but I couldn't resist glancing up at Thorne's expression, expecting to see World War III on his face.

But instead, Thorne smiled. "I learn of things that happen on the ground, far above and around the well. All the subtle vibrations in the tunnels change when a war begins, and I feel them. I hear people's wishes when they fall from the surface. I can read the roots that unfurl from the ceilings, and understand what happened above to make them this way. I have been like this for ages, and only recently did I hear of the family that defied Lord Falk and tamed the dragon. Even below Earth, you are legends."

Karina smiled. "Thank you. We didn't know we had such a reputation."

"You are mighty," Thorne said. "Young, mighty, and clever. Thus I wonder if you may be able to solve my current predicament."

Rina and I exchanged glances. I had a feeling I knew the predicament, but I also thought it would be super rude to make assumptions. Maybe Thorne was referring to his current form, but maybe he didn't see being made of brambles as a problem at all. Maybe he'd been born that way and never knew any other way of being.

"I'm not sure I'm following," I said.

"But we'd love to listen," Rina added quickly.

Thorne took a deep breath. Every inhalation made the vines around him swell. When he breathed out, they constricted just a little bit. I thought of my old science classes and found myself wondering if he actually breathed in oxygen, or if he breathed it out.

"I have little memory of my mortal life, dear friends. Of life above the well. But I suppose I must've had a long one, because I remember the sun. I remember the days where I felt that I was close enough to hold it in my hands . . . to squeeze the light into a jar like the juice of an orange and share it with the people around me." The Bramble King smiled, and though he didn't have lips, his smile was as real as any grin I'd ever seen. He closed his eyes. "I remember standing on two legs on a sunny day . . . leaning over a particular wishing well and clutching a beautiful red coin, prepared to make the wish of my heart's desire."

"What was your wish?" I blurted.

Karina nudged me. "We talked about this, Charlie. It's not right to ask about wishes."

The Bramble King laughed, rippling the vines around us. I kept a nervous eye on them, willing the thorns not to prick me if they came too close. "Contrariwise, Miss Rosas, I believe sometimes wishes can be much more powerful when they are shared with people you trust. You see, wishes possess a peculiar energy. If you share that energy with people who love you, it grows stronger. I want nothing more than to share my wish with you, friends, but I've forgotten what that was, for I no longer have a heart."

No heart? I supposed that made sense, but the idea still made me sad. And I had no idea how to talk about it. So I settled for a simple, "Oh. I see. So you were human once?"

"Yes. That much I remember. But I never made my wish, you see. Before I could drop my coin, I fell into the well. And I took this cursed form of brambles and roots, never to see the sun, never to touch the snow, to know a human's embrace, or feel the beat of my heart again."

"I'm sorry," Karina said. "That sounds like it's been lonely."

A wayward tear slid down my cheek. I hadn't even been aware of the emotions. I caught the teardrop on my finger and sucked in a breath. I couldn't imagine The Bramble King's curse. Karina and I had only been down here for maybe a few hours, and I already missed the warmth of the sun. As a Tucson boy, I needed sun like a fish needed water. Like wolves need the moon.

"Charlie," Karina gasped.

"I'm fine," I insisted. I was surprised by my feelings, too. I mean, it's not like I was heartless or incapable of empathy, but I'd be the first to admit I wasn't really the feely type. Something about Thorne's story had really plucked my heartstrings. Maybe I was afraid of ending up just like him—cursed to stay in the bottom of the well. Which led me to wonder . . .

"Who cursed you?" Karina asked.

I had a feeling I already knew. And I didn't want to suffer that same fate.

Thorne shook his head. "It was the overlord himself. The man you've already once defied. Falk."

A nervous breath escaped from Karina's lungs.

"I knew it," I said.

I put a hand on my belly. Mom always told me stress was stored in the gut, and that putting a hand there would relieve some of the pressure. She was usually right.

"It's a good thing Falk's in prison then," Karina said.

Thorne smiled. "That is why you bring me hope. You've already defied the overlord once. Maybe you can defy him again by setting me free and ending my curse. There is a special power that exists in this world. There is a stone that rested within the Wheel of Fortune. Surely you know of it." He paused. "There is a stone that negates curses of my nature. You have this power in your possession now, do you not?"

My heart plunged into my stomach. How could I tell Thorne everything that was wrong with this picture?

First, we didn't have any of those stones anymore. A smoky red genie disappeared with them and left us empty-handed, and that was why we were here. In his temple of wishes and thorns.

Second, we could never give it over, even if we found it. The only place where it belonged was on the Wheel of Fortune. With Lady Mirabelle. But I didn't think getting defensive with Thorne was a good idea. I liked him. If I had the orb with me, withholding it from Thorne and keeping him cursed would've been a hard thing to do.

I looked down at my feet. "We don't have it with us. I really wish we could tell you differently."

The vines on the walls writhed like wild tentacles, one even jerking so hard as to slap me in the face, grazing my cheek with a thorn.

"Ow." I stepped back and put my hand up to the wound.

A bit of sap leaked from Thorne's eye. "I see," he said. "I'm so sorry for nicking you, Charlie. I cannot always control the vines. I'm afraid they're growing at an alarming rate. Within the next twenty-four hours, I fear they'll fill this entire network. If only my curse could be ended."

Karina wrung her hands. "I'm sorry we don't have the crystal on us. We really do want to help you. Maybe you know a way for us to get out of the well so we can find you some help in a different way?"

"I do have an idea," Thorne said. "I cannot get you out of the well in my current form, but if you can find a way to break my curse, perhaps I can get us all out of here. I think that maybe there is another solution that may solve my ailment . . . a token of a different kind."

"We'll do it," I said all-too-quickly. "What kind of token are you looking for?"

Thorne's dry lips turned up in a rough smile, releasing clumps of dirt and moss in the wrinkles of his cheeks. "Perhaps you can bring me the ungranted wish I made a long time ago. My heart's desire. I think that maybe if I can remember my heart's desire, I'll reclaim my heart. And if I can reclaim my heart, maybe my curse will end."

An ungranted wish. Perhaps a coin The Bramble King lost somewhere in the underground? As if he'd been reading my thoughts, Thorne nodded.

"Yes. You can bring me the coin I wished on years ago. If it works, I could release us. I would owe you a great debt."

I wrinkled my brow, running through the possible scenarios and questions in my head. I was sure Karina found Thorne's second option to be much better than the first, but she wasn't ready to commit yet. "Looking for any one specific coin down here is like looking for a needle in a haystack, though. How would we ever find the one you're looking for?"

"You'll know it if you see it. The token is one of a kind," Thorne insisted, "a custom craft forged by a dreamsmith in Grimm's Hollow. You shall know it by its crimson hue, true as a rose, and the great weeping duskwood stamped into each side."

Great weeping duskwood.

I'd never heard of a great weeping duskwood before, but if it was anything close to what it sounded like, Thorne's wish wasn't too far away from me at all. In fact, there was every chance I had already held it in my hand.

Karina and I swapped a knowing glance.

"These looks you share?" Thorne said. "You needn't be afraid to ask. The weeping duskwood is the official tree of Grimm's Hollow. As I said before, you will know it if you see it. Of course, the odds are against you. I estimate there are no less than a hundred *billion* coins down here—one for every wish, for every star in the sky. But if virtue won't lead you back to the Wheel of Fortune, perhaps fortune will lead you to my lost wish."

"We'll get it for you," I said. "We've seen it."

Thorne leaned forward, eyes gleaming with interest. "You will help me?"

"Yes," I said. "In fact, we'll be right back. Before we go, though, we have a question. Our friends are missing. Niraya. James. Zid. And the Queen of Florindale, Rosana. Have you seen them? I know I heard Niraya's voice before we fell down here."

Thorne worked his jaw, appearing deep in thought. "No," he said. "You are the first humans I've seen in quite some time."

Karina hung her head. "Oh."

I bent over and made a funny face at my sister. "Hey, chin up, Rina. If we go find that coin and get out of here, I'm sure we'll see our friends again in no time. Right?"

Karina scowled. "Your optimism infuriates me a little." She bopped me on the nose. "But yeah. I guess you're right. Thorne, we'll be back. Just hang in there a little while longer."

As if on cue, the wall behind us crumbled, reopening the path that had been sealed when the thorns attacked us only moments ago. Thorne smiled. "Your hearts are true as diamonds, friends. Please, take your time."

"Take our time?" I scoffed before correcting myself and bowing for The Bramble King. "We'll get that thing back to you in like ten minutes."

Thorne nodded, the roots and vines growing and snaking into the tunnel. I was scared to think he might lose control of them entirely, and that if they grew too thick, they could strangle us down here. We'd never see Uncle Diego or our families again.

"We have twenty-four hours," Thorne said.

KARINA

THE HUNT FOR THE LOST COIN

⋅—◆—⋅

The scent of wet earth filled my nostrils as Charlie and I retraced our steps through the wishing well. We knew we wouldn't need a full day to find a coin we had just held in our hands probably less than three hours ago.

But I had questions. Reservations, even.

"What do you think Thorne's wish was?" Charlie asked, pulling the words right out of my brain. "You think he wanted like a new car, or to be a billionaire? A PS5?"

I rolled my eyes. My brother was such a boy. "Doubt it," I said. "Whatever it is, he thinks it's just as important as those pieces from the Wheel of Fortune. And people go *crazy* over those gems. What if that wish is something a little more destructive? World domination or something. What if Thorne is just like Falk and we're playing right into his hands?"

Charlie flicked a bug off his shoulder and made a face. "Really? You get Falk vibes from that guy? I mean, Thorne's weird, but I don't get the impression that he's half as bad as Falk."

"Less than half can still be pretty bad," I pointed out.

"Aw, come on. Don't make this complicated," Charlie said. "He's *off*, but we don't know that he's *bad*. I say we just give him the coin and leave him alone. He even said he can help us out of here. Then, he stays out of our way, we stay out of his, and we go back to our regularly scheduled lives, whatever that looks like now. We never have to know what he wished on."

Charlie's thinking could be so simple and black-and-white sometimes. He was looking for the easiest way out of here. I looked at this situation and saw a billion complications and ways this could all go wrong. Maybe I was paranoid; I don't know. I did know Thorne didn't deserve the Wheel of Fortune any more than Falk did. But I also knew I didn't want to be stuck down here forever, and that left one simple solution: We had to bring Thorne's coin back to him. I had to swallow my feelings and start thinking just a little more like Charlie.

I sighed. "Okay, you're right," I said. "But even if we find the coin, I still want those gems back. If we lose them forever, I will never forgive myself."

Charlie shrugged. "I'll forgive myself just fine. Hakuna Matata, Rina."

I backhanded my brother's shoulder, knowing he was telling the truth.

As soon as he said, "Ow!" which was ridiculous because I didn't even hit him that hard, a swirl of colored lights zoomed toward me from the depths of the tunnel and whacked me repeatedly on the shoulder.

It took me all of two seconds to realize the six annoying little pixie fairies had come back to assault me with their mischief. They didn't punch all that hard, but they pounded with just enough persistence to boil my blood. I reached up and tried to catch one in my fist, but they scattered and rushed to Charlie's side instead. The lavender one, also the biggest of the bunch, buzzed in front of my face before landing lightly as a feather on the bridge of my nose.

The pixie blew a raspberry at me, flew off my nose, and took a seat on Charlie's shoulder. Before I could make another grab for her, she curled into a little ball and snuggled up on his shirt. The act was so pure and adorable I almost forgot I hated pixies. On top of that, another one sat on his head, and the rest wrapped their tiny arms around his thumb, giving the appearance that he was wearing tiny glow sticks on his finger.

"Looks like those things have a crush on you." My heart softened for the pixies. But only a little bit.

Charlie studied the fairies on his thumb. "Weird," he breathed. "I mean, I know I'm handsome and everything, but—"

"Okay, let's not get crazy here," I said.

"Better be nice to me," Charlie warned. "The little pixies might attack you again. They're protecting me from you." He stuck his tongue out at me and made a nasally *nnn* sound.

I rolled my eyes, wondering what it would take for me to have a tribe of possessive fairies protect me. And when I thought about being protected, I should've been happy, but even the word *protecting* painted a sad, recent memory in my head. I let out a sigh that weighed my shoulders down, and spoke my mind. "I miss our wolves."

Charlie lowered his hand back to his side and nodded. "I do too," he said. "Oliver and Nella. Do you think maybe they're still alive?"

I wasn't ready to answer that. The most I could do was shrug, not because I was indifferent or because I didn't know, but because the probable truth cut too deeply to speak out loud. When we left the base of Mount Blackburn, most of the area was in charred, ashen ruins—a product of Verdoro's fury, or more accurately, of the puppet master who controlled him. Most of the wildlife, from the spiders to the ogre tribe of the area, did not survive. The sad, cold truth was that Oliver and Nella probably didn't either.

In fact, everything we left behind was a mess. In the village of Jericho Harbor, werewolves ran rampant, cursed to transform under the full moon. And all along, I'd had the power to break their curse and help them revert back to their true form. Well—not *me*, exactly. But Uncle Diego's pendant did, and I never did stop asking myself if I was wrong to keep it from them. Failing to help them was the same as cursing them, but I also knew it was too dangerous for any one person to have that pendant.

We also managed to burn down a sacred palace in the snowcapped mountains of Kesterfall. I blame the yetis for that one, but still, when tallying up all the destruction that followed us, it was hard not to feel like *we* were the curse. Like we doomed Nella and Oliver, and we were bound to burn everything else in our path.

Just give us one win, I thought. *Just one. Let's find that coin.*

"You remember what it looks like, right, Charlie?"

"Yup. I know I can find it again if I see it." Charlie slowed his steps, scanning the ground. "And this should be the area, too. Let's look." He sifted through the tiny mounds of coins, brushing them aside with his toe.

I followed my brother's lead. With every sweep of the heel, my foot created ripples of silver and gold. Maybe I was imagining it all, but it really seemed like there were twice as many coins at my feet as there were the first time we passed this spot. Like they'd multiplied during our visit with The Bramble King. "You know something?" I said. "I bet there's more money down here than there is in any bank in the world."

"Or *every* bank. Combined, even." Charlie paused mid-sweep, letting his foot hover above the ground for a minute, and a dangerous gleam sparkled in his eye. "Imagine if we had a way to bring all of this home. We'd be rich forever."

I pictured my brother and myself trudging up to our doorstep, dragging truck-sized sacks full of coins behind our shoulders like Santa's magic bag and shaking them open in the middle of the living room floor. Mom and Jorge would either freak out or celebrate forever. Probably both, and maybe even in that order. The idea made me smile. "We could buy a new house for our family. Somewhere closer to Uncle Diego."

"Or we could quit school." The light in Charlie's eyes grew brighter. "Oh man, I could do some serious shopping with all this dough."

The word *shopping* filled my head with images of my future dream home, complete with a movie theater, a collection of books that would rival the Library of Alexandria, and an Olympic-sized swimming pool. I was pretty sure Charlie was thinking of things he wanted now—clothes, a TV bigger than I was, and a library of movies ready to stream, a juiced up laptop he could play video games on . . . I knew my brother.

Eventually we both got on our knees and scrubbed through the hoard of coins, rattling off our shopping lists to each other to pass the time.

"I want a new dog for each person in our house, and a sweet robot pal that can make my bed and do homework," Charlie said.

"I'll adopt five horses and a llama, and buy my very own ranch to take care of them," I said.

We sifted through a few hundred coins.

"I'm gonna find an electric guitar and a drum set signed by all my favorite bands."

"Hmm, I'll find a huge writing desk that tilts into a drawing table, and then I'll take art lessons and become the next Bob Ross."

We sifted through a few thousand coins, still unable to find even a speck of red.

"I wanna buy my own Nike store and have a basket-ball court built in my name."

"I'll buy lifetime passes to Disneyland and privileges to get in after hours."

We sifted through more coins than we had ever seen in our lifetime. We went back and forth for so long that our lists got a lot less fun, and it was obvious we were running out of ideas. Where in the world was that medallion?

Charlie sat cross-legged on the ground, halfheart-edly picking up coins and tossing them over his shoulder one by one. His eyelids drooped a little, and even all the pixies that had been following us had curled into tiny balls and went to sleep. "I want some new Vans, and I want to eat a twelve-count thing of chicken nuggets. And a soda." He spat out the last word, throwing his coin overhand at the wall for emphasis. "Gosh."

"You don't wear the ones you have. And I just want some chocolate already." I tried to rub the heaviness out of my eyes. I wasn't exactly tired, but I was so bored I could have slept for fun. And it was starting to make us both cranky. "You don't remember what the coin looked like, huh? You forgot already."

With a shake of his head and an exaggerated scoff, Charlie said, "No, I didn't."

I raised an eyebrow. "Describe it to me."

Charlie yawned and covered his mouth with a fist. "Blue—"

"*Nooo.*" I threw my hands up, and my shout caused the pixies to stir in their sleep. "See, I knew it. That's not it at all."

Charlie flicked a copper medal at my leg. "I'm play-ing. Duh."

"I'm officially not in the mood for playing right now." I flicked the coin back at him.

In response, all the little pixies sprang up from their nap, and each started chucking coins of their own at me. I put my arms in an X to shield my face and turned away, wondering if I could use another coin to wish the little pests away. I couldn't even taunt my own brother anymore, and that was the one comfort I had down here.

I was ready to wage full-on war with the little crit-ters when a new voice, raspy and old, called from the dark. "Can you noisy kids cut out that racket down there? I'm workin' over here."

The pixies scattered, leaving us all alone again.

I couldn't immediately identify the source of the voice, but at first I imagined a mobster plucked straight out of an old gangster movie, talking with his hands and shaking his finger at me and my brother. *I'm workin' over here, capisce?*

Charlie and I exchanged a glance. What exactly did work look like in a wishing well?

We listened for footsteps or more voices but only heard the clinking of coins and the soft crackle of the flamed torches on the walls.

"Did you hear me over there?" the voice continued. "Good. Thank you for your silence. Can't get more than two minutes of peace and quiet down here with those pixies loose. Two. Minutes."

Well, at least the mysterious voice and I were on the same page about something.

A puffy body of smoke moved out of the shadows and grimaced at us, shutting down every image I had of an Italian mobster roaming the halls.

Another genie.

She was no Godfather mafioso—she was a cranky receptionist type with a tall silver beehive piled on her head, triangular glasses the color of a jalapeño, and a fiery smudge of lipstick that somehow clung to the lavender cloud of her face.

An enormous fishing net rested over her shoulder, sagging from the weight of the coins stashed inside. She tossed the bag on the ground and gave me a disapproving look. She reached into the holster of her leather toolbelt that served zero purpose given that genies didn't wear pants or even really have legs. From her holster, she pulled a yellow scroll, snapped it open, and studied its contents.

"Two-Euro coin, *Fontana di Trevi*, year twenty-oh-seven, hall three-oh-nine B . . . which one are they talking about?" She raised her gaze to the ceiling and shouted at nobody in particular. "You gotta give me more information, here. Every other wish down here is a two-Euro coin from two thousand seven. I swear they don't pay me enough for these shenanigans. I need another job."

The crabby genie stooped down, inspected a Euro, and then flicked it over her shoulder. The coin clinked into the fishing net, and the genie consulted her scroll again. "Peso, Fuente de Cibeles, twenty-thirteen. Hall three-oh-nine B . . . give me a break already." She pushed her glasses up her nose and sneered. "What are you kids lookin' at? Can't you see I'm workin' ova here?"

"What kind of work are you doing?" Charlie asked.

"What does it look like I'm doing? I'm prepping wishes for the factory line. Wanna slow me down even more?"

I swear this lady was crankier than my Nana Imelda. But her words *did* pique my interest, and I considered them as she bent over and picked up a dull one-peso coin for her net.

"Factory line?" Charlie continued.

The genie sighed and put her hands on her hips, disturbing the smoke below her belt. "Yes, the factory line, where all the wishes go for inspection and processing. I don't make the rules; I just bring in the coins. Any other questions?"

Charlie raised his hand. "I actually have all the questions. What do you mean by inspection and processing?"

The genie launched into a long speech that might have been an actual explanation, but by the sheer volume and biting tone of her voice, I suspected it was more of a cranky tirade about Charlie asking so many questions. I don't know. I can't actually say because I stopped listening. I was too busy reading her scroll, which was labeled the *Map of Dreams* and contained a whole list of coins and denominations both new and familiar to me. Yen. Cents. Pounds. Rupees. Ducats. Gold. Some were as recent as this year, and others were older than America.

And I wanted to know where all of them were going.

I needed to know because when the genie swung the fishing net over her other shoulder, a shining glint of strawberry red flickered toward the bottom of her pile.

My heart stopped for a second then sped to a gallop.

"There," the genie finished. "Are you finally done asking stupid questions yet? Can I work in peace now? Is that okay with you? Good. Now go play somewhere else and shoo." She rolled up her scroll, waved it in our direction, and then turned her back to me.

I tugged on Charlie's sleeve, put a finger to my lips, and then jabbed my finger toward the fishing net. *She has the coin*, I mouthed.

It took my brother a few seconds to understand and to connect my lip movements to what I was trying to show him, but I knew he had caught on when he let out a yelp. When I hushed him, he clapped his hands over his mouth, eyes wide as plates.

"Ma'am?" I called, the word tumbling from my mouth before I could stop myself. But I had to know if this was worth a try. "Could we possibly see one of the wishes that's going to the factory?"

"No," the genie roared. "No kids in the factory, no touching the wishes, no disturbing production, no nothing for you. So shoo. Shoo!"

When the genie was out of earshot, Charlie slumped back against the wall. "Well, that failed."

"Did it, though?" I asked. "Did it fail? We know where the coin is now. We know where it's going."

"She *super* doesn't want us to follow her," Charlie said.

I gave Charlie the side eye. "And you care?"

"Absolutely not. Are you kidding me?" Charlie put a fist in the air. "That cranky lady's leading us to a wishing factory. This we've gotta see."

CHARLIE

I own it: I'd make a terrible bank robber. I wasn't blessed
with whatever gene there is that makes people sneaky.
Even when I wear socks, my footfalls sound like pedals on
a bass drum. I've never been compelled to sneak out of my
bedroom window or try to ditch class or anything, but I did
stage a mini-heist to steal a cookie from Mom's sacred cupboard one night. There might as well have been a spotlight
and a rock-and-roll drummer following me all the way to
the kitchen, because as soon as I peeled the cupboard open,
Mom appeared, hair in rollers and eyes red with sleep.

Needless to say, there was never a next time.

So it followed all the logic of my life that I felt incredibly awkward trailing the angry purple genie to the wish

factory. I knew she was going to turn around and scream at me to *shoo!* I took careful steps to make sure I wasn't stepping in places that would jingle the coins on the ground or make audible ripples in the water, but I'm just not discreet. Unlike Karina. She could probably find a way to swipe a pair of sunglasses right off someone's face without them noticing. That's how sneaky she is.

The genie complained to herself the whole time, grumbling about coins that looked alike, about the humidity in the well, about me and Karina asking her so many questions earlier, about nothing at all . . . so it surprised me to learn her real name when we reached the factory.

The genie veered left at a fork in the tunnel, and Karina and I pressed our backs against the wall and waited for her to disappear. In the distance, hums and whirs, clicks and clacks, and all kinds of bangs echoed down the hall, threading with the jangling of coins and tiny splashes of water. The smell of boiling metals hung in the air. The factory awaited.

And a male voice sounded, "Daisy, our top collector. Welcome back."

Daisy the Crabby Genie.

We heard the fishing net hit the ground, rattling all the coins, and Daisy answered, "Payment?"

"Why, not so fast, Daisy," the other voice said. I couldn't see who was speaking, but whoever it was, his singsong voice reminded me of a really happy nurse—the kind who makes a game out of eating vegetables. "You have the joyous privilege of training the new girl on sorting today. Lucky you."

A long, airy sigh trailed down the hall. "Yeah, lucky me. Come on then, new girl."

For another few minutes, Karina and I didn't hear another voice, so we followed the hall and tiptoed into the wish factory.

My jaw dropped. We'd entered a room twice the size of an IKEA or a Costco, or even a concert hall. Inside was an impossible labyrinth of water wheels and stone aqueducts pumping streams of water, vine-laced walls, and a series of gears, levers, and pulleys manipulating the room. And suspended in the center of it all, the world's biggest lens and the world's biggest cereal bowl hung from a network of braided vines. As far as I could tell, the water flowed into three separate streams, each of which ran out of the factory chamber and continued into a separate part of the wishing well. Somewhere deeper.

This well was absolutely infinite.

All above us, genies hovered around and poured coins into buckets and tubes. Dwarves and little green men I'd never seen before pulled levers, made notes on parchment, and called orders to one another.

This was like a cross between a water park and Willy Wonka's factory. Except this was a sad Wonka factory—one where adult America threw up on Willy's instructions to let a smart kid named Charlie run the place.

"Speed it up, airheads," a cranky dwarf barked from a walkway over our heads. "Or no one gets paid."

Suddenly I missed the happy nurse voice guy.

"But we're so bored," a bright-blue genie complained. "My bones hurt."

"Pah. You haven't got any bones, airhead."

I elbowed Karina, my eyes searching the factory *Where is Waldo* style. Somehow, we'd already lost Daisy in the maze of water tubes, genies, dwarves, and gears. She might as well have vanished into thin air. With a prickle of concern, I wondered if that was something she could do. "We've gotta find that coin."

Karina gathered her hair into a ponytail, putting on that famous Rosas concentration stare. "Any good ideas? We're not even supposed to be down here, and this place is crawling with workers."

She had a point. We stood out like red M&Ms in a bag of trail mix.

Instinctively, I reached for an orange vest hanging from a peg on the wall. Inscribed on one of the pockets, the name BOB stared back at me in white thread, and a helmet, goggles, and leather belt hung from the peg below. I thrust the vest into her hands. "Here. We're gonna have to blend in with the workers. Oh and look, donuts!"

Karina took the vest and dangled it by one finger. "Can I not be Bob?"

I grabbed the vest on the peg next to it then crammed a chocolate donut into my mouth.

"Well, it's either Bob or Spike," I mumbled.

Wrinkling her nose, Karina slipped the vest on over her shirt. "Do we really wanna blend in here?"

I wrapped Spike's tool belt around my waist, having to tighten it by at least a foot. Above our heads, a dwarf screamed for everyone to stop slacking and work harder. "We can turn around whenever you want," I said. "You want to get the coin."

Thankfully, the helmet wasn't as heavy as it looked, but seeing Karina in an overgrown hardhat and a pair of thick plastic goggles, I understood what a stretch it was to believe we could actually blend in down here. We still looked nothing like dwarves, genies, or whatever other creatures lived in the well. Karina and I were the archduchess and the crown prince of Humansville.

By the hopeless expression on Karina's face, she knew it too. "Okay, here goes nothing," she sighed. "Just keep your head down, Charlie."

I pointed my nose at my toes and followed Karina up a stone staircase. "It's *Spike.*"

"I swear if you start calling me Bob . . ."

I smirked. "Bobriana? Bobette?"

I couldn't see her face, but Karina probably rolled her eyes. One day they were gonna roll right out of her head like bowling balls.

"There's Daisy," she said.

Carefully, I lifted my chin and followed Karina's gaze, past a genie who poured from a bag of glittering dust and stirred it into the water stream, past a dwarf who surfaced from the water with a scuba mask and a net full of everyday objects like sunglasses and car keys, past a woman who controlled a lever and changed the speed of the water flow. Above a narrow stone walkway, Daisy and a bright-pink genie hovered around, tipping coins onto a large, stone disk the size of a wagon wheel.

"Okay." Daisy sighed. "This here is a wish load. It's supposed to represent many places, many timelines, and many kinds of requests." She picked up a penny and slid it under a lens. "This is from a New World child, four years old, metro. Tossed in Bethesda Fountain one week ago. *I wish for a pony.* Bad. You throw this in the *no* stream. Got it? Think you can do it yourself now?"

The pink genie wrung her hands. "Oh, I don't know. Why is it a no for the pony? I'm not sure I fully understand yet—"

"Great. I'll be going home then. Happy first day." Daisy turned around, and I swore she looked directly at me.

I lowered my head and tried to look busy, hand on a lever and making mechanical noises with my mouth.

The pink genie spoke again. "But um, where is the no stream? Where does it go?"

Daisy clapped a hand to her forehead. "That's the no stream. It goes to secondary review. If secondary review says no, it either goes to the melting pot for reforging or it gets spit back out of the well for someone else to claim or do their laundry. Yes wishes go to inspection, record-keeping, then to bottling and shipping. Got it? Great. Bye."

"Can you show me just one more example, please? I'm confused."

Daisy sighed again, louder and longer than ever. She slid a gold coin under the lens. "Florindale Square, two days ago, dwarf of indeterminate age. *I wish for a baby dragon of my own.* Fine, whatever. Probably a kid, thinks he knows what he's getting himself into. He can have a dragon. We aren't responsible for any damages." She flicked the quarter into the yes stream. "Okay, bye."

Karina and I watched the "yes" coin float down the tube until the stream carried it through the wall. A neon sign above that tube read *Wish Processing.*

With that, Daisy hovered away like a motorized ghost, speeding out of the factory in a blink before her colleague could ask any more questions.

"This place really needs to work on their training," I muttered.

Karina put her hand over her heart. "That poor girl. Should we offer her some help? At least until we can get the red coin in our hands? We know it's somewhere in that pile."

I scratched my head. "Do you understand the job now?"

"I mean, from what I gathered, all we do is read the coins and decide yes or no. Either way, somebody else reviews it after so it's not a lot of pressure. I think it'll be kind of cool, don't you?"

"Okay. I'm right behind you," I said.

After watching Daisy for two seconds, I understood nothing. Why was it that a little girl couldn't have a pony, but when somebody asks for a dragon, their wish goes in the yes stream? By that logic, nobody could wish for a dog, but maybe they could wish for a flying alligator. How did that make sense?

By the time we got to the pink genie, she was an anxious, tear-streaked mess, sifting through the coins and letting them fall back onto the stone disc. I truly felt sorry for her. Daisy wasn't nice to her at all.

"Hi there," Karina said, using her sweetest *oh poor baby* voice. "How's your first day going?"

I gave Karina the eye, hoping she would remember she wasn't supposed to sound like a sweet twelve-year-old girl. After puffing up my chest, I introduced myself in the huskiest, gruffest voice I could manage. "Uh, good day. I'm Spike and this here is Bob. Working hard or hardly working, eh?"

The pink genie wiped her eyes, blending a dark smudge of mascara into the smoke that made up her body. "Oh. I'm Cloud. I'm working, it's just that I don't really know what to do, and my trainer just left me here. I'm so sorry."

Karina cleared her throat and spoke with a deeper voice. "We'll make sure we have a talk with Miss Daisy about her training methods."

Cloud didn't look very relieved. "Oh, I hope I didn't just get her into trouble on my first day. Truthfully, I'm having second thoughts. Do you think there's anything over in record keeping? I think I would feel more comfortable there."

Karina and I looked at each other, stalling.

"Well . . ." I drawled.

"So . . ." Karina raised an eyebrow. "You know what? We'll look into it. Take the rest of the day off, Cloud. We're more than happy to cover your workload today."

Cloud bowed. "Thank you so much."

"Of course." I returned Cloud's gesture.

When Cloud hovered away, I considered the setup in front of me. The large stone disc and the thick lens suspended above it. The two streams of water pumping in opposite directions. With a deep breath, I reached for a silver coin and slid it under the lens, hoping I could learn as I go.

When I peered at the coin through the glass, something about it had changed. A block of flowery text hovered just above it, like a golden hologram.

I wish I never had to clean my room again.

Russell, age 9, Buckingham Fountain.

"Okay." Karina peered through the glass. "See how we can read the wish now? This was made by a nine-year-old boy who doesn't want to clean his room anymore. This is a good one. What do you think about this one, Spike?"

I did a double-take. "Me? What do *I* think?"

"Yes."

In a few seconds, the weight of the world fell on one tiny little silver coin. How was I supposed to make the sole decision on whether or not he should ever have to clean his room again? Sweat slicked my palms. I was pretty sure I'd made this exact same wish before when I was his age. Heck, I probably made this wish a few days ago. What kid hasn't? I hate cleaning my room.

"I say heck yeah, man." I pushed the coin toward the *yes* stream. "Because cleaning is boring and playing video games is fun. Duh."

Before I could tip the coin into the stream, Karina swatted my hand and slammed the silver coin flat on the disc. "No."

"Ow!" I complained, more annoyed than hurt. "What'd you do that for?"

"Because people have to be careful what they wish for," Karina said. "Sure, cleaning is boring. Cleaning *your* nasty room is probably the worst. But we don't know how granting this wish will actually change this boy's life. What if he never learns responsibility and he can't get a job? And he lives with his parents forever?"

Leave it to my sister to throw all the responsibility on me, and then come up with a million reasons to fight me.

I shrugged. "Well, it's Russell's wish. Would that really be so terrible, having his parents cook for him forever? Free rent and all that?" I dragged the coin back toward the yes stream again. "I say yes."

Karina thumped the back of my hand, her blade of a nail leaving a mark. "Wait. But what if some other awful thing happens, and he becomes homeless so he never even has a room to clean? Or what if he dies tomorrow?"

My jaw dropped. "Dang, Rina. That's awful."

"Well, he'd technically never have to clean his room again. It'd be all our fault." Karina chucked the coin into the no stream. "No. And that's final."

I clapped my hand to my forehead. "If we're going to say no for Russell, we might as well say no for everybody. Because what if something awful happens?" I said in a mocking voice. "You're being a Negative Nancy. Er, uh—Negative Ned, Bob. What about secondary review? They can always overturn us."

Karina jerked on my sleeve and pointed to a red smoky blob floating in the distance. "Look. There's Groff, the one who took the Wheel of Fortune stones."

I blinked, watching the smoke figure take the shape of a floating man. "Are you sure? There could be a hundred red genies down here."

"I'm positive." She put on that infamous Rosas stare, pointed and unyielding. "That's him."

I nodded. "Then let's go get him."

Karina looked down, the Rosas stare melting into a frown.

"Rina?" I cringed. "*Bob.* Why are you making that face?"

"Because we can't both go after Groff. We have two tasks to accomplish now. We have Thorne's wish to find, and we have to get the crystals back. We know the coin is somewhere around here, but Groff . . ." Karina pointed to the genie again with her elbow. He oozed toward a dark hallway, one of probably a million in this network.

A cold weight settled in my stomach. "Don't you say what I think you're about to say."

Karina swallowed and put her foot down. "We have to split up. I'm going after Groff, and you need to stay here and find the red coin."

My lungs deflated, and I fell into a slumped posture. "You said it." I took off my helmet for a second and clawed my fingers through my hair. "This is going nowhere good. We have no idea how huge this labyrinth really is, and we still don't know what else actually exists in this world. The whole time we were in Kesterfall, we never split up. What if we get horribly lost and we're never able to find each other again?"

Karina didn't say anything for a minute. Maybe I'd actually changed her mind.

"Am I right?" I added for emphasis. "Say yes."

With those three words, Karina snapped out of her silence and said, "Then at least we'll know we tried. It'll be on me."

Seriously? "Not the response I was going for. If we get lost . . . How would either of us explain it to Tio? To Mom and Jorge?"

"How would we explain it if the wrong person gets the Wheel of Fortune and the world ends tomorrow? Hmm? Who would we have to explain anything to?"

I could see I had already lost the argument and that my sister wasn't going to change her mind. But I made one last attempt and said, "I'd still be here. I would understand. We'd still be familia no matter what. We don't have to do this. You think it's our responsibility, but it's really not."

All I ever wanted to do was rescue Tio from the dragon and go home and eat Oreos. We did exactly what we were supposed to do already.

"Charlie, you don't know that," Karina said, dropping our pseudonyms. "I really feel like we're supposed to do everything we can here. And as for us still being familia, you don't know that either. What if the Wheel of Fortune changes our reality and we aren't brother and sister anymore? Or what if the Wheel erases our lives completely so that neither of us exist? Have you thought about that?"

"Yes, I have," I said hotly. No, I hadn't. "But . . ."

"But what?" Karina shot back.

But I'm afraid.

Out of pride, I couldn't bring the words from my heart to my lips. I've never really been able to admit when I was afraid. Nervous, maybe. But fear was a lot more difficult for a Rosas to own up to. Not because we didn't feel it, or that we believed it was a bad thing.

We're just taught to break through it somehow, and the best way I knew how to do that was to pretend it wasn't there. I shook my head as if to dump out all that fear, curled my hands into fists by my side, and said, "But nothing. Leave, then. If we never see each other again, then it was nice knowing you, Rina."

"Charlie, wait."

"Nope." I turned my back to her. "Go on, then. I hope you get your wish or whatever. Because for me, this was never about the stupid Wheel of Fortune, you know. This was about wanting to be on an adventure with you. *You* cared about the Wheel all this time. And I guess you care about it more than your family. It's fine. I'll just be the same with that stupid red coin."

I picked up a dime and dropped it on the stone.

I wish I had more friends.

Riley, age 12, La Joute.

"I bet you want me to say no to this one too, huh?" I said.

But Karina didn't answer. She was already gone, and so was the genie.

She left me all alone.

KARINA

DORIS AND BOOGIE

The thorns and vines in the well had spread like wildfire since Charlie and I first entered, sealing the route from which we came. I wasn't sure how long we'd been here, but I worried about our twenty-four hour window to find Thorne's coin. I had no watch or phone, and without sunlight, we had no way to track our time.

Please, Charlie, I thought. *Find that coin.*

And maybe forgive me, too.

Splitting up from him wasn't an easy thing to do. All this time, we'd never been apart. We battled werewolves and yetis together. We faced Falk together. And I knew I'd made a risky decision. If I turned back, not only would I lose Groff, but I'd have no idea how to find my way back to the factory room. This maze could swallow me whole, and Charlie would never know.

Uncle Diego would never know.

Mom would never know.

I missed her questions. Her food. Her stories. Even when they were meant to scare me, like La Llorona.

And I wished Niraya were here. She would've gone after the genie or the coin in a heartbeat. She never would've wanted my brother and me to split up. We were stronger together.

Enzo even made us promise to stick together, and now I'd broken the deal.

I wiped grime off my face. This place was taking a toll on my hygiene. I couldn't wait for my next shower.

We will see you next week, Mama, I thought.

But first, Groff.

When I thought the red genie might never stop moving, he finally picked a room: Wish Processing 1, according to the floating sign above the door. The problem was that this was a wooden door the size of my house, chained and padlocked and covered with brambles. Not a problem for a genie that could pass through any surface at will. A big problem for a human Karina Rosas who definitely couldn't do the same.

Groff passed through the door with a soft little *swish,* and I followed right behind and rattled the door a bit. I gave the padlock a good yank. I jangled the chains. I kicked the hinges. And ultimately, I slumped against the wall and lowered my head to my knees.

I lost Groff again. I know exactly where he is, and I can't get to him.

I picked up a holographic coin and chucked it against the wall. I'd never had a stronger wish for superpowers.

Superpowers.

A dark thought crossed my mind.

What if I turned back, found the wish factory again, made my own wish, and tossed it in the *yes* stream myself?

I rubbed my chin. I could wish for the ability to walk through doors. To break chains with my bare hands. Maybe invisibility. And while I was at it, I could throw in some bonus wishes. I'd wish the Wheel of Fortune was whole again and that only Lady Mirabelle could use it. I'd wish Lord Falk could never escape from Florindale Prison. I'd wish Charlie and I could travel with Uncle Diego whenever we wanted—without the danger—and Mom and Jorge could come too. I'd wish for a new puppy and all the books I wanted and—

And this wasn't right. I could throw a hundred coins into the *yes* stream and I would never fix my problems by wishing them away. No matter how careful I was, there would always be another loophole somewhere. Another wish to be made.

The padlock taunted me from the door. The contraption was so small, too. The kind I'd put on a secret diary—not a huge wooden door.

Think, Rina. The door is right in front of you. You just need to find a way in.

I stood, yanked a pin out of my hair, and marched up to the door.

"I'm onto you, stupid genie." I jammed the hairpin into the padlock and wiggled it around, conscious of the fact that I had zero experience picking locks. All I knew was it looked super easy in movies.

But lock-picking was just another one of those things the movies lied about, because as much as I shimmied and twisted the hairpin, it did not want to be in the padlock. In fact, in only a few seconds I'd snapped the pin into two pieces and was left holding half of it while the other remained stuck in the lock.

I kicked the door and huffed under my breath. The only thing left for me to do was to wait here until Groff came back out. If he even came back this way.

"Bob!"

A tall, clumsy sort of figure in a hard hat and a vest came lumbering down the hall, and I quickly lowered my head and pulled the neck of my shirt up to conceal the bottom half of my face.

"Uh, hi," I said in my deepest voice.

I realized with some alarm that the figure who approached me was an ogre, just like the ones I'd seen in Kesterfall. *Not these things again.* The ogres in Kesterfall were terrifying, eight-foot tall brutes who carried dart shooters and loved to throw things around. They also threw a massive fit when I wouldn't play with them. Though I supposed that meant they had a soft side somewhere deep down, I wasn't really in a position to test that theory.

The ogre spread his arms out, expecting a hug.

I stepped back and put my arms up in an X in front of me. "Hey, uh . . ." I snuck a look at his name tag, sure I was misreading it. "*Boogie.* I'd give you a hug, but I think

I might be contagious." I pretended to cough. "That's why I'm covering my face."

Boogie scratched his head, not bothering to remove his helmet first. "Oh. Okay. I'm sorry." He pronounced it *sowwy*. "I tink da genie flu is still going awound. Say, Bob, your hair looks kinda diffewent."

I twisted a strand around my finger. The pink highlights were starting to fade. I knew nothing about Factory Bob, but I doubted he was a hot-pink highlight person. I cleared my throat. "I, uh, dyed it," I said.

Boogie grunted. "Oh. Dat's cool. Da blue looks good."

Blue? As big as all their heads were, ogres didn't seem too bright. "Thanks, Boogie," I said. "I actually have a question. Do you have the key to get in here? I seem to have lost mine, and I don't want to be late for work."

"Weally? I didn't know you was in Pwocessing now," Boogie said.

My heart quickened a few paces. *How much does Boogie know about Bob?* I figured it was probably best to say as little as possible before I blew my cover. "Yep. I'm just as surprised as you are."

"I lost my key again, too." Boogie stepped up to the door. "But I'm afwaid if I tell them, I'll get in twouble." With that, he seized the padlock and ripped it off the door with one tug. The chains fell away, and the vines slithered apart to clear the door. Boogie tossed the broken padlock over his shoulder and opened the door. "We can go inside now."

The padlock thumped my hard hat then bounced onto the ground. I kicked it aside and followed Boogie through the doorway.

"Thank you," I whispered.

The room ahead was smaller than the door led me to believe. I'd been expecting another wish factory. Instead, this area reminded me of my dentist's waiting room, complete with a water cooler, all kinds of weird plant life, and a receptionist: a tall elf woman in big square glasses, scribbling notes behind a desk. A tube of water passed over our heads, and I watched as it deposited a single coin into a large gold cauldron in the corner of the room. What surprised me the most was the fact that it didn't dump any water along with it.

The elf woman stood up and made her way toward the cauldron, peering at me and Boogie out of the corner of her eye. "Good day." Her gaze lingered on me much longer than I was comfortable with. "Checking in for work?"

Boogie waved. "Hi, Doris. Yes, we's going to work."

I looked at Boogie. "I forget," I whispered. "Do we have to sign in?"

The ogre nodded and took out a plastic square he kept in his vest. "You hafta slide your worker card with Dowis."

My stomach tightened. "Uh-oh."

The elf woman reached into the cauldron, plucked out the newly deposited coin, and made some notes on her clipboard. "You don't have your card, hon?"

I pretended to feel around my vest. "I must've lost it recently. It's been a rough day."

Doris slid Boogie's card and handed it back to him, along with the coin she had just taken from the cauldron. "Here's your wish, Boogie. As for you, Bob?" She clicked her tongue while she consulted her clipboard. "I don't see you on the schedule today, but that's okay, hon. We'll just have you sign in here before you go inside, and the boss will follow up with some instructions later."

I nodded, sweat coating my forehead. This whole operation was a time bomb. Sooner or later, somebody else was going to find out I wasn't *Bob*, and this whole tapestry would unravel in my hands.

But as long as I got the crystals and Charlie got the coin before everything went wrong, I couldn't care less.

"Just gonna need you to sign here." Doris rifled through the sheets on her clipboard and passed it to me, along with a good old-fashioned quill. She blew a large bubble with her gum and studied her fingernails, lavender with holographic runes.

I took the quill. "Go on inside, Boogie."

Boogie scratched his head. "You sure?"

"Yep. I'll be okay."

"M'kay. It's good to see you, Bob."

"You too, Boogie."

As the ogre disappeared behind the next door, I scratched a fake signature on Doris's clipboard. A swirly capital B, a tiny cursive o, and a jagged ugly swoosh back through the whole thing. Good signatures weren't supposed to be legible.

I handed the clipboard back to Doris. "Thank you."

She peered at me from over her glasses. "Mhm, you're welcome, dear. Let me get your temporary badge." She tore the page off her clipboard and fed it into a slot in the wall: *Inhuman Resources.* "Strange day all around," she said. "We're so much busier than usual, and then there's all these thorns everywhere. Must be something in the water."

I hummed under my breath, unsure how to respond. "So weird."

Doris walked behind her desk and handed me a sticker with a gold cauldron on it. "Here you go, dear. Have a good day at work."

I slapped the sticker on my vest and booked it for the door. "Thanks."

The next room was a lot more like what I'd been expecting, but my imagination still didn't match reality.

It didn't even come close.

NIRAYA

What can I say? I'm a pirate. We're not exactly known for our honesty.

"This is dishonest," Rosana said. "I'm having second thoughts. Tricking people into thinking we've gone missing is a horrible thing to do, and speaking from experience, Enzo's not going to stop looking. He probably has the Rosas family involved, and I just don't like this. But I digress."

I did a little hair toss, one hand on top of my hat. "Then we're just going to have to stay ahead of Enzo. Trust me, Rosana. It's safer that they believe we're missing. Safer for them."

Zid put his foot down. "Harrumph! Captain Storm, you will address Her Majesty as Queen, and I agree with her."

"Zid, my dear, there's only one queen on these waters." I tugged on the collar of my jacket, the leather soft on my fingers. Never mind the fact that we'd already been off the water for a while and venturing deep into the heart of Malumbra. I smirked at Rosana. "No offense."

"That's treason. Disrespect. Sheer villainy, I tell you." Zid swung a fist in front of him. "Niraya Storm, I swear this is the last time I accompany you on your horrid escapades. When we return to Florindale, I boycott you. I strike your name from my memory!"

I raised an eyebrow. "On your honor?"

James turned on his heel, stopped, and directed his famous, handsome little scowl at the group. "Next one of you to question my lady will feel the wrath of my hook." He waved his arm in the air, a rusty metal appendage protruding from his jacket sleeve. "Any questions?"

"You, sir, are hardly more intimidating than a wee newborn Pegasus." Zid held his hands about a foot apart to emphasize the length of his imaginary pet.

As much as I appreciated the timeless banter between Zid and James, I rolled my eyes. "Didn't a Pegasus give you a nasty bump on the head one day, Zid?"

Zid narrowed his eyes at me. "Harrumph!"

I cleared my throat. "Before we proceed, I need your word. Iron bound. On your honor, you will not attempt to contact Enzo or the Rosas family. We will only put them in greater danger if you do. This is *our* task, understood?"

Zid tugged on his beard. "They would want to be involved. Why the soft spot for the younglings, Storm?"

I fidgeted with one of my bracelets, a braided leather cord secured with a wooden bead. *Because they feel like family. Because Gran's gone, and it's up to me to carry the legacy of the woman who sailed the* Burning Lotus. *Because . . .* "Because it's the honor code."

"Maybe Niraya's right. Maybe they shouldn't be part of this," Rosana said. "I don't like it, but I understand it. Enzo needs to be in Florindale right now. Especially the way Falk's been behaving. You all didn't see him before we left. One minute he's pacing like a caged tiger. The next he's way too calm. Smug. The guards won't say it, but they're spooked. They need Enzo there. We'll be most helpful doing our part here."

A light gleamed in James's eye. "And the Rosas crew . . . the lads and lass deserve their rest. The fight with Falk is sure to have poked some holes in their sails. Asking them to remain a part of this would be a cruelty."

"The wildlings will always be a part of this," I said. "Of that I'm sure. Karina, Charlie, and Diego are more than capable, but it is not our place to meddle with their lives." I pulled a compass out of my pocket and flicked the trinket open. "Instead, let Fortune be their guide, and we shall all meet again in due time. Perhaps soon."

"Harrumph." Zid huffed through his nose. "Let's just get on with it, sea dogs. Lead us to Wyvern's Keep so we can finish this once and for all."

"Tame those wild waters in your head, dear Zid. Be patient. Before the wyverns, we need to visit an old friend of mine. There's a boy from my childhood who has something we need."

James's jaw dropped. "Boy. From your childhood?"

"Ha!" Zid ground his knuckles into his hips. "Ho, that's rich! Jamesy, are you feeling well? Because you look a little green, sea dog."

"Belay your yappin'," James growled.

I put an arm around James's shoulder. "The boy in question," I said, "is Jasper Livingstone."

James frowned. "Jasper Livingstone? You mean—"

"The Wraith," Rosana finished. "Jasper Livingstone is a *wanted man* in many places, Captain Storm. You know he stole one of the bells from Clocher de Pierre long ago?"

"Impressive, no?" I said. "Livingstone has his ways, and I suppose he also has his reasons. I'm not saying they're always right. But if you're concerned with catching outlaws, you might as well hand me to the queen of Malumbra while we're here."

Rosana narrowed her eyes. "What do you mean?"

I flicked my wrist in the general direction of a large tree, where a thick, crinkled sheet of parchment had been tacked to the trunk. Despite the fact that the artist had made my lashes too short and my nose too big, there was no mistaking the face. For me, it was like looking in a mirror.

"Wanted for theft." Zid blinked, processing his own words. After a minute, he shrieked, "Really, Storm?"

"Pirate, remember? Thievery is in the contract. I only steal from people who truly deserve it, but—"

"But you're a wanted woman on this island?"

James scratched the back of his head. "You failed to mention that minor detail to me, m'lady."

"That's because you just said it perfectly yourself, Jamesy." I gave his cheek two quick pats. He'd recently shaved for the first time in ages, leaving his face smoother than a windless night on the Joringel Sea. "It's a minor detail."

Rosana tilted her head back. "Then what are we doing here?"

"*You all* are going to wrangle some wyverns," I said. "That's why sweet Zid is here—to lend his expertise in befriending strange and terrible creatures."

Zid scoffed. "And you, Storm?"

"With Lady Fortune's grace, I shall tap into *my* expertise. I'm going to play cards with The Wraith."

"Why are you going to play cards?"

"Because Jasper has something we need." I patted the map in my pocket. "And before we make our journey, we must gather our assets."

"Like the Rosas family," Zid grumbled.

I yanked the map out of my pocket, rolled the paper into a tube, and whacked Zid on top of the head. He knew I adored the Rosas family—Charlie and Karina, the strongest, most resourceful, clever younglings I'd ever known, and Diego, the man who tangoed with dragons. People were already telling their stories in Florindale Square, and there would be more. But in the heist I had planned, I knew there was a great chance we wouldn't all survive. I refused to put the Rosas family in harm's way.

I explained my plan several times as we navigated the winding roads of Malumbra. Our timing would be vital. James and the crew had to free the wyverns just around the time that I bested Jasper Livingstone in a good ol' fashioned card game. Too early or too late for either one of us, and things would get blustery.

So when I stood at the front gates of Jasper Livingstone's old home, I wasted no time dismissing the crew.

"Remember," I said. "You're back with the wyverns when the sun touches the horizon. Not a second later. Not a minute earlier."

Zid, James, and Rosana each gave me their own brand of sendoff. For Zid, it was a crisp salute. "Wyverns," he said. "This shall be child's play."

James leaned in for a quick, little kiss. "Don't get too far from me again, Ms. Storm."

I rejected the kiss and dug my nail into his chest. "I choose to remind you that you got carried away last time. Literally. Keep your head on your shoulders this time, love. Don't provoke Fortune. I won't lose you again."

James made a heart shape with his fingers and his hook, and Rosana spun him around and led the crew down the road to Wyvern's Keep. "Forward, comrades. We have a mission."

As did I.

I secured my hat tightly to my head and slipped through the gates of Livingstone Manor, a place that might have rattled my bones as a young girl. Father Time had not been kind to this place, or perhaps Jasper just hadn't maintained it well. Two headstones leaned in the yard, cracked and faded so as to be impossible to read. Red weeds clawed out of the earth and bent toward the gates as if begging to escape the manor. The house itself was the pallid color of a hound's tongue, though I suppose it might not have been much more welcoming in its original color: blood red. The pale-white columns reminded me of fangs. I wondered if maybe Jasper wanted to give people the illusion that the house would swallow them if they went inside.

And I also knew better: all the good stuff was on the inside. Specifically, the one thing I came for.

I marched up the steps and raised my hand to grasp the knocker. The door swung open before I could touch it, and there stood The Wraith, a handsome, red-haired man in a crisp white shirt, a vest of crimson velvet, a matching eyepatch, and pants blacker than my soul. Time had been kinder to him than to his home.

Jasper Livingstone flashed an impish grin. "Ahhh, look what washed ashore today." He looked me up and down, rubbing his chin. "Niraya Jane Storm, Queen of the Seas. Shall I be afraid?"

"Are you even surprised?" I stepped through the doorway without an invitation and caught a whiff of burning cedar wood. Jasper's fireplace glowed in the back of his den, illuminating an eccentric collection of trinkets all around his home. Here was a man who loved the pirate life, filling his house with expensive metals, shiny gems, intricate tapestries and velvet upholstery, fine leather goods that still smelled brand new, ceramic containers polished to a high shine, jars of rare spices, and even exotic wildlife he couldn't possibly have found in any town market. Black scorpions clicked around a large glass cage. One look at them, and an unsettling tingle buzzed on my neck.

I tossed my hat on a coat rack that already occupied several coats and a black boa—live, not feathered. "Charming little place you've got. Mind if I look around?"

"Please, do come in." Jasper pulled the door shut behind us and gestured to a small round table set with rubies and pearls. He pulled up a chair and plucked a wayward tarantula off the cushioned seat. I watched with curiosity as he dumped the creature into the glass scorpion cage.

"Those critters get along well?" I asked, taking a seat at the table.

"Spare me the small talk, Storm. You're not here for tea and biscuits. What are you really here for?"

I let out a chuckle. Straight into business. "I'm glad neither of us is going to play naïve today. That should make this venture simple and clean. So tell me, Jasper. Years ago, I gave you a little trinket. Told you to keep it safe. What became of it?"

Jasper leaned back, gesturing to his walls. "A trinket. Can you be more specific?"

I held my thumb and finger about an inch apart in front of my face. "You know. Translucent little crystal the color of a cherry? Fits in the palm of your hand?" I leaned forward and rested my elbows on the table. "In fact, it looks an awful lot like the figurehead in that bottle over there. The one with the striking model of the *Burning Lotus*. When did you start building tiny ships instead of conquering real ones?"

With a slow, exaggerated sweep of the arm, Jasper dragged the model of the *Burning Lotus* away from me. "Don't touch, Niraya."

"That's a very dangerous thing to keep out in the open." I was inches away from Jasper's face now, smelling his pungent beard oil. "I want to believe if you knew what it really was, you would've put it away. Buried it, even. But to glue it to a ship in a bottle and display it on your mantle? You could've put our very reality in danger. Are you starting to catch my drift yet?"

Jasper's eye gleamed with something I couldn't quite pinpoint. Curiosity? Power? "I wish you *were* here for tea and biscuits."

"This doesn't have to be complicated." I took my elbows off the table and sat back down. "But you do know better. A pirate is always in business."

"Too bad you're no pirate." Jasper shook his head. "Careless thievery has never been your business. You play the dangerous damsel, but under the hat, you're different. You're an adventurer. A collector, perhaps. But if you're a pirate, then I'm Lady Fortune." He leaned back, a smug, annoying little grin on his face.

"The wanted posters all over this island suggest otherwise. But to each their own." I winked.

"I suspect there's more to the story behind those posters," Jasper said. "Is it enough to send you to Stelmorir if you're discovered?"

"Stelmorir?" I suppressed a shiver in my bones. "I hardly believe in fairy tales."

In *The Florindale Fables*, Stelmorir was an island formed from a fallen star—a prison for those who were too terrible for prison. The dead swarmed the island, every biological form bred to attack what it didn't recognize. Plants were predators. The fish who circled the island were known to crawl out of the water, walk on land, and consume the living, making escape nearly impossible. Resourceful survivalists hunted and cooked what they could find. They were always poisoned from within. Even the sun had all but abandoned Stelmorir. Night never ended, and stars were known to leap from the skies and consume the ground in fire. The evil always came back the next day.

"So what'd you do, Niraya?" Jasper asked.

"Let your imagination run wild. That story will have to wait another day."

Jasper popped a handful of pumpkin seeds into his mouth. "Do I have to rely on my imagination to understand why you're so interested in that little crystal again?" He rubbed his chin. "How much is it worth?"

"Just know I've come a very long way for it," I said.

"Oh? And thus I should simply hand it over?"

"Not if you're smart. Instead, I propose a game. Dead Man's Hand. The winner keeps the trinket."

Jasper spat a mouthful of seed shells into his palm then cast them into his fireplace. The gleam in his eyes grew brighter. "Two pirates wagering over cards." He walked to an ornate writing desk on the other side of the room, plucked a spider off the handle, and opened the drawer. He returned with a pack of hexagonal playing cards wrapped in a sheet of leather and tied with a black ribbon. "Astounding possibilities."

I peeled off my gloves and set them on my lap. "Oh? Thought I wasn't a real pirate."

Jasper unwrapped the cards and shuffled. "You're not one to steal, but you *are* one to lie. How is either of us to be trusted in a simple game of cards?"

"We're not. Just know that one way or another, I'm walking away with what I want."

"Shall we make this more interesting?" Jasper asked. "Because I see a one-sided wager right now. If you win, you leave with something more. If I win, I see no profit. What if we modify the stakes?"

"Ah. So what do you propose, Jasper?"

Jasper raised a brow. "If I win, I give you to the queen of Malumbra, and I collect that handsome bounty on your head."

I crossed my arms, hiding my sweaty palms. *You wouldn't,* I thought. *You couldn't do it. Not after all we've been through together.* Once upon a time, Jasper Livingstone and I were a true team. Scoundrels at sea. We used to spar together and share our worries and dreams of the future. Never did those dreams consist of hunting for the Wheel of Fortune, a piece of which we'd both had our hands on before.

But I was certain. Without a doubt, the gem in the bottle was one of the seven pieces belonging to Lady Fortune, and I was going to take it back. Not only that, but with Rosana, James, and Zid, I could free Lady Fortune from the cloud she was shackled to. The story I'd grown up with would end with me. I would finish it for the Rosas family, or I would let Jasper Livingstone turn me in for trying.

Taming the currents of adrenaline in my veins, I shook Jasper's hand. "Now we're talking."

PART THREE

THE TRIALS OF THE WELL

KARINA

11:11

I pinched my own arm twice. Somehow that had to be enough proof that I wasn't dreaming.

The wish processing unit was sensory overload in the best possible way. Suddenly, I felt like a kid in Santa's workshop, and my heart was full. In fact, I was so excited that I forgot what I was looking for in the first place.

For one thing, this part of the factory went on forever. I couldn't even see the ceiling—just an endless wall of square portals, like windows, most of which appeared to be filled with water. I resisted the urge to put my hand in one, not knowing how the water managed to remain in place without a glass or something to keep it from spilling onto the floor.

Some of the other squares depicted starry skies in full motion, comets blazing and clouds swirling. In one portal, beautiful arcs of green-and-purple light twirled above a snowy mountain, and I was sure I was looking at the Northern Lights.

In another pane, white fuzzy dandelion seeds hovered endlessly over a beautiful field.

Yet another showed a weird pyramid-looking thing bouncing around in some blue liquid, almost like the inside of a magic 8-ball.

And some of the windows weren't windows at all. They were doors decorated to look like birthday cakes, technicolored, speckled, and adorned with tiny little lights that blinked on and off. Some were painted with princess decorations and blasted with glitter, others decorated with footballs, assorted cartoon characters, or fireworks.

"Wow," I breathed. *I could stare at this wall for hours.*

The center of the room was just as mesmerizing. Green conveyor belts zipped around the factory, all transporting cardboard boxes or bottled substances that looked positively magical. I couldn't get close enough to read any of the labels, but I saw a lot of shimmering mist, brightly colored liquids, and some bottles that didn't hold anything at all.

Elves, genies, and goblins bustled about the factory with clipboards in hand, while ogres and dwarves carried sacks of jingling coins over their shoulders and fed the contents into a large black machine. The machine would think for a minute, jingle and crank and shimmy, then spit out a box, a bottle, or a long slip of paper, which the worker would take to yet another room.

"Heads up, folks," one of the dwarves called. "The 11:11 batch is coming in again."

Grumbles erupted throughout the room.

"Is it ever *not* 11:11 somewhere?"

"Don't people know it doesn't mean anything to us?" someone added.

"Nope. If it did, I would wish for them to stop making so many wishes at 11:11."

I pulled my hard hat low over my eyes and moved around the room with confidence that I didn't feel. Maybe if I looked busy, I wouldn't be questioned. When the awe wore off, I refocused. I had to find Groff.

The terrible idea came to me that maybe he went through one of the portals. There must've been a portal for every birthday cake in the world, along with every shooting star or stray eyelash that ever existed.

What if somebody else already wished for the Wheel of Fortune stones? An icy tide of dread flooded into my body. *What if Groff is granting somebody's wish right now?*

And what if it was Falk?

Silently, I prayed that whoever was guarding Florindale Prison hadn't served Falk a meal with a wishbone at its center.

I strode up to a random dwarf, feeling brave because he looked like Zid—and someone who looked like Zid couldn't be all that bad, right?—and I cleared my throat. "Excuse me, uh . . ." I squinted and read the name tag. "Rinn. Have you seen which way Groff might've gone?"

Rinn reached up and clapped me on the shoulder. "I'm so glad you're here, Bob. Word in the well is that there's trouble brewing in secondary review. We're still looking into it and waiting for the official word, but we may need you to do some damage control." He gave me a pleading look. "Can we count on you?"

I looked around for a flash of red smoke. "Um, yes, but—"

"Oh, thank the stars." Rinn let out a sigh of relief. "I'll let them know you agreed."

Great. "Um, before anything, I really need to know where Groff is. It's urgent."

Rinn stroked his chin. "Groff. Hmmm. You know, this is a big factory. I still haven't learned everybody's names. The name Groff isn't ringing any bells. I'm sorry."

"Big red genie," I said quickly. "Please."

A crashing sound echoed behind me, and Rinn clapped his hand over his mouth. "No!" He shoved me out of the way and ran for one of the conveyor belts. A collection of bottles had piled up, spilled on the ground, and shattered, releasing a bright-yellow cloud of smoke in the air. "Oh no, oh no, oh no. Not good. Someone needs to get me a mop and a broom and a very big vacuum."

I wasn't sure what it meant when bottles broke, but the way Rinn was flapping his hands and pacing all around the mess, while also taking measured steps to avoid the yellow cloud, I had a feeling that it wasn't good. I stepped closer to get a better look at one of the labels, and while I was finally close enough to see things clearly, all I could see was a bunch of weird little squiggles and symbols. Not a single word of English, though I did recognize the red exclamation point. A warning label, maybe?

"There's a jam somewhere." Rinn cupped his mouth with his hands and shouted, "Pause production. Turn off the machine."

On cue, a lanky ogre stabbed a big red button with his pointer finger. The machine thought for a moment then ground to a slow, steady halt.

Rinn put his hands on his knees and breathed a sigh of relief. "Thank everything."

A team of workers climbed onto the machine and moved along the conveyor belts, armed with wrenches, screwdrivers, hammers, and what looked like packs of chewing gum.

And among the climbers, I recognized a crimson cloud of smoke thundering around and pouring coins into various entry points.

Groff. My heart skipped a beat.

I looked at Rinn. "I'm, uh, gonna go investigate the problem," I said. "Hopefully someone brings you that broom as quickly as possible."

"I sure hope so," Rinn said. "Because if someone is tampering with the wishes, then that means—"

But I didn't get to hear what that meant, because I was already hoisting myself up onto the conveyor belt and analyzing the best pathway to Groff. He must've been a hundred feet high, and this machine was a labyrinth of belts and junctures. I could spend hours trying to trace the belts to any one point in the machine, and I wasn't sure I had hours. The genie could get away again, or—

"Thorns," someone called.

I looked to the door. The brambles were spreading along the walls, covering portals and creeping along the floors.

We're running out of time, I thought.

Not to mention the fact that climbing a huge mechanical beast like this was incredibly dangerous.

Rina, what have you gotten yourself into? I asked myself. I chose a path and began my trek up the conveyor belt, taking care to avoid stepping on bottles as I made my way up a steep incline.

It's a good thing you just climbed a mountain recently, I told myself. The dull ache in my calf muscles would be back soon. Only this time, there were no freezing temperatures, yetis, or hunger pains to deal with. Hopefully.

I reached the first juncture, a tall gray tower looking thing, and took hold of the red ladder on the side.

"Hey, Bobbo," one of the workers called from somewhere in the other direction. "The jam's this way."

I started up the ladder. "I believe in you, boys," I said. "I have some routine maintenance to do somewhere else."

After I reached the top of the ladder, I clung to the next conveyor belt. This one was even a little steeper, but luckily, steeper put me on a quicker pathway to Groff. I kept one eye on him the whole time, looking for patterns in his movement. But I also made the mistake of looking down when I reached the third conveyor belt.

How did I get up this high so fast?

I clutched my stomach, shut my eyes, and took a deep breath. *You've done hard things before,* I told myself.

I would need those affirmations when the belts started to move again.

They lurched beneath me, jumped like a car that wasn't sure if it wanted to start or not, and then took off at twice the speed they'd been moving in before.

"No!" I threw my arms out to my sides in a sort of surfer pose, trying to find my center of balance as the conveyor belt rocketed me forward toward another large tower. *Oh no!* When I was little, I used to watch a cartoon about a man who lived in the jungle and liked to swing on vines, but he was always crashing into trees. This was going to be me.

Below me, somebody screamed. "We weren't ready for the belts yet."

"I didn't start it up," the ogre by the red button yelled. "There's a malfunction somewhere."

"Then find it!"

The tower loomed in my vision, growing larger by the second, and this time I didn't see any ladders or places to catch the next belt. My only option was to turn around.

I spun on my heel and raced the other way, fighting the conveyor belt's momentum. This time, I *did* end up kicking over bottles and boxes, and the people at the bottom would just have to deal with the mess. The problem was that I was fighting a losing battle. I wasn't as fast as the conveyor belt, and I could feel myself being pulled back with every step I took. Any second and I would crash into the looming tower.

Against my better judgment, I took a second look down, scanning for conveyor belts that I could jump down to.

And just below me, an elf on a ladder looked up from a large printout that had come out of his tower, and his eyes were wide with fear.

"I've identified the problem," he said. "The boss has gone mad!" His words began to come out between heavy, staggered breaths. "Up in the chamber . . . doing secondary reviews and . . . these wishes should never be granted! Terrible wishes. Oh, it's a mess."

Charlie? My mind fizzled. *My sweet, wonderful, ridiculous brother. What are you doing over there?*

But secondary review? I remembered seeing that sign in the factory, but Charlie and I never went in that chamber. The story didn't fit.

As I ran for my life, I didn't have the stamina to ask what kind of wishes or what the elf meant. I kicked one of the boxes, hoping to toss it aside, but it was much too heavy. My toe throbbed in protest, and then the box bounced back. It bounced a full foot in the air, shimmied a bit, and then a long white horn burst from the packaging. When I heard a noise that sounded a lot like a horse, I knew I was in trouble. The hooves appeared next, stamping through the box and facing me as the white horn glowed a hot, electric blue.

A unicorn? Any other day, I would've been ecstatic. How many times in my life had I wished unicorns were real? Somebody out there must've wished it into existence. But boxes were tearing all around me, and I had to wonder who could wish for the monstrosities that were appearing in the factory.

Things like a twenty-foot giant made of volcanic rock and veins of molten lava.

A mad titan with ember eyes and fire in its mouth.

A stone beast that roared like a thunderstorm as it tore through the brambles on the ground.

Those kinds of wishes.

All things considered, I was lucky to be in front of a furious unicorn instead of a mad titan, but I had a feeling that horn wouldn't feel very good if it decided to skewer me, and right now, the hooves were working the way a *toro* does when it sees red.

Trapped between a horned animal and a tower that was about to flatten me, I did the only thing I could think of to escape.

I jumped.

And not a second later, something caught me.

Something red, soft, and smoky.

CHARLIE

A fter Rina left, I spent most of my day rejecting wishes. I was basically Santa Claus in an angry mood, and everyone was on my naughty list.

I wish for a new puppy. "No," I said.

I wish to box with a kangaroo. I smirked. "That actually sounds really fun. No."

I wish for a lifetime of chocolate for free. "Chocolate," I said. "Yeah, no."

I wasn't trying to be mean, but Rina had made some very good points before she left. By her logic, it seemed dangerous for me to say yes to anything at all. Even when I wanted to say yes, there was always a way to darken the wish. The person who wished for a puppy could've been allergic, or I could've granted her a rabid dog. I certainly couldn't win a fight against a kangaroo. I was fairly certain Tio discussed kangaroo boxing on his TV show, too. The moral of the story was he didn't recommend it, which was disappointing. And the chocolate thing? Well, I personally didn't see a way chocolate could ever be wrong, but it seemed like a bad idea to say yes.

"Sorry, people," I said to no one in particular. "My sister's just not that fun sometimes. She ruined your wishes, and she ruined my day. She ruined this whole vacation to Switzerland by jumping down this stupid well."

I poured a batch of coins into the *No* stream and watched the water carry them all away to Secondary Review. There had been some real weird ones in that batch—things like, *I wish for a rock giant pet* and *I wish for my own all-powerful lava monster*. One had to wonder what kinds of movies these kids were watching before bed.

"I can do things without Rina," I continued. "She'll see. Tio, too. I'll get that stupid coin back without anybody's stupid help."

Except I'd been digging through this factory for what felt like ages and still hadn't found the red coin. I did need help.

"Where are you, stupid wish?" I muttered, scrubbing through every glint of red I could find. "Stupid, stupid, stupid." I knew Daisy the Crabby Genie had dumped it somewhere in this room. Maybe it had already been sent to the *No* room.

We'd put too much trust in The Bramble King. What if we found the red coin and it turned out to mean absolutely nothing?

"Rina, you put way too much trust in me," I said.

And to my horror, a raspy voice behind me answered, "Yes, she did."

I whirled around and came face to face with Ryvendor, the elf who had chased Rina and me through Switzerland. My heart responded with a leap against my rib cage, and I took a giant step back. Had I stepped back by even another inch, I would've fallen off my platform and tumbled to the ground. "You," I said. "What are you doing here?"

Ryvendor flashed a creepy grin, his eyes devilishly red. "I know what *you're* doing here," he sang.

"I don't have your stupid fortune stones," I said. "Get off my case, jerk face. There's no reason for you to be following me around right now. Or my family."

Ryvendor shook his head. "But it's so fun to brag! I'm so excited to tell you that I have something you don't. You'll be following me before you know it. See how fast the Wheel of Fortune can change direction?" He clapped his hands twice then pinched at the air somewhere over his head. He reminded me of Tio when he does close-up magic, plucking coins and Oreo cookies out of people's ears.

I used to think it was the coolest thing in the world when Tio did that. But when a shiny red coin appeared between Ryvendor's fingers, my lungs swelled like hot air balloons.

"Looking for this?" Ryvendor asked.

I lunged. "Give me that."

Upon impact, Ryvendor burst into a cloud of black mist, and I scraped my knees on the ground.

The mist gathered behind me, and Ryvendor reappeared. He wagged his finger and clucked his tongue. "Ah, ah, ah. You'll have to work harder than that. How badly do you want this, Charlie? Do you even know what it's for?"

I climbed back to my feet and smacked the dust off my knees. "Why do you care so much about it?"

"Because our master cares about it," Ryvendor said. "In fact, Falk will be free from his prison any minute now, and I can't wait to tell him that I played a role in outsmarting the kids who put him there. Think of the rewards. The riches!"

"Falk doesn't care about you or anyone."

"Then what would *you* give me?" Ryvendor asked.

I raised my fists. "How 'bout a fresh knuckle sandwich?"

Ryvendor took a step back, dangerously close to the edge of the platform. He dangled the coin over the side, raising an eyebrow at me. "That doesn't sound like a fair trade at all. You have to want it more. How far will you go for a magic you don't understand?"

I closed the gap between us, knowing how pointless it would be for me to reach. Ryvendor had at least two feet on me. Even if I made a jump for it, I'd just lose my dignity and possibly my life. "*Please* give it to me," I said. "I don't have much to offer, but I'll give you whatever you want. The King of Florindale once posted a reward for the Dark Dragon of the Old World. What if I convinced him to give that to you?"

Ryvendor laughed. "Silly boy. I don't want the king's fortune. I don't want anything you can give me. I just want Falk to know you finally lost. And you will lose, because you're not brave enough to follow me."

He put one foot over the edge of the platform, letting his leg dangle fifty feet off the ground.

My stomach dropped. "Ryvendor, stop."

He snapped his fingers, and there was a loud sucking sound somewhere beneath us. Coins rained down from the different levels of the factory room, and workers turned to look at us.

I peered over the ledge. A large, dark circle swirled underneath us, like a vortex in the middle of the air. The coins stormed into it and disappeared on impact, and the wind tugged at my clothes. My shoelaces came undone and wriggled in the vortex's direction. "What in the world?"

Ryvendor cackled. "Are you brave enough to jump in, Charlie? Because this particular wish is about to be denied!"

He snapped his fingers, popping the red coin into the air.

My soccer legs sprang to action. I shoved everything aside and made a mad dash for the edge, my vision laser focused on the red coin. Nothing else seemed important while that was falling through the air, even as Ryvendor stepped aside and shoved with one quick push, forcing my momentum over the ledge.

"Bye-bye," Ryvendor said.

My heart jumped into my throat as I toppled feetfirst toward the dark portal. The red coin seemed to be falling in slow motion. It grew farther and farther away from me, tumbling and turning in mid-air. If I caught it on video somehow, I'd want to watch it frame by frame, because the split second it touched the vortex, it disappeared.

And that meant I was going to do the same.

I reached up and gave Ryvendor's ankle a harsh tug. "Fine. You're coming, too."

The elf lost his balance just like I hoped and tumbled face-first over the edge of the platform. We were going to the same place, wherever it was.

I knew I was in serious danger when he screamed, "I can't go back there. Anywhere but there!"

KARINA

HICCUPS IN THE FACTORY

When I first entered the wish factory, all of its mysteries felt like a beautiful dream.

Now all the horrors and malfunctions were creating a nightmare.

Terrible things were clawing and biting their way out of boxes all around me, bottles were tumbling to the floor and releasing oddly colored vapors, and elves and goblins panicked as the maze of conveyor belts zoomed them all around the chaos.

Meanwhile, Groff had grown so big he could fit me in one hand, and he was so much scarier when he had me in his fist. Even though he was made of vapor and smoke, his hand was as firm and real as my own. He held me up to his face, and his eyes were all yellow.

"You should not have followed me here, foolish mortal," he thundered. "The ways of the wish granters are not yours to know. Perhaps you choose to spend eternity here."

I squirmed in his fingers while my heart writhed in my chest. "I have a right to be here," I said as calmly as I could. "Why are you doing all of this?"

A hornet the size of my head buzzed around, zooming so close I could feel one of the fuzzy legs get tangled in my hair.

"You're granting things that shouldn't be granted, aren't you? And you stole my crystals. Those belong to Lady Fortune."

"Foolish mortal," Groff said again. He bared his teeth, each as big as a gravestone. A sword appeared in his monstrous empty hand, looking more like a toothpick against his palm. He pinched the handle between his thumb and finger, and I thought for a second that I was about to lose my head.

"Please, no," I pleaded.

Groff wrinkled his brow. "You don't want the sword? Then what will you fight with?"

He held the sword out for me to take.

I gulped. "You're not going to hurt me?"

"I could have ended your fragile existence without conjuring a blade. Right now we need to save the factory from these abominations."

My brain danced between *fragile existence* and *save the factory*. On one hand, I was incredibly offended and feeling petty. "Fragile existence?" I questioned. "At least I'm not made of smoke."

"Smoke implies fire, and I am made of neither. Can we be mature yet?"

My brain switched back to the *save the factory* part. "Wait. You mean you're really not the one causing this?"

The genie sighed. "I'm not sure why I expected you to be intelligent. You jumped down a well, and you're a terrible listener. Use your critical thinking skills, human. I'm trying to save the factory. Of course I didn't cause the damage."

Groff's snark was beginning to boil my blood. To insult my existence was one thing. Stealing the Wheel of Fortune stones was a huge offense. But to insult my intelligence? That was the last straw. I reached for the blade. "Gimme that sword, you jerk."

"Wise command." Groff set me on the ground and passed the sword to me. "After we clean up this mess, we may confront the boss together."

I wrinkled my brow. "Boss?"

Whether Groff answered me or not, I didn't know. I was too distracted by the fifty-foot rock monster ambling toward me. Although he didn't move particularly fast, those legs scared me, his calf muscles made of dry mud and his feet so big he could bury me under his little toe.

A sword was not going to help me here.

"Run, foolish mortal," Groff said.

Evading a slow, giant rock monster was a lot more difficult than I expected. I dashed away as fast as I could, my legs feeling like jelly.

The fact that Groff was a genie was completely unfair. He didn't even have legs. Did he ever get tired hovering around?

The giant hornet returned and made a dive for my head. I raised Groff's sword and brought the blade down in a diagonal slash, more of a frantic flailing than a carefully planned swing.

"Go away," I squealed.

To my wonder, the hornet plummeted to the ground, still very much alive and scrambling to crawl toward me. A large, translucent film with the texture and color of an onion skin floated to the ground and covered the hornet's head. I'd severed one of its wings.

Watching the hornet crawl toward me, panic bubbled within my stomach. This factory was like the jungle of Kesterfall all over again—the horrible goliath spiders, the ogres, the dragon . . . And of all the horrible things that could try to kill me, giant bugs freaked me out the most. Regular sized bugs in Arizona were horrible enough. Who in their right mind wished that hornets and bees would grow as big as a pick-up truck?

I pointed the sword straight in front of me and took slow steps back, my arms shaking as the hornet stared me down.

"Stay away," I said, wondering if it could even understand. "I mean it."

A shadow spread over me and the hornet, and my throat dried up like a cotton ball.

"Better move, foolish mortal!" Groff said.

I looked up and gulped. A mass of dried mud towered over me, dirt trickling into my hair as the rock monster prepared to bring its foot down on my head. *Uh-oh.*

I turned to run away, but found myself flat on the floor, burdened by a tremendous weight on my back, my ears ringing from my head's impact with the ground.

I shut my eyes. *That's it,* I thought. *I've been crushed by a rock monster.* Somehow, I figured it would hurt more.

Hot, moist breaths poured down my neck, followed by the sound of a deep, friendly voice. "You was gonna get cwushed, Bob. Dat was a cwose one."

I opened my eyes. "Boogie," I breathed, my heart soaring. "You saved me."

The rock monster's foot came down inches away from my head, shaking the ground and unleashing a rain of dirt clumps into my eyes.

Boogie patted me on the head, each tap just a little more forceful than I cared for. "Of couwse I saved you. Yaw my fwiend."

The rock monster lifted his foot again, and my adrenaline surged. Sticky hornet guts oozed from his mountainous heel.

I coughed, rubbed my eyes, and grabbed my sword, struggling under Boogie's weight. "Can you stand up, Boogie?"

The ogre obliged, stumbling to his overgrown feet before reaching down and picking me up with one swift, strong pull.

In a move I'd rather not tell Charlie about, I reached up and kissed the ogre on the cheek. "Thanks for saving me, Boogie. And I'm not Bob. My name's Karina Rosas, and I will always be your friend. But listen, I think you should get out of here."

The rock monster's shadow loomed over us again, and I grabbed the ogre's hand and pulled him back into the light. Confusion riddled his face, his eyes a bit wider and his brow creased with questions. "Not . . . Bob?"

"No," I said quickly. "Karina. Listen, Boogie. Go and tell Doris there's a problem in the factory. Tell her they need to call all the backup they can get down here. Somebody's tampering with the wishes. All these workers are in danger, and so are you."

Boogie was eerily, disturbingly quiet at this request. Every inch of my being hoped that he wasn't mad at me for pretending to be someone else. I didn't need another ogre against me—not after he just saved my life.

"You gave a lie," Boogie said. "I twusted you."

The rock giant's foot came down beside us again, nearly knocking me off balance. This thing's footsteps had to have registered on the Richter scale. I looked down and realized I still had Boogie's hand, and he was tightening his grip at an uncomfortable rate. His mouth curled into a full-fledged frown, his breaths hot and heavy.

"*Boogie*," I said, filling my tone with every word I didn't have time to say. *Please. I'm sorry. Thank you. Help me. Get out of here. The list went on.*

"I twusted you," the ogre repeated.

My bones throbbed in Boogie's grip, and the rock monster was already lifting its other foot. The room pulsed with activity. Panicked workers. Thundering unicorns. Breaking bottles. Monsters bursting out of boxes.

"Boogie, you need to let me go," I said. "Now."

The ogre jerked his hand away from mine and let out a *humph* sort of noise through his nose. "Sowwy I helped," he said. "Bye fowever."

Without another word, the ogre turned around and ran away.

Groff zoomed over to me and waved his arms above his head. "Stop worrying about the ogre. He can get workman's comp anyway. Your life is in danger, foolish mortal. Help me. And whatever you do, do *not* breathe in the gas from the black bottles."

I looked around the room, my mind buzzing like one of those hornets. "There's too much," I said. "Do I really have to kill the unicorns?"

"You don't have to kill anything," Groff said. "Just defend yourself from the things that attack you. I'll figure everything else out later. Right now I need to stop the boss from corrupting anymore wishes. Can you keep the monsters distracted until I come back?"

A huge roach scuttled under Groff's tail and ambled toward my foot. I plunged my sword into its back with a nasty crunch like dry cereal between the teeth. I waited until its wiry feelers stopped writhing before I pulled the blade out and flicked the juice into the distance. "Ugh." I wrinkled my nose. "The boss is doing all this? Really?"

Groff pointed to a window high over our heads, where a short, shadowy silhouette danced in the amber light. "Just look. She's gone mad with power. She's the one who pulls all the levers and makes the final call to overturn denied wishes."

I squinted at the dancing shadow. There was something oddly familiar about that silhouette, and the attitude behind it.

"Go figure," Groff continued. "She comes back from her vacation—wherever she went—and she's a totally new person. She's actually dancing. Joyful, even. All because she's doing something evil . . . worthy of old man Falk himself. Step to your left, by the way."

I side-stepped as the rock titan stomped his foot yet again. Blood rushed to my ears. "Tell me her name," I said.

"Clova," he said simply.

My throat tightened.

"Now, will you do something about these monsters so I can go deal with her?" Groff asked. "It's high time I filed a labor complaint."

Clova. One of those Fortune Guard cronies that chased me and Charlie out of Switzerland. Looking at her made my blood boil. She'd been so mean. So colossally rude. So determined to derail my family from protecting the Fortune stones. And here she was, dismantling this beautiful wishing factory. I couldn't wait to see her face when she failed.

"How 'bout no?" I said to Groff. "I think you should keep the monsters distracted. I want to go after Clova."

The genie blinked a few times. "Excuse you?"

"You heard me," I said. "That woman ruined my summer vacation. She's the one who came after me and my family to get the Wheel of Fortune stones, which for the record, I'm still mad at *you* for stealing. I'm gonna go make her put a stop to all of this, and then I'm coming back to have a little chat with you. Because guess what? You're gonna give those crystals back and return me to the surface. You are a genie, aren't you? That's my wish. Get to work."

Groff looked down at his thumbs, eerily quiet.

I hated the silence.

"Perhaps you *are* more fit to face Clova," he said.

Me? More capable than an all-powerful genie? I had a feeling someone like Groff could snap his fingers and hex Clova into doing whatever he wanted. So why did he agree so easily?

"Really?" I asked. "Wait—"

Groff shrugged. "Far be it from me to stop you." He pointed at a rather large mosquito that hovered down to him, and a beam of red light shot out of his fingertips, obliterating the bug in a puff of smoke. Sweat welled up on Groff's forehead and he wiped his brow. "Whew."

My jaw dropped. "Did you just blow up that bug with your finger? Can you do that with anything?" I looked at the rock giant.

"Nope. Not enough power. I just *hate* moskeeters." Groff conjured a sword just like the one in my hands and pointed up to Clova's shadow dancing in the window. "You'd better get up there before this gets worse. And remember: Whatever you do, don't ever breathe in the smoke from the black bottles. Good luck, mortal. May the light be with you."

"What's so bad about the black bottles?" I asked. But Groff was already gone, zooming around and chipping at the rock monster to little avail. *This is a total metaphor for my life right now,* I thought. *Trying to protect the Wheel of Fortune and get out of this factory is just like trying to kill a rock titan with a sword.*

I climbed up on the conveyor belt, sword in hand, and rode the machine toward the boss's office. "May the light be with *you*, Clova," I muttered.

CHARLIE

I hit the dark vortex with a splash of all things, sinking back-first into a warm liquid. I hadn't been falling for more than a few seconds, so I didn't have much time to build expectations, but I wasn't expecting a splash. Looking at that swirly black matter, I think I had been preparing myself for a splat, or to pop up in outer space and float forever. How could I know how these swirly things worked?

The liquid folded me in as I swallowed a mouthful of warm water. My eyes shut when I hit the surface, but after a few seconds, I forced them open, surprised to take in a burst of sunlight rippling somewhere over the water. But then the panic set in.

Water.

My lungs turned to iron, and I imagined a thousand tentacles pulling me deep into the abyss. I fought the water with everything I had, my arms and feet writhing and flailing as I fell deeper and deeper, the sun growing farther away and the water growing darker. My hard hat and orange vest only weighed me down more.

I attempted to cry for help; only a mouthful of bubbles burst from my lips and let another stream of water into my lungs.

Where was the coin? Where was Ryvendor?

Where was I?

Ryvendor had been royally freaked out about falling through his own portal. This couldn't have been a nice, happy place, wherever I was. Maybe I'd never know. I'd probably drown before I'd ever know where I was.

Rina would be on her own.

Don't fight the water, Charlie.

Oh man, get out of my head, Tio.

You need to calm down. Stop struggling, hold your breath, and get ready to swim up. The average human can survive for three minutes without air. You have about a minute and a half, mijo. Relax your body. I know you can swim. Come on, follow my lead.

Leave it to Tio to insert his TV show lessons into my head right when I'm about to die. He'd probably been in this exact situation before. Well, minus the elves, the mystical currency, and the dark portals to wherever.

I unfastened my hard hat and let it sink. My head felt ten pounds lighter already.

Smart call, Charlie. Now get moving. You don't have much longer.

I focused on the sun, relaxed my muscles, and pushed.

And with a bit more clarity, my struggling and flailing morphed into kicking and paddling. The sun grew bigger and brighter again. My lungs tightened and my heart sped up, but I knew I was moving in the right direction.

Push, I told myself.

I pushed and pushed until something started to pull, like an invisible hand tugging on the neckline of my shirt. Luckily, the invisible hand was tugging me in the right direction. Up. *Am I being pulled up to the clouds? Did I run out of my three minutes already?* Time seems to work differently when we're struggling. If we're really in pain, three minutes could feel like forever.

When I came up for air, large ships bobbed around in my field of view. The sun blasted my vision, and the light had never been more welcome. I coughed and sputtered and finally muttered a quiet thank you to my tio, wherever he was.

"Well, well, aren't you the catch of the day?" a woman said.

I looked up at the source of the voice: a tall, red-haired woman with a fishing pole. What I thought had been some divine, invisible hand had really just been a hook on the back of my neckline. She stood on a rickety dock, and I had this weird sense that I'd been here before.

I smiled and extended my hand toward the angler. "Help me out, but please don't eat me? The last thing that ate me sneezed me back out."

The woman gave her fishing pole a superhuman tug, jerking me out of the water until my feet were dangling over the surface. We were nearly eye level, and she was glaring at me with so much heat I could almost feel my clothes drying. "You're calling me a *thing?* Do I have to throw you back in there?"

I clasped my hands as if in prayer, my heart pounding. "No, please, don't do that. You're not a thing; you're like an actual person. Thank you for pulling me out. Can you please set me down now?"

"Down?" She took her reel and lowered me a foot or so, drenching my boots.

"Please," I pleaded. "I, uh, come in peace."

The woman gave her pole another inhuman tug and did a one-eighty, flinging me onto the dock where I landed like a limp marionette.

I caught my breath, unhooked my shirt, and put my hands together in a steeple gesture. "Thanks, lady. I appreciate you. *Dang,* you're strong. What kind of pole is that?"

The lady tossed her pole aside and looked me up and down, the suspicion steaming off her brow. She was giving me almost the same stare the eighth grade cheerleaders would give me when I first started middle school, like I was the scum of the earth. I was toilet paper on her shoe just for existing.

And that's when it all came back to me. The impossibly strong, not-that-nice woman. The rustic fairy-tale buildings around me. The god-like statues towering overhead and cradling the sun. They stood with their arms of stone spread apart as if to invite Godzilla in for a hug, but this was the last place where anybody would greet me with open arms. I really had been here before. And I never wanted to come back.

This was Jericho Harbor, the town where the werewolves lived, and I'd never let anyone forget that werewolves were the second creatures to try to eat me.

"Uh-oh," I said.

The woman's arm was a blur as she reached behind her, unstrapped a bow on her back, and before I could say *full moon*, she had a steel-tipped arrow pointed straight at my head. "Carlos Rosas. You are the enemy of our people, and you should never have come back here. You should've known better."

She was studying the space between my eyes like the center of a dartboard.

"I, uh, really don't plan on staying. Maybe you can help me, actually. The sooner I get what I'm looking for, the sooner I can get out of here and leave you all alone. Preferably forever this time?"

The woman bared her teeth. "Why would we help you? You brought chaos to our village last time you came here. We took you in. We fed you. We clothed you."

"And then your innkeeper went full *Teen Wolf* in the middle of the night and tried to hurt my family," I said. "Don't act like he didn't have a choice or anything. We didn't provoke him. Everything that happened in that forest is because he made a choice."

"Well, now *I'm* gonna make a choice." The woman shook her bow, as if she really needed to emphasize the fact that she had an arrow aimed between my eyes.

"Neoma," a man said. "Easy."

I could hardly believe my eyes when Io, the inn-keeper of the Golden Gibbous, emerged from the trees and gripped the woman's elbows from behind. He had gentle, young, Hollywood-good looks in his human form, a stark Jekyll-and-Hyde difference from the animal that attacked me and Karina last time we were here. He had a similar effect on the woman, who deflated from rabid, angry ninja to quiet, meditative lily. Her breathing slowed, her gaze softened, and she surrendered her bow to Io.

Io pocketed the arrow and clapped his hand on Neoma's shoulder. "This isn't our enemy."

I did a double-take. "Wait, really? I'm not? Because last time we saw you—"

"Speak no more," Io said. "The next full moon isn't for another fortnight. My actions are my own, Carlos. As long as the sun shines, you'll continue to talk to the man you see in front of you. We are but puppets of the lunar cycle until somebody breaks our curse. You have my sincerest apologies for the way we treated you, but I suggest you finish your business here before the corn moon flares again."

I let go of the tension in my shoulders. At least I wasn't about to be skewered, but I was still skeptical. "So you also apologize for stealing my uncle's pendant?"

Io tapped his thumbs together. "That is much more complicated. The pendant was never truly his to begin with."

I wanted to open my mouth and yell *Yes, it was.* But Io actually had a point. The pendant never was my tío's. He stole it from an Egyptian pyramid, where the crystal landed after Lady Fortune destroyed her own wheel. I had no real argument against Io.

"However," he said, "I do acknowledge my actions against your family as irrational and selfish, and I never should have deceived you for my own personal gain. I am ashamed of the hurt and disgrace I have caused my people."

Saying sorry is the easiest thing in the world. Not everybody can actually mean it when pride is so much stronger.

"Yeah, yeah," I said.

And *yeah, yeah* was where I planned to leave it until Io dropped to one knee. He lowered his gaze, chin against his chest and a humble sigh escaping his lungs. "On your knee, Neoma," he said. "Redemption starts here."

"Redemption from what?" Neoma spat. "They locked my sister in a wardrobe and left you for dead in the forest."

These were half-truths. Yes, Niraya shut one of the guards in a wardrobe last time we were here, but that guard was in full raging beast mode at the time, having sprung through a window to attack her. And while we did leave Io behind when he was injured, we offered to help him back to the village. Karina insisted on helping him a million times, and he refused. But I didn't have time to argue with Neoma, and Io wasn't having it either.

"Ahem." Io reached out and tugged on Neoma's sleeve. "On your knee."

"But—"

"Knee."

Neoma dropped next to Io, and my jaw fell with her. Either one of them was about to propose to me, or they were about to start begging. I didn't want any of those things. I just came for some help. "Uh," I said, "This really isn't necessary. You can stand up."

"On behalf of the residents of Jericho Harbor," Io said, "I apologize for deceiving your family and for the theft and violence committed against you."

When he finished speaking, there was an awkward pause. Io cleared his throat and thumped Neoma on the elbow.

"Your turn," he whispered.

Neoma spoke in a swift, choppy monotone, the words falling out of her mouth. "As a token of our remorse, you are entitled to our aid and protection, and we humbly grant you a favor of your choice to be redeemed before the next full moon." I'd never heard somebody sound so bored. I could almost hear her rolling her eyes. "The end."

I wondered if this was some sort of ritual conversation they started with every family they attacked during the full moon. Every family that came back, that is, and who would actually want to?

"Can you accept our apology and our favor?" Io asked.

Neoma started to pull herself up, but Io put a hand on her shoulder. "Not yet," he told her.

"Do you mean it?" I asked.

"Yes. On my honor." Io looked up, and we made direct eye contact. I was no psychologist or FBI agent, but I did know people's eyes and faces carried a lot. Sure, this was complicated and risky—it's not like I saw the deception in Io's face the first time I met him—but I did see a lot of depth when he looked up from the ground. The gleams and angles of his eyes, the tension in his lips and the creases in his forehead? It's hard to fake remorse on that level.

Neoma didn't even bother trying.

"She'll come around," Io added. "Honor is everything when we make this vow. Can you forgive me?"

I forked my fingers through my hair. By the time the full moon came back around, I would be long gone and hopefully reunited with my sister. I had no pieces of the Wheel of Fortune with me, and very few possessions of value worth stealing. Lastly, I really did need some help. Io knew Jericho Harbor better than I did, and I needed to find that red coin again.

"Accepted." We shook, and I helped Io and Neoma back to their feet. "We're cool."

Please don't let me regret this.

"Wonderful," Io said. "Now, tell us what you need."

I told Io and Neoma everything. How we confronted Falk himself in Kesterfall then put him in Florindale Prison. How we divided up the known pieces of the Wheel of Fortune with King Enzo. How Karina and I went back to our world, only to get yanked back when Falk's people came after us. How we threw ourselves down a well to protect the orbs in our hands. How we encountered The Bramble King and listened to his request to find the red coin, and how the underground seemed to be working against us along the way.

"And now I'm here," I said. "That elf pushed me into a portal, and I landed here." The fact that I hadn't seen Ryvendor yet had me on edge. "We need to either find Ryvendor or the red coin."

"I suppose you're in luck," Io said. "We haven't seen this Ryvendor anywhere, but shortly before you arrived, the townspeople noticed an unusual amount of coins flowing through the water network in the harbor. It's quite likely your red coin is in one of our streams. But if you want to trace those streams, there's some b-bad news."

I didn't like the quaver in Io's voice. What could a werewolf have to be afraid of besides Captain Niraya Storm? "You can just point me in the right direction if you want," I said. "You got a map or something I can take? Something that highlights all the rivers and lakes?"

"No maps," Neoma said. "We forbid them in Jericho Harbor. In any case, few people visit and even fewer stay. I'll tell you one thing though. If you intend to go splashing in the water around here, you'd better be ready for what you'll find."

I had a feeling she wasn't talking about algae or cute little duckies.

"I'm ready for anything," I said. *As long as it's not another kraken.* "Even if you just point the way for me, I'll take it."

"You have two options if your token surfaced in Jericho Harbor." Io pointed behind me. "The harbor itself"—he turned and gestured to the forest—"or the lake. We'll have an easier time if it's the harbor, where the piranhas live."

Gulp. So I'd almost been piranha food?

"And if it's the lake?" I asked, fighting to sound calmer than I felt.

"You already know what's in the lake," Io said.

Another memory flashed in my head, this time of a silvery woman with wild hair rocketing out of a shimmering lake and hovering there to give us a test.

"Lady Constance," I said.

Io nodded. "The Spirit of the Broken Forest, and all she commands."

Lady Constance was the woman who cursed the residents of Jericho Harbor. People encountered her on the trail to the mountains, where she offered them a difficult choice. I didn't know if it was always the same, but for Karina and me, it was a test I nearly failed. *Take the shortcut to your uncle at the expense of an innocent life, or take the long way and suffer with no guarantee of seeing your uncle again.* Those who passed the test continued along the trail. Those who failed were confined to Jericho Harbor and forever cursed to transform into a terrible creature when the moon was full.

I never wanted to see Lady Constance again. She freaked me out. She gave harder tests than my last history teacher. What if I had to pass another one to get the coin back?

Or what if the coin *was* the test? And maybe I already failed by leaving Karina behind.

Yep, I definitely already failed. And with my luck, the lake was exactly where the coin was headed.

"I can take you to the harbor if you'd like to check there first," Io offered.

"No," I said. "There's no point. I know my luck. It's going to the lake. You don't have to come with me if you don't want to. You can stay here."

Io flashed me a sad smile. "The fact that you would even suggest such a thing is exactly why I must come with you. I owe you a debt, and I intend to pay."

"Do you really want to play her game again, Io?" Neoma asked. "How much more do we have to give? Our limbs? Our lives?"

"I have another job for you," Io said. "Go and search the harbor instead. See to it that nobody stands in this boy's way. We've put him through enough already."

"You want me to leave you alone with this thing?" Neoma said. "I don't trust this. Something smells, Io."

Dang. This lady wasn't even *kind* of interested in my feelings.

"I'm not asking," Io said. "Leave us. Search the harbors. Return to the Golden Gibbous at sundown."

Neoma scoffed, throwing up her hands. "Fine. But if you're not back there waiting for me, the vow is off." She stared daggers at me, curling a thumb in my direction. "And I'll be coming for you, boy. Are we clear?"

I made a pair of finger guns at her and clicked my tongue behind my teeth. "Like water."

But as Io led me back into the Broken Forest, that evergreen prison I never wanted to see again, something gnawed at my gut. And I always trusted gut feelings.

Like the feeling that Neoma's attitude was the least of my problems to come.

KARINA

I always thought a giant maze of conveyor belts sounded like fun, but it really, really wasn't. Especially not in a malfunctioning wishing factory, where the belts switch directions, stop, and speed up at random. I didn't know how long I'd spent trying to reach Clova's little hideaway at the top of the machine, but she wasn't making it easy. I wondered if she knew I was coming for her.

The climb was a lot like navigating an obstacle course. There were times when I had to jump, there were ladders I had to climb, and the higher I got, I even had to walk across some narrow metal beams. All of this while bats and giant hornets flew around the factory, the rock monster stomped around shaking the floor with every step, and who knew what else was coming out of all those other boxes?

How the heck did Clova get up there? I wondered. If she was the boss, then she probably had to do this climb every day. How did such a terrible, villainous person even become the manager of a magical factory?

I got at least one of those answers when I got close to the window. Clova's hideaway was a large plastic dome overlooking the factory floor, and she was almost completely enclosed from the bottom except for the little trapdoor in the center, where I needed to get in. She either climbed in the hard way, or she dropped in from the top. A thick metal chute fed into a round hole at the top of the dome, but I had no idea where that chute led because clouds obscured everything above. I'd officially reached the limits of what I could see in the wishing factory.

I clung to the lower rungs of a ladder, my sword strapped across my back. Clova's shadow continued to dance around in the window. If she saw me, she didn't acknowledge me. She was too busy cackling, throwing levers and pressing buttons. Every action triggering a new anomaly in the factory. A change of direction on the conveyor belts. A fresh new delivery box falling from the clouds. Did I dare look down and see how things were going on the floor? I sure hoped Groff was okay.

I studied the trapdoor beneath Clova's hideaway. I'd climb the ladder all the way up, pull the lever on the door like one of those emergency exit switches, and slip in. The entrance wasn't exactly discreet. But if I could at least be quick, I could reverse whatever Clova was doing and go back for Groff.

Maybe the climb down would be easier somehow?

Rung by rung, I climbed the ladder, feeling a bit like Jack on his beanstalk. Only in this story, the giant was below me, stomping around and shaking the ground, sending humming vibrations through the ladder. And Groff had my magic beans. Perhaps that was for the best until I finished things with Clova.

When I reached the top, I squeezed my eyes shut and took a deep breath. "This is it, Rina," I told myself. I grabbed the lever, using the other hand to cling to the ladder for dear life. Clova's menacing, shrieky cackles cut through the trapdoor, and I wished I'd brought some ear plugs.

The lever was heavy and my arms were numb, but inch by painstaking inch, I unlocked the trapdoor. The final inch made me cringe as my heart leapt into my throat, because the door let out a rusty screech and a loud click. Clova had to have heard me. The door popped up a few inches, casting a wedge of fluorescent light on my face.

So much for being sneaky.

Knowing my cover was blown, I shoved the door open, scrambled up the ladder, and pulled myself into the room, expecting to find Clova in defense mode. But to my surprise, she hadn't seemed to hear me at all. When I shut the trapdoor behind me, Clova's back was to me as she stood against one of the domed walls, punching buttons on her control panel while belting a tune I vaguely recognized. She wore ugly brown earbuds shaped like mushrooms.

"When you wish upon the dark," she sang, *"makes the nightmares sing and bark! Anything you truly fear will come*

find you!" She belched, uncorked a bright-purple bottle, and chugged the contents. When she finished, she tossed the bottle behind her, and it shattered on the ground.

The whole control center was a mess of those bottles, the same kinds I'd seen on the conveyor belts below me . . . yellow, red, blue, pink, almost every shade possible. Luckily I didn't see any black ones. Groff told me to avoid those at all costs.

I could've spent ten years flipping switches in this room and never quite figure out what everything did.

Behind me sat one of those dishes Charlie and I had used to read the wishing coins, complete with a giant lens and a handful of coins, dandelion seeds, golden paper cranes, and most horrifying of all, some eyelashes. I wondered if these were truly bad wishes, or if Clova was up here turning the good ones into nightmares. Either way, I had to put a stop to this.

I cleared my throat. "Clova."

Clova ripped out one of her mushroom earbuds, turned her head slowly then scrunched her face when she saw me. She aimed a crooked finger at me. "You."

The venom in her voice gave me a petty sense of satisfaction.

"Whatever you're doing to the wishes," I said, "you need to reverse it right now."

The dwarf swatted at the air. "You really need to learn to pick your battles, sweetheart." She eyed my sword with a hungry gleam in her eyes. "You know how to use that thing on your back?"

Why did people ask that? Zid had once explained swords with brilliant simplicity: *Insert sharp end into bad things and remove. Repeat as needed.* I shrugged. "Ask some of the wasps you brought to life."

Clova cackled. "All smug. You must feel so clever and accomplished for making it all the way up to confront the mean ol' dwarf lady. But you must not have looked in a mirror in a while. You're a mess. Take a look at yourself. Go on."

She pointed to the giant lens on the wish granting column, where I caught a glance of my hair spidering out in wild tangles.

But I cared more about what I could see beyond the reflection. My focus shifted through the lens and at the tiny gold script hovering over an American penny.

I wish rock monsters weren't real.

Ryan, age 4

A hot, angry breath shot out of my lungs. "You're bringing kids' nightmares to life down here. Why would you do that? Do you feel like you're accomplishing anything?"

"Do you feel like you've accomplished something chasing that insufferable genie around all day? Splitting up from your brother to do Thorne's bidding?"

I stood a little taller. "For your information, I do. Groff is down there fighting your monsters. He's not on your side. But I'm on his. Between the two of us, you're never going to get the Wheel of Fortune. I know that's what you really want."

"So you befriended the genie who took your precious rocks," Clova said. "Congratulations, twerp. Take a deep breath and relish this feeling. Smile while you still feel like a hero."

I scoffed. "What are you talking about?"

"I slowed you down with my factory fiends." Clova punched another button. "You may have caught up to me, but you've accomplished nothing. I, on the other hand, have accomplished everything I set out to do today. And by this time tomorrow, so will Lord Falk."

My vision twisted. What did Clova mean?

Before I could say another word, she reached into her pocket.

My breath hovered in my throat.

As if in slow motion, the dwarf pulled out a silver pouch and shook it over her head.

The fortune crystals. The same ones Groff took from me.

My heart slammed in my chest. *How did she get those?*

"No," I said.

Clova grinned. "Yes. I have the upper hand now. If you leave here today, why don't you ask Groff how I retrieved the crystals? It's a painfully simple story. I'm sure he'd love to tell you."

I thought of Groff's strange behavior before I climbed up here. How he'd gone quiet and told me that maybe I was better equipped to confront Clova. I knew right away that something was off, but I never would've believed it was because he no longer had the stones. And just when I was starting to believe I was going to succeed. Had he betrayed me?

I unstrapped my sword and pointed it at Clova.

"Those don't belong to you." I could still win this.

Clova tossed the pouch up and down, taunting me. "Huh. I don't think they belong to you, either. What a dilemma. 'Round and 'round we go."

I took a step forward. "You know who they belong to."

Clova opened the pouch and shook out an orange stone. "There *is* something special about you," she said. "All that determination and drive, the annoying goodness and self-righteousness. You're so confident and heroic, and you don't even need any of this stuff to be the way you are." She gestured at the colored bottles on the ground. "I think that's why I despise you."

I froze. All these compliments she was tossing my way, and they were all reasons why she was so terrible toward me. My mom always said something similar about bullies. *They're mean because they're jealous of you.*

Clova squeezed the orange crystal in her hand, and the bottles on the floor changed color before my eyes. The yellows turned red. The reds turned purple. And within a few seconds, every bottle in the room had turned inky black.

My arms trembled. These were the bottles Groff told me to avoid. What did they do?

"Let's see how you do when you're at your worst," Clova said.

She picked up a bottle and smashed it on the ground.

A puff of dark smoke welled around the glass.

I lowered my sword with one hand and used the other to plug my nose. *Don't breathe it in,* I willed myself.

Clova laughed and picked up another bottle. "Good. Keep your nose plugged. See how much that helps."

She dropped the second bottle then crushed another under her boot. She pocketed the silver pouch, put her mushroom earplugs back in, and danced around the room, kicking and smashing bottles with every step. *"When you wish upon the dark . . ."*

"Stop it." My vision swirled, all the shapes melting together. I lunged for Clova, determined to go down swinging. She danced out of the way with feline grace. Meanwhile my own movements slowed, like I was pushing through a haze of peanut butter and carrying weights on my shoulders. I cleaved at the air, smashing something I couldn't see. More black smoke exploded around me, and the sword slipped from my fingers. "Stop," I breathed.

Clova picked up my sword and strapped it onto her back. "Thank you for the present." She sounded far away, as if speaking through cotton. "This will help me later."

"Clova." Color dripped away from the world. The pinks and yellows faded to cold, lonely grays.

My skin paled. Everything looked sad. Hopeless.

The way I was starting to feel.

Unable to support my own weight, I slumped down next to the wishing bowl and tilted my head back.

"I think it's funny." Clova picked up a quarter and tossed it in the air. "This was the wish you threw in the fountain only hours ago. You didn't wish to save the Wheel of Fortune or find all the orbs. That's how con-fident you were that you would win. And look what's happening now. You're *losing*. Ha!" She stood in front of me, pocket of stones inches away from my face. All I needed to do was reach up and grab the pouch, but my arms were wrapped in iron. We weren't going to win no matter what.

And I no longer cared.

I closed my eyes. "Leave me alone. I just wanna go to sleep."

Clova danced a little jig. "Hilarious. I'm standing right in front of you, and you're giving up. Do you remember why you're here? What you wanted to accomplish today? Or are you too exhausted to think?"

I curled in on my side. "I just wanted a nap," I said. "Everyone else can do whatever. This place is boring."

"That's the spirit, twerp," Clova said. "Sleep. Have your nap. Because after all your time here, it is the *only* thing you've earned."

CHARLIE

WEREWOLVES AND
BEARGOBBLERS

Karina would've been furious if she knew I was following Io into the woods again, tracing a thin, bab-
bling stream I hardly remembered from my last trip to
Jericho Harbor. But this time I didn't take my eyes off
the water; that would've been the minute the red coin
would float right past me. Ma calls that Murphy's Law.

Looking for the coin opened my eyes to everything
else I'd never noticed, and it was during the search that
I realized just how strange this broken forest really
was. Before, I thought the land was just full of squir-
rels, deer, and bears. But there were spiders that knew
how to swim, making them look like tiny hairy octopus
creatures. Certain kinds of plant life glowed in the dark

with unhealthy shades of neon green and moonlit blues. I swore the trees had eyes. The more time I spent in the forest, the weirder it became.

The worst of it all was a big green dome-looking thing, with scales and writhing Medusa tentacles, peeked out of the river and swiveled around as if looking for food. I had no idea how big it was beneath the water's surface, but this thing could've been the ugly cousin of a river kraken or a swamp monster. A scream welled in my throat and threatened to burst until Io clapped a hand over my mouth.

"*Shhh,*" he warned.

I swallowed my scream, nodded my head, and gasped for air when Io took his hand away.

"What the heck is that?" I whispered.

"That's a beargobbler." I hated how disturbingly casual Io's voice sounded. *Oh, that's just a rock.* Beargobbler? "One of Lady Constance's pets."

"A beargobbler?" What a horrible word, and an even worse creation. A slimy, tentacled beast that hides in rivers and eats bears. "Why would Lady Constance have a pet, uh, beargobbler? Isn't she all about nature and rainbows and protecting the wild?"

"*Beargobbler* is a misnomer," Io said. "It doesn't eat bears. It just has the appetite of a bear. It eats humans who disturb the forest. That, along with any plastic and metals it finds along the surface. People keep threatening our river with their trash. Think of the beargobblers as anti-pollution monsters designed to keep the water clean. I call it Lady Constance's warning to humanity."

I gulped. "People, plastics, and metals? It can't eat, like, pumpkin soup or something?" My teeth hurt just thinking about trying to chomp on a ball of aluminum foil. I put my hand up to my mouth, running a finger over my canines. "Weirdest diet ever."

"It is not particularly fond of pumpkin soup," Io said. "As for the diet, you've never seen us eat when the moon is full."

A shiver passed down my spine. "I'm guessing you don't eat Purina puppy chow?"

Io laughed. "Try to relax. I'm willing to bet this beargobbler can smell fear."

"Yeah right. Nothing can smell fear. Only cheesy comic book villains say they can smell fear."

"Well, I can, and it smells like chicken." Io shrugged.

I glared at Io. This was hardly the time for dad jokes. *What does anger smell like?* I wondered. *How 'bout knuckle sandwiches in your face?* But the only question worth my time was, "And if this beargobbler ate my coin? Because, you know, Murphy's Law and all that?"

"I don't know who Justice Murphy is, but if the gobbler ate your coin, then you need to make that thing spit it out. Or give up."

I'd already been eaten by one aquatic sea beast. Tonight I was putting my foot down: I, Charlie Rosas, would *not* be eaten again. "All right, then how do I—"

"Don't get its attention," Io said. "If we can avoid a fight with that thing in the first place, we'll be better off, and who knows? There's a chance your token is still floating down the stream somewhere."

Yeah right. There was also a chance King Enzo was the son of Pinocchio. Neither chance was particularly large or worth betting my life on.

"Io, what do we do?" I asked.

Io picked up two broken tree branches, inspected the ends, and tossed one to me. "We'll use these to comb through the water, like this." He dipped his branch into the river and made slow, cautious swirls. A pearly pink fish leapt from the water, startling me more than I was proud to admit. "Go slow and keep your distance from the gobbler. No splashing."

I dunked my stick in the water as Io instructed, keeping a few feet behind him.

We traced the banks for quite a while, the time impossible to determine based on the shadows of the forest. Did the ground ever see the sun here? I wondered how the flowers grew in their vibrant, bountiful colors, and the plump fruits managed to thrive. Magic, I supposed.

Speaking of magic, we lost the beargobbler almost right away. I'd been determined to keep one eye on that domed, writhing mess of tentacles, and I swore it had vanished into thin air. The hairs on my arms stood straight up when I realized I'd lost sight of the monster. "Does that thing have camouflage or something?"

Io waved his hand as if to shoo away my fear. Ineffectively. "Worry not, friend. I would smell it if it were on the hunt. He's long gone by now."

"You'd smell it? Even when you aren't in wolf form?" I wondered if that was a rude question. I wanted to stay on his good side, especially with that monster around.

"Because I didn't smell anything when he was here. Also, how do you know the beargobbler is a he?"

"Just trust me, okay?"

A tall order from someone who tried to eat me once, but I didn't argue. *Good side*, I thought to myself. "Did you really try to kill Verdoro?"

Io froze, his tree branch swaying idly in the water.

Maybe this *good side* thing wasn't going too well. I vowed not to ask any more questions.

"Sorry," I mumbled.

"Yes."

Suddenly I felt like a teapot, all the questions building up like steam until they threatened to spill out and relieve the pressure. *No more*, I told myself.

"Many people intended to destroy that dragon." Io's voice was low and gruff. "For fame. For fortune. For the lofty goal of conquering something bigger than themselves. There are very few dragons left in Kesterfall, you know. I was taught that those that remain are bad luck. They bring death to all who have seen their shadow. What happened to Kale and Helene was all the proof I ever needed."

Now it was my turn to go quiet. Kale and Helene? *What did Verdoro do?*

"My brother and sister." Io had a faraway look in his eyes. "Helene was much younger than me. She was the baby of the family, the one I always wanted to protect even though I knew she was the strongest of us all. So pure and joyful, like a moonflower. That's what I called her, you know. Moonflower." He sat on the riverbank, swirling the stick around the water. "Kale was the best friend I ever had . . . the man I wanted to be. He was a blacksmith, the breadwinner of the family. And the pumpkin soup I make at the Golden Gibbous? That's his recipe."

I took a seat next to Io. "Dude. That pumpkin soup is, like, divine."

"And I don't even do it justice." Io looked down. "Those two always thought dragons were divine, too. They loved dragons. They were enamored the day Verdoro first passed over our heads. It was a harvest day. Mom and Pop dropped everything, and I mean everything. Fresh eggs broke all over a newly scrubbed floor. Our father nearly severed his foot when he dropped the scythe in the wheat fields. The dragon was an omen, Mom said. He would bring us terrible luck. He was a symbol of Lord Falk. They stopped everything and made me hike to Chandler Springs and do a peace ritual. Kale and Helene didn't believe our parents, and so they stayed at home that day. The last day."

I swallowed. "And what happened?"

"They died in their sleep that night." Io let his stick go. "Turned out they'd caught some form of a plague. We called it the Last Flame. Kale, strong and healthy the day before, snuffed out like a match. And sweet Helene."

A sinking feeling gnawed at my stomach, mirroring Io's stick as it sank to the bottom of the river. On some level, maybe Verdoro was a bad omen. A curse of some sort. After all, he'd been unlucky enough to be Falk's chosen puppet, and my whole family became tangled in all the terror that unfolded beneath Verdoro's wings. I did feel for Io when he told his story. I had the horrible thought that if anything ever happened to Karina, it'd break me, and sure I probably would've condemned the dragon, too. Whenever I was hurting, the pain felt lighter when I had something to blame, like Falk, or the weather, or the Wheel of Fortune.

But if the Wheel was destroyed ages ago, then that meant that bad luck just happened from time to time. There wasn't always a reason to it. Sometimes it was just a coincidence, or the hand we'd been dealt in the Uno game, as Karina and I once said.

I sat there feeling a little awkward and picking at blades of grass. "Io, I'm awfully sorry about your brother and sister. It makes me sad." I cleared my throat, surprised to feel that a knot had been building there. "I have to admit, I'm not really good at knowing what to say in these situations."

I didn't just mean when a werewolf opened up to me, which had never happened before, but when *anybody* was real with me. Honest, emotional conversations never came up with my friends, especially my "bros." As a guy, I wished we could be more genuine and stop being so weird about having feelings. Like, I cry way more than Rina does, and I'm not ashamed to admit it.

Io nodded at me, the smile slowly coming back to his face. "You're a good listener. You don't have to know what to say if you know how to listen." He sighed. "I haven't spoken about Helene and Kale in ages."

I set my stick by my side. "Thank you for sharing that with me."

Io sat up on his knees and leaned over the water. "Guess I need another stick now."

I tossed him mine and stood, beating clumps of mud off my knees. "I'll go grab another."

In a place like these woodlands, a good stick wasn't hard to find. I only needed to walk a few yards, following the riverbank and keeping one eye on the water. When I wasn't messing with the river—when I let it flow—I could see clearly. Past my reflection, I could make out the rocks and the fishes, the grains of sand, the clumps of plant life . . . the glint of red metal . . .

Wait a minute.

I shook my head, wondering if I had imagined that flash of crimson. We'd hardly spotted a single coin on our walk through the forest. I was starting to think the beargobbler had eaten them all.

Taking a knee, I leaned over the water and searched for that speckle of red again.

Sure enough, wedged in between two rocks and nested in a clump of weeds, a red medallion sat on the riverbed while the current fought to pull it free.

Not just any red coin. *The* red coin, stamped with— what was that tree called again? I felt like I hadn't seen The Bramble King in ages. The action of these past few hours had reduced Thorne's story to the barest of details: He needed it to reclaim the wish of his heart. A strange thought came to me: Rina and I only really wanted to help because we wanted to get out of the well. I *did* get out of the well. Maybe I could find another way to pull Karina out, and we could forget all about the creeptastic underworld of wishes.

But my Rosas pride demanded that I finish what I started. "Io." I pointed to the coin.

"That's the one?" Io planted his stick in the ground.

"The actual one." I remembered holding that coin in my hand only minutes before meeting Thorne. The metal called to me like my bed after a soccer game, demanding my undivided attention. Without another thought, I sat down, pulled off my boots, and then put them side by side. "I need to get it out of there. You'll cover me, right?"

Io rolled up his sleeves. "Right behind you. I'll pull you out if you need. The water may look shallow, but it goes deeper than it appears."

Luckily in a river like this, my feet could touch the bottom and I'd still be able to keep my head above the surface. The water would barely come up past my knees. I balled up my socks and tugged my shirt off, just in case. "Rina's not gonna believe I'm getting back in the water."

I couldn't believe I was getting back in the water. Not just any body of water, either. A river, where La Llorona liked to hang out. My mom would never let me forget that if I talked back or didn't clean my room, then the crazy crying ghost woman would show up in the night and zoom me away.

She can't hurt you here, I thought. *She's not real. She's a bedtime story. Like dragons and genies.*

I took a breath, and with newfound confidence, I eyeballed the coin, stepped into the river and—

Plummeted.

Not just past my knees. Waist. Shoulders. Head.

I let out a panicked scream, but all that came out was a mouthful of bubbles, scaring away a school of koi that definitely weren't there before. In fact, the river was filled with new things. For starters, way more space than I was expecting. Above, below, all around, the water surrounded me. This wasn't the thin little riverbank anymore. This was basically a canyon.

Coin. I looked down, disheartened by all the metal that lay on the riverbed. I had sworn there had only been a single red coin tucked between a pair of rocks before. Now, there were pocket watches, necklaces, bits of copper and silver, and even forks. But as my lungs tightened in my chest, I noted that I couldn't make out a single flash of red.

I kicked and pushed my way back up, starving for air. I was afraid. Io's comment about the depth of the water had been a massive understatement.

When I broke the surface, I took a deep, exhilarating breath, while Io looked on with wide, hopeful eyes.

"Did you retrieve it?" he asked.

I glared at Io. "No." I shook the moisture out of my hair, treading water. "What was that, man? I wasn't prepared to do a deep sea diving adventure." I looked down, the illusion of the shallow riverbed still intact. From above water, it looked like my feet were touching the ground. "A little heads up would've been nice."

"I told you it was deeper than it looked."

I scoffed. "*Thanks.*"

"Just swim straight down. If you saw it from up here, it's down there."

And that was the trouble. Looking down from the surface a second time, I didn't see the red coin anymore. Had I hallucinated? I sighed. "I'm gonna try again. Remember, keep an eye—"

I plummeted again, this time pulled by something that had a tight, slimy grip on my ankle. Sadly, I knew from experience that it had to be a tentacle. *Llorona! I* thought, kicking and struggling against her grip. *This is the end.*

Except La Llorona wasn't supposed to have tentacles.

Hesitantly, I spun and faced my captor.

I shouldn't have been surprised to see the tentacles attached to the big green dome that was wandering the river earlier. Only now that I was close enough to see the beargobbler's eight blurry eyes, the mouth as big around as a trash can, and the *teeth,* I hated everything. Some of its teeth were sharp and pointy, partly because most of them were broken. Living on a diet of metals and bones was bound to be a dental nightmare.

Being consumed by a beargobbler was my nightmare, and I'd lived one just like this before.

The monster let out a roar, flooding every rational part of my brain with fear.

Oh god, I thought. *The beargobbler can smell all the chicken right now.* I had to override the fear. I had to think rationally. I had to trust my instincts and remember what the great Diego Rosas would do. As the gobbler pulled me in and opened its mouth, I channeled my tio.

Pop quiz, Charlie. We don't have much time, but you've seen this before. I wrote about it in my diary, remember? Do you run or play dead?

Not great options, Tio, I thought. *Do you see what's happening right now? I can't run from this thing. A: I'm in water. B: This jerk has a tentacle on my leg. If I play dead,*

I'll just make it easier for him to eat me. Any chance this thing's allergic to grapes? Oh wait, I don't have any grapes.

I squeezed my eyes shut. Imaginary Tio had just asked me a trick question. There was a third option, but it would require me to do the bravest thing I'd ever done. No fear. No chicken. Okay, a *little* chicken.

If only I weren't underwater, I could've said something epic and heroic right about now. Something like, *Not today, jerk face.*

I swam *toward* the open mouth, made a fist, and punched that beargobbler in the face. Once above its mouth. Once on top of the dome.

Twice in the eyeballs.

Black, cloudy ink squirted from—well, I couldn't really tell where—but I was pretty sure I had won. Even if I hadn't gotten the beargobbler off my case, at least it let go of my ankle, and that's when I booked it. I headed for the surface as fast as I could, channeling my inner dolphin.

Thanks, Tio, I thought. After all, his diary taught me to punch a shark in the snout if I was ever up against one. I figured the beargobbler was in a similar category.

I gasped for air when I reached the surface, extending my arms high over the water. "Io, pull me out. Please. The gobbler's in there. He's after me, and I just made it super mad." I looked down, my heart racing as I gulped in that precious air. Again, the illusion had returned. From above, all I could see was the pristine, crystal river, gobbler free without a single drop of ink. But I knew better. The river was not my friend. "Please."

A cold hand closed around my wrist and pulled. I vowed not to take my eyes off the water until I was dry again. The last thing I needed was to let my guard down and lose a foot.

"Thank you," I breathed as my waist came out of the water. Then my knees. Then my feet. I could have hugged Io for helping me out of the river.

Except when I looked up, the hand that had grabbed me wasn't Io's. In fact, Io was nowhere in sight.

I gasped. Io had left me. After all the effort I put into trusting him, he abandoned me at the river.

With the beargobbler.

And with the person who pulled me out, someone I wished I could be happy to see. But I was terrified. My heart crashed against my bones as I studied the light-green gown, the elfish pointed ears, the long silvery hair that swirled about in every direction and wavered as if submerged in water. Worst of all was the stern, cold expression of disapproval—the flat, thin lips and hard green eyes.

"Hi," I said awkwardly, wiggling my free hand.

Lady Constance, the Spirit of the Broken Forest, said nothing.

KARINA

———•———

When I woke up, I remembered everything, and I hated myself.

I'd had the perfect opportunity to turn the tables—to stop Clova—and all I could do was sleep. The black bottles didn't necessarily make me sleepy—they just made me feel so sad and heavy that all I could do was give up. Like no matter what I did, everything was pointless and gray. I wasn't sure how long I'd been asleep, but when I sat up, Clova was gone. My sword was gone. The machines in the control room whirred and grinded. Over time and with a shake of my head, color returned to the world. The blacks and whites fizzled into vibrant shades again, but every last drop of liquid in those bottles was gone. I'd probably inhaled it all.

I used the column with the wishing bowl to pull myself up and shake off the last remnants of sleep. I rubbed my eyes and looked out the window. Smoke, chunks of glass, and scraps from the conveyor belts littered the old factory. A few coins showered the ground, while others clung to the walls and the floor in unintelligible puddles of molten goo. The portals in the walls seemed to flicker like bad reception on a TV. There was no sight of the rock monster, or Groff, or any of the monstrosities I'd left behind.

Thorns riddled the factory ground. I wondered if my twenty-four hours was up. Had Charlie found the red coin yet?

It was only then that I saw the big red button labeled *Reset! Press in case of emergency.* I smacked the button with all my might, fully aware that I was already too late. This factory would take ages to clean and repair.

The mechanical whirs and grinding noises stopped, submerging me in silence. I was alone with my thoughts and failures, a dangerous place to be.

A dozen terrible scenarios flashed through my mind when the trapdoor clicked behind me. Clova was coming back. Maybe even the rock monster, or Falk. My adventure was coming to an end.

I picked up a shard of broken glass, ready to defend myself from my intruder.

And I wept with joy when Groff, Doris, and Boogie entered the control room, all three lightly bruised and scraped. I rushed to hug Boogie, pleasantly surprised when he hugged me back. I even hugged Groff. As for Doris, we weren't quite on that level yet, but I gave her a handshake. She sprang into action rushing around the control room with a clipboard and cataloging everything she saw.

"This is an Inhuman Resources nightmare," she said. "We've never had a day quite like this in the factory."

Boogie smiled at me. "Kawina," he said. "I'm glad you're okay."

His kindness only made me cry harder.

Groff studied the control room, his lips tight. "We've been betrayed today," he said. "I feel responsible for all of this. The malfunction in the factory. If only I'd known. Karina, did you retrieve the pouch from Clova?"

"No." I hung my head. "She took them all. Groff, why did she have the fortune crystals?"

Groff kneaded his forehead. "Because I gave them to her."

My heart sank. "What? *Willingly?*" I turned away. "And to think I was starting to trust you!"

The genie sighed. "The Wheel of Fortune is in great danger. We are all in great danger. Now it is clear: The Fortune Guard has been corrupted from within."

I took a step back. "You've been part of the Fortune Guard all along." I felt like the walls would fold in on me and my skin would unravel. "But they're the bad guys. Is Clova a part of the Fortune Guard?"

Groff crossed his arms. "Tell me what you think you know about us."

My words came out in frantic breaths. "I know you kidnapped Niraya Storm and nobody knows where she is, and you work for Falk and he chained Lady Fortune to a cloud and—"

Groff held up a hand. "Stop. We hardly believe in *good* and *bad*, dear girl. But let me summarize what I gather from you: You think The Fortune Guard intends to reassemble the Wheel of Fortune and hand it over to Lord Falk so he can steer our world into chaos. Yes?"

I swallowed a tickle in my throat. "Well, yeah."

"You have it all wrong, mortal. Well, mostly."

"Then explain it to me," I said. "Why are you working so hard to keep those crystals away from me?"

"We do not serve the master you think we serve," Groff said. "The brute you refer to as *Falk* is a lazy, wrathful individual who doesn't know why he wants the Wheel of Fortune. He is like many people in your world, seeking power for the sake of power, wanting to create chaos for the sake of chaos. We do not serve this agenda."

"What do you serve, then?" I asked. "World peace and love? I doubt it."

"You doubt correctly. We serve neither the hand of chaos, nor the hand of peace." Groff brought his palms together and intertwined his fingers like vines. "We serve a harmonious balance. We serve the cause of luck rising and falling in true, unbiased randomness, as it was always intended to flow."

I lowered my arms, feeling my guard coming down as well. "What do you mean?"

"Why do you think Mirabelle poured her fortune into a wheel, and not, say, a line, perfectly straight and narrow?" Groff put a finger in the air and drew an imaginary line in front of his face. "Or how about a tower with all its levels and stairs, a foundation firmly planted in the ground? Certainly nobody can walk away with a tower and abuse it for their own agenda, hmm?"

I tried to wrap my head around the metaphor. "What do you mean?"

"A tower ascends from ground to sky. By its very nature, there are rooms at the top and rooms at the bottom. Highs and lows. Good luck, bad luck. But a tower is also rigid and unyielding. A cellar will never become a balcony. Fortune should not be rigid, however fervently Falk would argue differently. In a true and meaningful life, fortune should rise"—Groff swirled his finger in a circle, clockwise in front of him—"and, unpleasant as it may be, fortune must also fall. How else would we be challenged to find strength within and grow on our own? That's why luck is a wheel. Every point along its edge will reach many apexes. It will touch the ground just as often. And at any given point, it is far more likely to be somewhere in between."

I took a second to think. *Unpleasant as it may be, fortune must also fall.* I wanted to argue with Groff and say nobody should ever have to deal with their lows, but he was right. I considered my time in Kesterfall with Charlie. I'd been scratched by a werewolf. Charlie had been swallowed by a sea monster. Sure, I would never wish these fates on us again, but I knew we had all completed our travels stronger than before. Because if we couldn't choose to be lucky, we could at least choose to be strong.

"Falk would undo this perfect system so that he is always on top, and everyone else is always at the bottom.

He succeeds in wealth, in love, in happiness, at the expense of all others' chances for any of the above. We, the Fortune Guard, oppose this. We seek to reconstruct the wheel as it was intended to exist."

"So, you're on Mirabelle's side? You want to help her?"

Groff nodded. "Of course. We intend to see Lady Fortune freed from her chains so she may conquer Lord Falk. Surely that prison cannot contain him forever."

I'd never seen Florindale Prison before, but truthfully, I had a feeling it would barely contain Falk for one more day. Before Charlie and I left Enzo, he made a joke to us about how Florindale Prison couldn't even contain his parents. I knew nothing about Enzo's parents or whether they were evil sorcerers or tiny little bread bakers, or even whether they had help breaking out. Falk almost certainly had someone else helping him from within the prison, and he was no tiny bread baker.

My knees buckled as I processed all these thoughts whirring through the gears of my brain—a hundred tiny wheels powered by a million neurons.

"Clova was once a trusted member of the Fortune Guard, right up until today. And this, mortal, is why today's events are my fault. 'Twas I who gave her the stones today, before I realized she had switched sides."

I shook my head. "I worked so hard to keep those from her earlier."

"Yes, and that's why I chose to let you face her. You saw through her facade. I did not." Groff sighed. "My dear girl, perhaps you are a better member of the Fortune Guard than I. And still, I worry about Clova's betrayal. She and the other members, myself included, know the Wheel better than any other beings in all the worlds. Can you guess why?"

I shrugged. "I have no idea."

Groff arched an eyebrow, and the corner of his lips turned up in a sly, knowing smile.

"Because we helped Mirabelle build it."

CHARLIE

BROKEN FOREST

—•—

The first time I'd ever seen Lady Constance, she introduced herself by jumping out of a lake, snapping her fingers, and yelling, "Stop." In the moment, I had been so mesmerized by the fact that she seemed to stop time itself that way. The wind had stopped blowing. The animals stopped moving. We were the only moving life in the forest.

But whenever I looked back and thought about that again, I thought Lady Constance's introduction was super rude. "Stop." A command without a "please" or a "hello" or anything. If I spoke to my mother that way, she'd ground me so fast my head would spin.

Lady Constance's introduction tonight was even ruder. Minutes of glaring and silence, followed by her first words.

"Clothe yourself."

I shook some water out of my jeans while I pointed to the river, the remarks and questions spewing from me without a filter. "I'm still wet, ma'am. Also there's a beargobbler in there, and where's my friend? Io was just with me. Did he leave me?"

Lady Constance drew in a deep breath, held it, and blew. In perfect unison, a powerful gust of wind whipped through the forest, wicking away every drop of moisture on my body. Unfortunately, it also had the unpleasant side effect of blowing my socks away. I ran after them, hopping wildly as I treaded on bits of pinecone, the true LEGO bricks of the forest.

While I put my shirt on and laced up my boots again, the questions kept coming. "Ma'am, are you here to give me another test? Can you help me get something from the riverbed? Seriously, where's Io?"

"Io has disobeyed me." Lady Constance hovered to a thicket of strawberry bushes, where a baby wolf cowered in the shrubs. She crossed her arms and shook her head, clucking her tongue at the wolf. "I warned you. I warned you all."

I clapped a hand over my mouth, too surprised to stand up. "That's . . ." *That's him?*

The Spirit of the Broken Forest shot me a warning look, and another pinecone plummeted from a tree, thumping my shoulder.

I gulped. "Lady Constance," I said. "Why did you pull me out?"

"Because you're a threat to my forest," Lady Constance said. "You come back from your first quest, and this time, you pollute my river with your man-made metals. You jump in for a leisurely swim. You assault my gobbler! What shall your punishment be? I can turn you to metal and leave you for the other gobblers in the river, or perhaps you shall become my next pet. You hardly have enough eyes to be a gobbler, but even that's an easy fix."

I shook my head so hard I saw two Lady Constances. "No," I said. "Please don't. I'll spend a whole Saturday cleaning your river if you want. I'll apologize to your gobbler if you promise it'll be nice to me, but honestly, ma'am, that thing assaulted *me*. I'll—"

"*Enough.*" Lady Constance towered over me. "You don't get to decide your fate. Your place is to be silent while I decide your punishment."

To my horror, the beargobbler crawled out of the water, eyes still intact, and waddled to Lady Constance. I could have sworn it shot me a dirty look when it passed by, and possibly even stuck its tongue out. And Lady Constance scooped it up and cradled it in her arms. Where it had looked massive to me before, now it looked like a spoiled toddler.

I'm not okay with this, I thought. *She's totally going to turn me into a werewolf. And Io! The poor, poor man. He's just a little pup now.* With one eye on the beargobbler, I went to the bush, where the little Io whined under the strawberries.

"Do not touch him," Lady Constance said. "Stars, the folly of humans! I am at a loss for what to do with you, Carlos Rosas. Despite all warnings, you polluted my forest. You are not a friend of nature."

I threw my hands up. "See, you don't know the whole story," I said. "I didn't pollute your river. There's something at the bottom that I need. I'm on a quest."

"A quest." Lady Constance sneered. "You still mean to kill the dragon of Kesterfall. And here I believed you were pure of heart."

Her words were arrows to my heart. I thought of the last time we'd been here, when Verdoro was considered a danger. Karina and I thought there was a very real possibility that we would've had to kill the dragon, not that we were ever sure we could have. Now, that time seemed so long ago. Verdoro was my friend now. Man, I missed him.

I shook my head. "Lady Constance, no. We would never hurt Verdoro. Not now or ever. We're trying to protect the Wheel of Fortune."

Lady Constance tilted her head toward me, her expression dark and reserved. The wind howled as she narrowed her eyes. "How do you know about the Wheel of Fortune?"

"I mean, it's mostly my sister's idea, but it's the right thing to do. That's why Verdoro's still alive, you know. Falk was using the nature stone from the Wheel of Fortune, and he was controlling the dragon. We got the stone away and set Verdoro free."

Lady Constance set the beargobbler down, and it used its tentacles to latch on to the tree above her, swinging from branch to branch and chasing a pigeon. "So you did." Lady Constance's expression softened. "Surely you remember my test. I laid two paths before you, one of which was meant to be easy. You would reach your kin. You would set him free before your predator caught up to you. You would return home happily ever after. And the other?"

I kneaded at my forehead. I would always remember her test. "An innocent life would need our help. Our enemy was sure to catch us. There would be no guarantee of our safety."

Lady Constance nodded. "Yes."

"You weren't talking about the baby wolf." A pang of sadness settled in my stomach when I thought of Oliver. "When you wanted us to save an innocent life, you meant Verdoro."

"You had to bond with the pups before you could respect the dragon," Lady Constance said. "But yes, that was my overall intention . . . that you might save the beast everyone is so quick to judge, to threaten, to place under a target for their burning javelins, and worst of all, to control for their greedy pursuits. You, Carlos Rosas, proved yourself to be different. You ventured through with the sole priority of saving a life. All others marched forth with the intention of taking a life. So I keep them here. I make them spend eternity as the half-men—the *beasts*—they already were inside, mourning the ivory moon and cursing the day they ever put a toe in my forest."

My mind spun. Lady Constance wanted us to save Verdoro all along. Her test was so much bigger than I understood, and her punishments far more enduring. I understood her logic, but when I thought about how Io had worked so hard at redemption, I didn't think Lady Constance's sense of justice was fair. The way she made the people of Jericho Harbor suffer, she wasn't really any better than the werewolves themselves. As my brain cooled, a question entered my mind, and it took me by surprise. But once the thought came, I had to ask.

I took a deep breath. "Did you create that nature stone?"

Lady Constance hovered closer to me, her eyes bright. "Yes."

My mouth dropped open. "Really? I mean, that was just a total guess."

"Your intuition—it grows stronger." Lady Constance took a knee and placed one palm on the ground. When she pulled her hand away, a single rose unfolded from the soil. "It is not in my nature to construct such an arti-fact to control that which will not be tamed. And indeed, Falk used it for all the wrong reasons. He befouled the very meaning of nature. My intention for the orb was to heal. To bring peace to that which suffers when the pain is too big for my abilities. My reach does not extend beyond this forest. The stone can be anywhere. The error is that the stone always falls into human hands, which will never be tender enough to wield it. Only one like Lady Mirabelle can be trusted to hold the crystal and turn the Wheel of Fortune. Its pieces are delicate, but humans even more so." She sighed. "So if you find it, you'd better put it back."

I gulped. She would never have to tell me anything twice. "We're trying," I said. "There's this one obstacle in our path. The Bramble King. My sister is stuck at the bottom of a well right now. It's a long story, but one of Falk's people opened a portal there, and all those coins that spilled into the river? They came from that well, and so did I. I've been after one specific coin to help the king, and I think that coin is at the bottom of the river. That, or uh, your beargobbler ate it."

I looked cautiously at Lady Constance's pet. Strangely, it actually looked cute swinging from the trees. Sure, it was still ugly, but it seemed so joyful. So carefree.

A new voice sounded behind me. "Oh, Charlie. You naive, foolish boy."

Io growled. Lady Constance raised her hands and aimed a glowing palm at me. I turned around, and there stood Ryvendor, the dark elf who had led me here, looking smug as ever. He twirled a staff in his hands, and between that staff and Lady Constance's death glare, I'd never felt more vulnerable. I ducked and side-stepped out of the way.

"Ryvendor," Lady Constance said. "You have betrayed the Fortune Guard."

The dark elf grinned. "Lovely to see you, Constance." He bowed. "And so, Charlie, have you figured out the trick yet? Have you given up your search for the red coin?"

My fists shook at my sides, my teeth grinding. I was so angry I didn't even know what to say to him.

Constance snapped her fingers, and the beargobbler jumped down from the trees to pose at her side. "Leave this boy alone. I have deemed him a worthy ally of the Fortune Guard. He has my full protection. Whatever is lost shall be returned to him at once."

Ryvendor threw his head back and laughed. "That's just the thing. I never had the artifact Charlie seeks. The little red coin he's dying to possess? It's not here."

I shook my head. "What are you talking about? I saw it. More than once. I've been chasing that coin for hours now!"

"You've been chasing an illusion, little Charlie boy." Ryvendor grinned. "And a very convincing one at that. Now you couldn't possibly be farther away from your sister, or your goals. You are failing your quest, and in a matter of minutes, the master is going to be free." He clapped his hands and danced a jig in the grass. "I simply cannot wait until he knows about this!"

No, I thought. *There's no way all of this has been a waste of time. He lured me away from Rina, and it was all for nothing. No, no, no.* "No!" I lunged for the elf, and before my hands could connect with his throat, he disappeared in a cloud of smoke.

"Over here," he said, reappearing behind me.

Lady Constance raised one arm and dropped it by her side, releasing more pinecones and debris from the trees. I hadn't been expecting a person to fall with them, but Neoma leapt out of the branches, her bow drawn and swiveling between me, Lady Constance, and Ryvendor.

"What did you do to my friend?" Neoma sneered.

"Silence." Lady Constance snapped her fingers.

Neoma's bow fell from her hands. Within a few seconds, she had morphed into a little wolf pup and charged for Ryvendor.

"Oh, that's adorable," Ryvendor said. "The master will like you." He scooped the Neoma pup into his arms, flashed me a grin, and vanished in another puff of smoke.

His laugh echoed through the forest long after he vanished, the trees trembling as if in fear.

My knees hit the ground, and the loudest, longest scream I had ever let out escaped my throat, a cathartic release of every bit of anger I'd stored in my heart since the day the Fernweh Express crashed and blew me and Karina into this world. I pulled at my hair. I beat on the grass. I picked up a pinecone and flung it into the water.

Io trotted to me and rested a paw on my lap.

Lady Constance sat beside me, not saying a word. I thought she'd lecture me for tearing at the grass or throwing pinecones into the water, but she simply sat in silence. The grass grew around us, greener and crisper than it was before.

And when I had finally stopped crying, she offered me a rose.

I had more questions than ever now, but none of them seemed important anymore. The red coin didn't seem important anymore. All I wanted was to get back to Karina.

When I stopped sniffling, Lady Constance said, "The beargobbler has decided to forgive you."

I gave her pet the side-eye. The green dome bobbed up and down as if to be nodding.

"That's great, I guess," I said.

"Ryvendor and I were friends once. Perhaps one day I will forgive him for his betrayal. I cannot always know the future, but my intuition has told me these things: That Ryvendor will come to experience much pain soon, and that he was correct." Lady Constance wove her fingertips together. "Just a few moments ago, Florindale Prison experienced a breach. The opponent of the Wheel of Fortune will soon be freed. I am afraid you, your family, and the Wheel are no longer safe. I fear the most for the Lady Mirabelle herself. This is the path that has unfolded. It was always foreseen. I did not know it would arrive so soon."

I put my head in my hands, my temples pulsing in my fingers. Of course I knew Falk was going to escape one day, but I hoped we'd at least have a little more time. Or that at the very least, Rina, Tio, and I would all be together when it happened. Now, we were all apart, each fighting our own battles. Maybe Rina was winning hers, but I had lost before I began. The red coin was a fake.

"I think I'm going to be sick. What's going to happen to Neoma?" The wolf pup rested his head on my knee. I scratched him behind the ears, an idea forming in my mind. "Would you forgive them?" I asked. "The people of Jericho Harbor?"

Lady Constance narrowed her eyes. "Tell me, why would *you* forgive them? After all they've done?"

I thought for a moment. I didn't want to push too hard and risk becoming a monster myself, and I didn't trust Lady Constance to contain her wrath if I upset her.

"Because we're not our mistakes. Because people learn and grow and do good things. And the way the people of Jericho Harbor helped me when I needed them today? I think that means they deserve another chance. Maybe even a chance to help people in other parts of the world, too. I think I can make them see the good in Verdoro. Maybe I can save Neoma, too."

Lady Constance grimaced, wrinkling her nose as if I'd just spat something sour onto the ground. I prepared for the worst. I'd made her mad. My life as I knew it was over, and my next life as a werewolf would never end.

I hoped my wolf form would at least be cute. If not, epic and terrifying. "Am I in trouble now?"

"No." Lady Constance shook her head. "You've only caused me great frustration. Of all the people who come to me, you are the first to pass a test I never even offered you. You bestowed forgiveness on somebody who I could not."

I said nothing, but a small wave of relief surged through my bones.

"I . . . I shall free Jericho Harbor of the lunar curse." Lady Constance narrowed her eyes.

Io wagged his tail, and my own heart did a funny leap. Was this really happening?

"Really?" I asked.

"Yes. But it will take some time. And if Io and the people of the harbor disappoint me—if they do not tread lightly in the Broken Forest—then you shall suffer the consequences."

"Me?" I asked. "Like, become a werewolf?"

"Worse," Lady Constance said. "You will be a wolf forever, with all the memories and thoughts of your human mind locked within. You will recognize your sister but never speak to her. You will remember walking on two legs but never stand upright. You will rue the day you wasted my time."

I gave Io another pat on the head. "You can thank me later, dude," I said. "When you're human again, you can see the world. Just don't ruin it, okay? My life's on the line."

Io whined and gave me a little nod, a small reassurance in the grand scheme of things.

"Guess it all means nothing if I don't survive what's coming next," I said.

"Indeed. But I have a funny intuition you might. To assist you in your battles, I offer you one aid, but you must go to it." Lady Constance pointed to a clearing in the forest, and the moon illuminated the trail. "Your path is open, Carlos. May the light be with you."

KARINA

THE NATURE OF WISHES

◆—————◆

"You *built* the Wheel of Fortune?" Even as I said the words, I didn't believe them.

Groff, arms crossed over his chest puffed with pride, nodded once. "Yes, we did. We poured our very essence into that wheel. We have limited freedom to leave our posts, but we want to defend Lady Fortune to our last breaths. For this to happen, the Wheel must either be restored and bound only to her, or destroyed entirely so that none may ever misuse it. I take it you mean to help us?"

I studied Groff, someone I was so willing to fight when I first came to the wishing well. How could I have known they built the most important artifact in history? I knew somebody must've built it, but I wasn't expecting such a group of . . . well, misfits. Misfits like me.

"After everything that's happened to me and my brother, and my uncle, I feel like I'm meant to," I confessed. "We're the chosen ones, aren't we?"

Groff shook his head. "No. There is nothing chosen about you or your family. Fortune is random. It's the nature of the Wheel. But you can choose to be a part of this, and that ability to choose is far stronger than our magic."

I wasn't sure whether I felt more relief or disappointment. A little of both, probably.

"We already are a part of this," I finally said. "And I choose not to back out."

"At the expense of your safety?" Groff challenged. "This will not get any easier when Falk escapes."

Not *if*. *When*. An inevitability.

"We're going to live dangerously anyway," I said. "My uncle is an adventurer. I got that from him, too. You should know something about us Rosas. We don't give up. Ever. I just need to know where to begin."

"This began ages ago, Karina."

I was glad he finally stopped calling me a foolish mortal. "Then where does it end?"

Groff pointed to the ceiling.

"Back in Kesterfall?" I guessed. "Or Florindale Prison, maybe. We need to go there."

Groff ballooned higher off the ground, extending his arm far above his head. "You need to aim higher."

Higher? I thought.

"The clouds," I said. "Where Lady Fortune is."

Groff came back to the ground, a satisfied smile on his face. "You truly are a better guardian than I. You're smart. Clever. Driven. I'm glad you are part of this."

I thought of Clova's backhanded compliments to me before she knocked me out with the black gas earlier. Only this time, the words warmed me from within. I smiled. "Thank you, Groff. I'm honored."

Still thinking of Clova, I picked up one of the shards of glass, the paper label etched with random gold symbols. "What do all these bottles mean, anyway? The symbols?"

Groff picked up a pink label. "Ah, this is the real question. Each label represents elements of a wish, but they are only decipherable to wish granters. They come in almost an infinite variety of flavors. This one happens to be a Potion of Patience. Fittingly, it tastes strongly of passionfruit if you drink it straight." He picked up a bottle with the green label still intact. "Elixir of Imagination. There's also Concoction of Kindness, Brew of Brain Power, Flaming Philter of Fortune, Serum of Sincerity, Mixture of Mystery, and so on. We create new mixtures every day to suit new wishes, and then we send them out into the world."

I thought for a minute. "What about the boxes? The monsters and stuff?"

"All against our code, not to mention fueled entirely by nightmares and despair—the dark stuff. The bottles are the essence of the factory," Groff said. "You see, when mortals make wishes, we don't give them exactly what they ask for. We haven't done that in hundreds of years."

I shook my head. "I'm not sure I'm following."

"We have the privilege of reading the desires of mortal hearts every day," Groff said. "Mortals your age wish for all kinds of interesting things. They always wish they were skinnier, or taller, or better looking."

That wasn't surprising. I'd made those wishes before, more often to my reflection than into a fountain. Mirrors were magic because they knew everything about me—how I wanted to be prettier. Smarter. And I knew Charlie wasn't any different. He wanted to be stronger. Cooler. He played with his hair until we were nearly late for school sometimes. We both had our pressures.

"My brother and I can relate," I said.

"We know," Groff said. "But our rule is this: When a mortal wishes to be more beautiful, we will give them the opportunity to recognize how beautiful they already are. Aesthetic beauty can be taken away with old age. The beauty you find within cannot be touched. If a mortal asks for strength, we'll give them the chance to learn how strong they are. When mortals ask for love or for a friend, we give them the chance to show love and be a friend to somebody else. And all of this is why you see what you see on the bottles: courage, faith, persistence, love, a little luck . . . We don't give mortals friends or wealth or health. We give them what they need to make their own wishes come true. *That* is the secret of the well. Can we trust you to keep it?"

One of my stepdad Jorge's old sayings finally made sense. I once asked him for a grilled cheese sandwich, and instead of giving me one, he walked me to the kitchen and showed me how to make it myself. Then he said, "*Enséñale a pescar . . .*" Something about teaching someone how to fish instead of giving them a fish, and then feeding them all their lives. I'd been so confused, especially because there was no fish whatsoever in my sandwich, but it was delicious, and I never had to ask for one again.

Now I understood.

I raised my pinky and extended my arm. "The secret is safe with me."

Groff stared at my pinky, a quizzical look on his face.

"Watch." I grabbed his hand and pried his little finger open. "We go like this, and we lock it in." We interlaced our pinkies and shook.

The genie tilted his head to the side. "Why?"

I shrugged. "Because it's a promise, and when we do the pinky part it's even stronger."

"Why?"

"It just is."

Some magic couldn't be explained.

The secret of the well was a double-edged sword. I was hoping after all my work down here I could make an ironclad, loophole-free wish that would give me and Charlie the advantage again. I'd been thinking about it all along. I could've wished for Falk to stay locked up forever, or for the fortune stones to come back to me.

Now I knew none of those things were certain and that none of them could be given to me, and something about that hurt. There was still a long way to go, and our path was still uncertain.

But that also meant Falk and the traitors of the Fortune Guard faced the exact same problem. Sure, they had the upper hand, but they were not guaranteed success just because of a wish. They'd have to struggle just as much as me and my brother, and our poor sweet uncle. *God, he must be so worried right now*, I thought. Did he know I was okay? Or alive, at least? Because knowing him, he was probably looking everywhere, and in a place like Florindale, he was still a fish out of water. He didn't know the magical world like he knew the natural world.

Now that I knew the secret of the well, I knew I was capable. If I could be courageous, if I could be persistent, if I could be patient, I may not be guaranteed success, but I had a fair chance.

Groff and I unhooked our pinkies, and the genie turned to Doris and Boogie. "We have some cleaning up to do," he said.

"We have some paperwork to do." Doris removed a pen from behind her ear. "Six hundred and fifty-one pages of it."

I cringed. "Is there anything I can do to help?"

Groff shook his head. "You and I both know we have more pressing matters to attend to. I'm afraid I must remain here, but you have the opportunity to leave. I trust you know where to go."

The idea was dizzying. We needed to find Lady Fortune and warn her of everything that was coming. I didn't want to do it without my brother by my side, and I was incredibly unprepared. No sword. No orbs. Nothing. I didn't even know how to get out of here. And what about our promise to Thorne?

Groff nudged Boogie's shoulder. "You have a gift for her, no?"

"Gift?" I asked.

Boogie stepped forward. "I have a pwesent," he said. "Because we're fwiends now."

Groff nodded. "Boogie discovered something on his shift today, and given that you are friends now, he wanted to share a souvenir with you. I trust you'll know what to do with it."

Boogie held out a small leather pouch in his palm. He bounced the pouch up and down a few times, and its contents didn't make a sound. When he handed it over, I was surprised by how light it was. I peeled open the drawstring, looked inside, and gasped.

Groff winked. "So you *do* know what to do with that."

I straightened my back and pocketed the pouch. "I know exactly what to do with it." I gave Boogie a hug. "Thank you, my friend."

Boogie laughed, a joyful noise I wished I could bottle up for a rainy day. "My fwiend."

Groff pushed a button, and the metal tube above me made a loud sound like a vacuum. "This chute will take you back to the tunnels. I don't know when we'll see you again, but we'll all be thinking of you and wishing you the best. May the light be with you, Karina. We're all going to need it."

CHARLIE

I GIVE UP. THE END.

•————•

After a stiff, awkward hug with Lady Constance, and a hesitant pat on the head for her pet beargobbler, I didn't walk away. I sprinted. I wasn't exactly trying to get away from them, but Lady Constance had talked about our "funny intuition" and our relationship with nature—how mine was getting stronger every day. My funny intuition was giving me some ideas about what I might find in that clearing.

I had two guesses. The first was that I'd find a wishing well, round and streaked with vines that glowed under the moon. After all I'd been through, I didn't exactly feel like diving into another dark hole, but I'd make myself do it, and I'd cross my fingers that all the wishing wells in the

Old World were connected. They'd have to be if Lady Constance was pointing the way, right?

Ryvendor's appearance in the forest played on a loop in my brain. There was so much to decode between him and Lady Constance. How had they known each other? She said something about him betraying the Fortune Guard. But wasn't the Fortune Guard bad? And if so, did that mean Lady Constance was on the wrong side?

That can't be it, I thought, my funny intuition buzzing again. *We had it wrong somehow.* Lady Constance was fiercer than the lunch lady at my school, but I trusted both of them not to use the Wheel of Fortune for evil or orchestrate my ultimate demise. I mean, they'd both had plenty of opportunities by now, whether they were making me a lunch or pondering whether to make me *into* a lunch.

The more I thought about Ryvendor, the faster I ran. He was still out there somewhere, possibly even watching me run or planning his next attack against me. Didn't he have better things to do?

Of course Ryvendor had better things to do. He told me himself that his master was going to escape from Florindale Prison soon. Was Ryvendor going to be the one to release him?

I stopped and caught my breath for a second, resting my back against a strange tree that didn't fit in with all the others in the forest. This tree was shaggier and thicker, like a willow, but the leaves burned a bright shade of red. And I definitely would've remembered the drops of water that pooled at the tips of the leaves, dangled for a second, and dripped when they got too heavy.

I'd remember that the crystal water droplets evaporated before they touched the soil, leaving the trunk and the forest floor as dry as any other patch of ground. A single drop of water dripped onto me. My hair drank it up, and something about it made me sad. Like my heart had grown heavy, and I couldn't articulate why.

It's almost like the tree is crying, I thought. Like maybe it knew about Falk or Thorne or Lady Fortune, or even my family. This tree knew all the sorrows of the world, and it carried them all on its fragile leaves.

This was a great weeping duskwood.

"That's what it was called," I said to nobody in particular. "The tree on Thorne's red coin was a great weeping duskwood." And it seemed so fitting for his story. *If you're still down there, I'm sorry I couldn't help you. I'm sorry about all of this.*

So my second guess was that the gift in the clearing would be the red coin summoned by Lady Constance's magic, however it worked. I gave the tree a pat on the trunk as if to comfort it, and with hope in my heart I finished running for the clearing.

I knew my hopes had definitely been high: a red coin or a wishing well. Maybe both were too much to ask of anyone, even an elven forest goddess.

After all that hoping, I arrived at the moonlit clearing to find that I had been dead wrong. If there was a wishing well, I definitely would've seen it. If there was a red coin on the ground somewhere, it might've taken me hours to find among the rows of roses and moonflowers.

Flowers? Really? Lady Constance had said I'd find something to help me here. How were flowers going to do anything for me? I sighed. Of course this was another test, and I didn't have the mental strength to puzzle through this one. I had a feeling I'd be pretty disappointed if I did. *Roses for Rosas, like our family? Is this supposed to be a reminder that we're strong? Moonflowers just like Io's little sister? Am I supposed to be inspired? None of this is actually going to help me.*

I fell to my knees in the middle of the clearing. Everything was terrible. The moon was disappearing, strung with dark clouds that suited my mood. I didn't know how to find my sister. I didn't know how to find the red coin. I didn't know how to prevent Lord Falk's release. I didn't even know where our tio was, or what was going on with the crystals anymore.

I had nothing. Less than what I came here with.

I hung my head

"I need help," I whispered. "If anyone hears me out there or even cares, could you just send me a sign or something? Anything? Even just a little thing would do."

And then I sat and waited for that something. That anything. That little thing. A firefly or whatever. I had low expectations.

I give up, I thought. *The end.* I stretched out and laid on my back, figuring I'd just go to sleep among the flowers and let the clouds rain on me when they were ready. After a good storm, things couldn't get much worse. I'd just plant roots in this clearing and become a weeping duskwood or something. An elven forest hermit like Lady Constance. I'd be an urban legend. The new Llorona. I didn't care anymore.

"Good night, cruel world." I let my eyes drift shut.

Of course nobody answered. Not even Imaginary Tio with his annoying pop quizzes. Even my imagination had abandoned me.

So I didn't care about the whooshing sound far beyond the clearing and high over my head. I figured that was just my imagination flying away.

Except that the whooshing sound grew closer. And louder. And more distinct.

Whatever. It's definitely the wind. No. It's just a bat. It's a cicada. It's—

I sat up and opened my eyes. My brain processed the image in front of me in less than three seconds. *Gold-green. Ginormous. Scaly.*

"Verdoro!" I sprang to my feet with newfound energy and made wild Xs and Vs with my arms, my heart soaring in my chest.

I jumped up and down. "Verdoro! It's really you."

All I asked for was something little, and on the horizon, my best and biggest friend appeared. My flying death lizard.

The dragon shrieked, a ribbon of smoke curling from his nostrils and trailing behind him. I knew he'd seen me. He was coming.

Wait. A morsel of panic cut through all my excitement, and I stopped jumping. Verdoro had to remember me, right? And he would remember we became friends, right? And if that was the case, he definitely wouldn't try to eat me again.

Right?

My brain buzzed with what-ifs. What if Verdoro was under Falk's control again? What if he wasn't, but he still didn't remember me?

What if I'd just provoked him? Because with or without Falk's control . . . *you never provoke a dragon.*

Verdoro corkscrewed over the clearing, performed a flashy dive, and landed on the other side of the clearing with a ground-shaking *boom!* I wondered if Lady Constance would be angry about her flowers.

I kept a careful distance as I gazed at Verdoro. Gosh, he was incredible. I remembered Tio's first words ever to the dragon. *My, you're a beautiful thing, aren't you? Such a handsome, beautiful creature.* Back then, I thought Tio was crazy. Looking at Verdoro today, I saw through Tio's eyes. I saw every ounce of beauty in the dragon's glowing eyes, the leathery wings, the shining scales.

I smiled. "Hey there, big guy."

Verdoro snorted, smoke curling out of his nostrils while he bucked a few times like a bull. Zid had apparently fixed some straps and padding on his back, and all the bells and whistles of a domesticated dragon meant for human flight.

Would've been nice if we had all this the last time we rode on his back.

I spread my arms to show Verdoro I was unarmed, my gaze trailing to the scarred layer of skin on his belly side. Most of his body seemed coated in green-gold iron, tough and resilient, but his last "master" knew where his skin was most tender. I had no way of knowing what kind of memory a dragon had, but I imagined Verdoro had a pretty good concept of pain, and some kinds of pain chafe through more than skin alone. I vowed that Verdoro would never have another man-made scar again. Not on my watch.

"Do you remember me?" I asked. "You've seen my face before. You know me, right?"

Verdoro tilted his head like a curious bird, grunted, then hopped once, less like a mad steer and more like a playful horse. Or a puppy.

Well, he hasn't eaten me yet. That's a good thing.

I took a tentative step forward, watching to see if Verdoro's demeanor might change. "Can I come closer?"

As if he would answer. *Sure, bro, no prob.* Verdoro tilted his head the other way and flapped his wings once. I took that gesture to mean pretty much the same thing and inched forward by one more step.

"It's me. Charlie." I tapped my chest with my thumb. "You remember carrying me across the ocean? We had a fun time, right? Enough that you might wanna hang out again?" Regardless of whether or not he remembered me, I knew Verdoro could understand me. If not my words, then at the very least, my intentions. My tone.

And this time, there was no immortal overlord controlling him. Hashtag blessed.

"I need your help, buddy." I was finally close enough to where I could touch the dragon. I gave him a pat and rested my hand on his leg. "Florindale's in trouble. I think my sister might be, too. I don't know what to do, but I don't think I can save them without you."

And that was when I knew Verdoro truly understood, because he sprawled out on his belly, curling his legs beneath him, and folded his wings over his back.

His head came down as well, and with his chin touching the same ground my toes were on, his head was the same height as my entire body. *He's listening to my story, I realized.* He could have flown away, spewed fire, or ignored me entirely, but instead, Verdoro closed the gap between us and laid down to listen to me spill my vulnerability. He answered by being vulnerable himself—giving up his powerful stance, collapsing onto his belly, and getting into a position where he could fall asleep at any moment. How much trust did it take for a dragon to do that around a human? Around anything that could be both prey and predator to him?

I patted him between the ears. "You get it, don't you? Probably better than I know. You understand." I smiled. "Look. I don't want to turn you into my personal airline or anything. I don't want to turn you into a weapon, or even my pet. I want you to be free, the way you're supposed to be. Free from captivity, Falk, hunters, and whatever else is out there. But if there's any possible way that you can help me, I promise I will always do everything I can to protect you from all that." Before I could stop myself, I was hugging the dragon. A real hug, not one of those one-armed things. I had him in a full-on embrace, and it didn't even scare him away. He lifted his enormous head and nuzzled it on my shoulder. "I think I'd want to protect you anyway."

Verdoro made a low, soft noise from his throat.

"You're a big softie, you know that? Don't worry." I let him go and patted him between the ears again. "I won't tell anyone about this bro moment we're having. Until this Wheel stuff blows over, it's probably better if we let you keep your bad boy image and scare the bejeezus out of everyone. You still know how to be scary, right?"

In response, Verdoro lifted his head and made that gurgling sound again.

I laughed. "Oh, come on. That's not scary at all. I've seen baby kitties act scarier than what you just did." I took a few steps back and puffed my chest. "Come on, buddy. Show me what you've got."

Verdoro stood, unfurled his wings, and scraped one foot against the ground like a bull about to run for a matador. Suddenly it occurred to me I probably should've had a shield or some sort of armor with me. Here I was, a kid about as scary as chocolate pudding, provoking him on purpose. I trusted him, and as far as I could tell, he trusted me, too, but this was a beast that could do some damage. He probably didn't know his own strength.

But all he did was hop a few times and stretch his wings, making him look a bit more like Batman than a ferocious dragon.

I kneaded at the tender skin under my eyes. "You're gonna have to do better," I said. "We'll work on that."

Grawrrr!

Verdoro lurched forward and let out the most vicious, epic, mountain-sized dragon roar I had ever heard. Fire lanced from his throat and licked the air around me, and his eyes flashed from emerald green to a Martian red that drilled into my soul.

"Oh my god." My heart galloped out of my chest, and adrenaline sent me sprinting behind the thickest tree I could find. While the world glowed orange, I crouched into a ball and buried my head in my knees.

I pushed too hard, and now he was mad. No, he was *livid*. Why did I have to provoke him? That was hands down the stupidest thing I ever did, even more than the day I microwaved my socks after a day of running in the rain.

When the fire and the roaring stopped, I counted down from five, my heart slamming against my chest and squeezing the air out of my lungs. Finally, I bloomed out of my pose and snuck a peek behind the tree.

Verdoro was smiling.

He didn't have a full-on Cheshire Cat sort of grin, and most people would've argued that he wasn't smiling at all. But I knew by the thumping of his tail, the green glint in his eyes, and the way that low sound gurgled in his throat again. Tiny embers glowed on dead tree branches like fading birthday candles, and I could tell Verdoro was thrilled with himself.

I was pleased, too.

I shuffled out from behind the tree, a little embarrassed. "Yeah, you really did have me fooled," I said. If I kept talking to him this way, people would start thinking I understood his grunts as individual words, the way everyone from *Guardians of the Galaxy* seems to understand the talking tree. "You're kind of a prankster deep down, huh? I like that."

Verdoro craned his neck into the tree beside him and bit off a branch full of greens.

"Don't worry," I said. "I may know you're a softie now, but you're still crazy terrifying."

When you can hug someone, prank them, and promise to keep quiet about what a marshmallow they are under their scales, scars, and smoke, then you're best friends. It's just science.

And when you're best friends, sometimes you share food. Verdoro reminded me of this when he lowered his head and spat out a wet ball of leaves. It actually smelled a lot like mint. I didn't know whether the smell was Verdoro's breath or the plant's natural scent, but the wad in front of me had the slimy texture of canned spinach. At risk of offending my temperamental pal, there was no way I would ever touch it.

I wrinkled my nose and shook my head, wishing I had some Oreos to offer up in exchange. "No thanks."

So Verdoro bent down and consumed the ABC—already been chewed—leaves.

Learning that he was an omnivore filled my heart with pride. We could enjoy *so many* of the same foods that way. Maybe even pizza.

We spent some more time bonding in the clearing. I told the dragon all my troubles, what happened with Ryvendor and Lady Constance and the red coin, how worried I was about Falk escaping. I told tales of our short time in Switzerland, what we'd been able to do and what we still hoped to do. I spilled everything. And every time I shared something new, my heart felt lighter. I wondered if this was how Io felt talking to me.

I didn't know how long we were there, but we stayed until the rain started, fat drops thumping my head.

"You know," I said. "I'm not sure where we're supposed to go next, but I think we need to keep moving." I had two ideas. We could go to Florindale and defend the prison tower, as scary as it would be. We'd do our part to keep Falk there as long as we could, even though Lady Constance was certain he'd break out anyway.

"We'll go to King Enzo," I said. "He's probably looking all over for us, and he'll know what to do. Maybe my tio is still with him. Or that Pietro guy. Are you up for an adventure?"

Verdoro lowered his head, inviting me to climb up on his neck. Rain soaked through the padding and the straps already, but they still made the dragon a much more comfortable mount. I appreciated the bit of cushioning beneath me. The only trouble was, I had only flown Verdoro a short distance through the Kesterfall jungle, and that had mostly been luck. I wasn't sure I knew how to fly Verdoro all the way back to Florindale. I wasn't nearly as skilled as Zid.

I grabbed the reins, shut my eyes, and took a deep breath. "Okay . . ." I whispered.

And before I could get my bearings or breathe another word, Verdoro took flight at a terrifying speed.

DIEGO

MY CANCELLATION

There was one real advantage to befriending a king:
Even without the power of social media, hashtags,
or his own TV show, Enzo had massive influence. The
search started with a single command to one person:
Pietro Volo, the Flying Man.

"I need as many people as you can possibly get
looking for the twins," Enzo had told him. "Tell them
to pay especially close attention to any wells in the
area and leave no stone unturned. As for you? Search
the skies."

Within minutes, Florindale sprang to life. A search
party of three became three hundred. At least, it seemed
like three hundred with crowds venturing into the

Woodlands, knocking on doors, diving into the waters near Dickory Dock, and sweeping the skies.

These people knew the living map of Florindale, and that gave me comfort. In the one place where I ever truly felt lost, these people had written the churning alleys, secret crevices, and emerald heights into their bones. They breathed the mysteries of the land, both the hiding places and the vantage points.

One such point was Clocher de Pierre, the enormous bell tower that overlooked the town. Enzo led me up there, hoping I'd be inspired by the sight of all the ant-sized people scattered across the map, each aware that the famous Dragon Tamers from the New World had gone missing. He hoped I'd catch a spark of inspiration looking over the land—a hunch on where Charlie and Karina would be.

And in some way, Enzo was right. I did have a hunch. I just didn't like it.

"This land is nothing like my own," I said. "Where I come from—"

Enzo shot me a pointed look. I'd forgotten he grew up in my world, too. Somehow, he'd learned to wear rustic, whimsical Florindale like a glove, just as snugly as he wore the gritty modern world I came from. The one I loved.

"The world *we* came from," I said, "it's logical. It makes sense."

The king threw his head back in a rich, youthful laugh. "Modern day Earth makes sense? That place gets stranger by the day."

"You know what I mean," I said. "It has physics and stuff. There's no magic there."

"That doesn't sound like you," Enzo said. "Aren't you the guy who tells the world that magic is everywhere if you really pay attention? That your own backyard is full of adventure and all that? Didn't Diego Rosas climb Everest and spend all his free time exploring caves and jungles? Of all the people I know, you should call the New World magical."

"Well, I can adapt to a cave or a jungle. I trained myself for that. But not this place. The magic here scares me."

Enzo's grin melted away. "In what way?"

I laughed. "In what way?" I repeated. "There was something James told me when we were stranded in Kesterfall. It was one of the first things he ever said to me. I told him I would get us out of there. I told him I was trained to brave the elements—weather, hunger, fatigue . . . And then James said word-for-word, 'Magic. You aren't bred for that.' Even he didn't know his way around the unpredictable."

"And you both survived," Enzo said. "That's my take-away. Why are you still worried?"

"What's the strangest thing that's happened to you in this land?" I asked.

"Oh," Enzo said. "Well, there was the mirror, the Ivory Queen, the shadow merman, there was everything that happened in New York . . . hmm. Do I have to pick just one?"

I narrowed my eyes, unsure that I really wanted the details of these stories. "Do you see my point now?"

Enzo grabbed my shoulder. "Yes. Believe it or not, I really have been in your shoes, Diego. And I'm still learning. I don't even feel like I should be King of this place sometimes. James was right to tell you that magic is dangerous. You've already seen the things it can do. It can scatter ghosts to the mountains. It can curse harbors and make people thirst for the moon. It can drive an immortal overlord to spend ages hunting for rocks."

"So then, what in the world can it do to my niece and nephew? How do I know they're not stuck in some mirror or, I don't know, transformed into a tree somewhere?"

"We don't know," Enzo said simply. "I'm the last person who would tell you otherwise. It took me a long time to believe in magic, even while it danced in front of me. When I finally accepted it, it scared me for a while. But I stay here and I hold onto hope because I believe one important thing about magic, and everyone around here tends to agree with me. Do you want to know what I've learned?"

I nodded. I needed the hope.

"As easily as it can hurt you," Enzo said, "I think that it will always try to protect you, too. If it likes you, that is."

"If it likes you?" I repeated. Ridiculous. "You talk about it like it's a living thing. With feelings."

"Maybe that's what you need to hear," Enzo said. "You go out in your own world and tell people about how nature is kind to you if you're kind to it first. Not bears, not snakes, not poison ivy. Nature. Capital N. The sum of everything you know. You're out there teaching people to earn its respect, promising that it will respect you in return."

I thought for a minute. "You're saying your Magic, Capital M, is my Nature, Capital N."

"Kind of fits, doesn't it? If nature can learn to love you, magic can, too. James and magic don't necessarily love each other yet, so of course he was the one to tell you how terrible it is. Why do you think Falk has spent centuries looking for the Wheel of Fortune and hasn't found any success, whereas you and your family have come into contact with four fortune stones? I think it's because Magic must find you more deserving than it does Falk. Think of magic like a wolf. It's always capable of biting. But maybe if you develop a bond with it, it'll protect you first, just like the wolves that befriended Charlie and Rina."

I rubbed my face. Charlie and Rina were so disheartened every time they mentioned Oliver and Nella. They had all bonded so deeply, only for Falk's magic to turn the wolves against them at the last minute. And with the blaze we left behind in the jungles of Kesterfall, they couldn't possibly be alive anymore. "That's a terrible example."

"I may know a few things you don't know," Enzo said. "Let's just say I trust magic to do everything it can to protect your family."

A large shadow fell on Clocher de Pierre, eclipsing the sun. I thought it was just a cloud until a black chariot and two skeletal, winged horses descended in front of the balcony, wheels spinning and wings smoking. I had never seen a more nightmarish image. The chariot had no driver. Just an empty, crimson velvet seat and two horses that were glaring at me.

"Enzo?" I said, my legs turning to iron.

The king unsheathed his dagger. "We need to run."

He didn't have to tell me twice.

But when I turned to run, a large, brutish man was blocking my path.

"So," Lord Falk said, "who will protect you from me?"

NIRAYA

DEAD MAN'S HAND

I always learned a lot about a person when we played a game of Dead Man's Hand. Like Blackjack, it was one of those games that didn't require any particular skills in math, but instead demanded significant skill in reading your opponents. One always had a better hand than the other, but could they be cunning? In the tapestry of the mind, could a player identify and pull the loose end—the single thread that would cause the opponent to unravel?

Jasper Livingstone was good at this with most people. He could make any opponent sweat while he always remained impossible to read, and that was because everyone had a tell. A twitch of the eyebrow. A sweaty thumb. To his credit, Jasper was a master of disguise and of hiding his tells.

But I was better, right up to my last hand.

"Show." Jasper fanned out all of his hexagons facedown then made a show of turning them over one by one:

A rum bottle.

A golden sail.

A wheel. I resisted the urge to laugh. This was by no means a strong start for Jasper.

A bronze key.

A second golden sail.

A third golden sail. I bit my lip.

A bronze treasure chest. *No.*

Jasper let his hand hover over the final card, piercing me with his gaze. "Say hello to the queen when she arrives, Ms. Storm."

He flipped the eighth hexagon. A fourth golden sail.

I grabbed my hat and fanned myself with it, eyes closed as I released a slow, heavy breath. "Well," I said. "I don't believe it, Jasper. A Full Mast. Congratulations."

The Full Mast was nearly impossible to get. Out of seventy-seven playing cards, there were four golden sails. To end up with all four in a hand of eight was an impressive feat, but to add the bronze key *and* the bronze treasure chest made it one of the best hands in the game.

Jasper leaned back. "You've always been a great opponent, Niraya. I'm honored to be the one who finally beat you, with Lady Fortune's guidance."

"Lady Fortune certainly gave you a strong hand," I said. "You should feel proud."

"Perhaps not as proud as the one who taught me to play the game," Jasper said.

I spread my cards facedown in front of me, maintaining my forced look of defeat. "Then as the one who taught you, I hope you'll remember not to assume you've won until I show my cards."

Jasper laughed and reached his arm out to his side. The black boa I'd seen on Jasper's coat rack had been slinking around while we played and had made its way to the table. When Jasper put his hand out, the snake moved up his arm and wrapped itself around his shoulders, hissing its approval at the attention it was getting.

"Can you beat the Full Mast?" Jasper smirked. "That, I'd love to see."

I flipped my cards one by one and read the contents aloud. "The barrel. The tortoise. The tempest. The hook."

I paused, and Jasper leaned in, narrowing his eyes.

"The kraken," I continued. "The locker. The Silver Siren. And last but certainly not least . . ." I flipped the final card and revealed the skeletal, hooded figure on the other side. "The Scythe."

Jasper's lips curled into a scowl. "Impossible."

I tapped on the Scythe with a daggered nail. "Witness the Dead Man's Hand, Livingstone. The only one that can beat the Full Mast." I snuck a glance out the window. *Just a few minutes to sundown now.* And the clouds were assembling, thick obsidian puffs masking the horizon. "And that effectively ends our competition."

Of course, the game wasn't really complete. The real game had begun before Jasper unwrapped the cards. We'd already been sizing each other up, each trying to read the other and find that single thread. And it wouldn't end until I'd left Malumbra with what I needed.

"Niraya Storm." Jasper let the snake coil around his arm. "You wily, cunning woman. How have you managed to stay so sharp all these years?"

"Not from building ships in bottles." I winked then pushed out my chair. "But I appreciate the attention to detail on your *Burning Lotus*."

Jasper nodded. "Your grandmother conquered that one. Aurora Storm. That's where you got your brains."

I stood. "Naturally. My grandmother did take the original *Burning Lotus*, the ship that can sail anything. That was her style, and I carry her legacy in my bones. How poetic that I get to take *your* Lotus now."

When I reached for the bottle, Jasper made a clicking sound with his tongue.

As if in response, the boa lunged, snapping its mouth dangerously close to my wrist.

I jerked my arm back, heart pounding wildly in my chest.

Jasper wagged his finger at me. "Ah-ah-ah."

My hand raced for the dagger in my belt loop. I unsheathed the blade, took a step back, and pointed it in front of me, not sure if I should've been aiming for Jasper or his serpent. "We had an agreement, Jasper. The stone is mine."

My opponent stood and pushed in his chair, far too casual for a man at the other end of a blade. "I've known you thirty years, Niraya. You've acquired many things. You've given up many more. That's what makes you unique. No pirate in history has ever shared your generous heart." He cleared his throat. "But in all thirty years of knowing you, never have I seen you come back for something you were so determined to give up. What could possibly have caused the headstrong, impossible Niraya Storm to change her mind about something so simple? The gem you seek was a gift from Atlantis, no? For saving their people long ago? You knew this when you gave it to me. You knew it was one of the most valuable, precious objects one could have in possession."

I rolled my eyes. "And then you glued it to a ship in a bottle like an art vendor in a cheap bazaar."

Jasper waved my comment away. "So what reason does Niraya Storm have to come back for one of the most valuable gems in the universe, other than she's learned it was even *more* valuable than she thought? That it has utility and value beyond what she previously knew?"

I waved my dagger. "This would be a great time for you to stop talking."

A knock sounded at the door.

Jasper grabbed a sword from his wall and spun the blade a few times, taking extra care to avoid the boa on his shoulders. "It might not be a good idea for you to be holding that dagger when the door opens." He shrugged. "You're already a wanted woman."

The door thumped again. I peered out the window. White horses stood outside Jasper's home. Many of them had armored men and women on their backs, and I had seen that purple insignia before—the five arrows crossed to make a sort of wild rose.

I slammed the tip of my knife into Jasper's table, heart in my throat. "You summoned the queen's men? What were you thinking? We had an agreement!"

Jasper raised his sword. "Sorry, Storm. You should know better than anyone that I mean no ill will. Piracy is never personal."

"This sure feels personal to me," I said.

One more knock on the door.

"It's business, Niraya. Unlike you, I'm a true pirate, and I succeeded in finding the most profitable outcome of this game. Because now, I get to collect the full value of your bounty, and I also gain the opportunity to find out about this little crystal's value. In this game, Niraya scores zero, and Jasper takes all. I doubt you're familiar with Chess, Niraya, but if that had been our game of choice today, the name for this situation would be—"

"I know Chess, thanks." I clenched my fists. "This is treachery."

"This is checkmate," Jasper finished. "Now start walking to the door, or I'll have to open the scorpion cage."

I scoffed. "Please. That's hardly a threat." A sharp poke beneath my shoulder blade spurred me into action. "All right, all right. I'm walking."

Jasper's smirk seared into my back.

With a deep breath, I opened the door. Seven men and women stood in a line, horses at their sides and bows on their backs. One woman stood in front of all the rest, an officer with the queen's garish insignia burned into her armor. She held a scroll in her hand, and her silver hair was pulled in such a tight bun I wondered if her head hurt.

"Niraya Jane Storm," the officer read.

I did a sarcastic little curtsey. "Charmed."

Jasper poked me in the back again, and I shot him a death gaze as we both stepped outside his home. I raised my hands over my head for good measure.

"By the authority of the queen," the officer read, "I hereby place you under arrest for the crimes you have committed against humanity. You are accused of theft in multiple lands. You have stolen ships that did not belong to you. You have stolen royal artifacts, precious goods, and valuable time."

I rolled my eyes. "Seriously? Valuable time? How do I get *this* time back?"

The officer went on. "You are accused of using extreme sarcasm and an uncivil tongue in the presence of royalty."

If these officers didn't like the things that came out of my mouth, they certainly wouldn't've liked the thoughts I kept inside my head. Thoughts like, *Your queen is the stupidest woman who ever lived.* I raised a brow. "Is that it, then?"

"No." The officer shook her scroll, and it unfurled even farther. Down to the dirt. The tip nearly reached my toes. "You stand accused of conspiring with the Court of Thieves. You stand accused of fraud committed against The High Wizard. You stand accused of—"

Jasper interrupted the officer with a long, high-pitched whistle. "An impressive list, Storm. Even for you."

I kicked the tip of the scroll. "There's no possible way I committed that many crimes, least of all on a meaningless island like this one. Give me that and let me read it."

The officer flicked her wrists, and the scroll retreated in her hands until it was all rolled up again. "I think the point has been made."

"You're here to lock me up," I droned. "Fascinating."

"No," the officer said. "Niraya Jane Storm, you are being sentenced to exile on Stelmorir, effective immediately. We have come to escort you."

The skin on the back of my neck prickled, my ears ringing. "Stelmorir. So it exists."

"At long last," Jasper says, "something that scares the life out of Niraya Storm."

"At long last," I said, "a fitting challenge."

I had to admit: The idea of going to Stelmorir really twisted my stomach in knots. Out of every story I'd read in the Florindale Fables, none held greater power to give me nightmares. For the first time since I arrived at Jasper's home, I worried. *What if Rosana and the others didn't succeed?*

This whole plan had hinged on them. The simplicity of the logic was a real punch to the gut: If Rosana, James, and Zid ran into trouble with the wyverns, then tonight I would die on Stelmorir. If I died on Stelmorir, then Falk would seize the Wheel of Fortune. My life, and the world, was truly in Zid's hands. I'd been foolish to tempt fortune this way. Wyverns were volatile, headstrong, impossible creatures, notoriously unwilling to be tamed. If anybody could get through to them, it was Zid, and he had arguably lost some of his touch since his first encounter with Verdoro. Deep down, I knew the wild still scared him, and yet I had put him in charge of our fates.

I cleared my throat. "I'm not going anywhere until you finish reading all the accusations. I have a right to hear what I've done wrong. Every word of it."

Of course, I didn't really care about all the accusations, but maybe the list would buy me some time.

The officer tucked the scroll into her bag. "I'm afraid the knowledge won't change your fate, Ms. Storm. Your crimes and punishments are written in stone, and I have orders to take you."

"You've just told me that I'm going to die on that island," I said. "I think I deserve one last dignity. Read me all the charges, and I'll come quietly. Read me all the charges, or I promise I'll make this the worst ride of your life."

"I'm afraid we've wasted too much time already." The officer seized my wrists and trapped them in the metal rings, cold, heavy, and rusty. Only a few metal links separated the rings around each wrist, leaving me very little slack to maneuver my arms. The ankles would come next. I wondered if they'd leave them on me when they dropped me on Stelmorir. I'd be so trapped there that it wouldn't even matter.

The officer took a knee and fastened one shackle to my right ankle, tight around the leather of my boot. "Do you have any final words before we ride?"

I turned to face Jasper, the steel coating my stomach with every second that passed. "Watch—"

"*Ho, Captain!*" A stream of shadows passed over our heads, and my heart leaped at the sound of Zid's voice.

The officer looked up, the other shackle still in her hand. I relished the surprise on her face.

Three large, two-legged dragons circled overhead, and my friends looked down on me in triumph.

"What is this?" the officer yelled. "Shoot 'em down."

A storm of arrows and fire ensued, and suddenly I was no longer the object of the officers' attention. I only needed a second to break away from the one who cuffed me, but not before a swift kick to the chest. I ran for Jasper's front door, every step flinging a loose shackle all around my right leg, which was going to get old real fast. The last thing I needed now was to trip and smack my chin.

The queen's officer was an uncoordinated mess, not sure where she should keep her attention. She did a funny little side-run in my direction while shooting arrows at the sky, her eyes darting back and forth. Had she really never found herself in this situation before? A column of flame poured from James's wyvern, and the officer raised her shield. "Don't let Storm get away!"

When I made it back inside Jasper's home, I didn't bother shutting the door. I went in with a single-minded focus on the model of the *Burning Lotus*—the troublesome little trinket behind all this mess. Jasper tailed me inside and made a flying leap for my ankle, only to be conked in the forehead by my flying shackle. He landed on his chest, scowling and clutching his forehead.

"I should never have let you in my home," Jasper said. "Wyverns, Storm? You couldn't have settled for escaping on horses. You had to be theatrical."

I grabbed the ship in the bottle and stepped onto Jasper's back. "You're the one who called in the queen's guards. You were never supposed to see the wyverns. They were never a part of an escape plan. They were part of where I'm going."

James and Zid burst into the room, faces red and plastered with sweat. "Problem!" James said. "Hello, love, by the way."

Zid elbowed James in the gut. "Storm. The wyverns are dead. You failed to mention the little detail about the archers. They brought the poor beasties down."

My heart sank. "No," I whispered.

The reality of Stelmorir was looming closer and closer with every minute. How had we lost the wyverns already? I peeked outside and beheld flashes of green and red light, flying arrows, and three lifeless wyverns on the ground.

"Rosana is holding the queen's people back," James said, "but we need another plan."

"The plan hasn't changed at all." The queen's officer marched in with her bow raised at me. "Except that now, there are four of you going to Stelmorir."

Jasper squirmed under my boots, and my veins coursed with anger when I realized he was laughing. "Looks like your luck has finally run out, Storm. What did you do anyway? What dark sorcery are you meddling with?"

I shrugged. "Depends what kind you stored in this bottle."

And with that, I raised the ship-in-the-bottle high over my head and smashed the glass against the wall. My pulse pounded in my neck as the bottle exploded, freeing the *Burning Lotus*—and the fortune stone. I used my nail to pop the crystal off the model. I thought it might have felt special or heavy in my hands, but it felt like any other rock I'd held before. The ship, however, grew heavier.

I dropped the model of the ship and watched in disbelief as it transformed in midair. It fell as a compact model, but when it hit the ground, it had become something else entirely.

The whole time it fell, the *Burning Lotus* grew, multiplying in size by the millisecond. It had barely left my hands when it swelled large enough to shove me aside, throwing me off Jasper's back. The wood creaked and the sails crackled, and the tiny anchor on the side plunged straight through the floor with the deafening shatter of hardwood. The figurehead knocked the bow out of the officer's hands, firing her arrow into Jasper's poor, cracked ceiling. My vision went black before the transformation was complete.

When I opened my eyes, stars exploded before me. I'd conked my head on Jasper's floor and a startled tarantula scuttled around before me. When my ears stopped ringing, Zid's voice swam in and out of focus as he shook my shoulders. "Captain Storm. Captain, we gotta go!"

I sat up, my head fuzzy and sore. "Go where?" I looked up at the full *Burning Lotus*, a behemoth of a ship that had split Jasper's house in two. Livingstone and the queen's officers all lay unconscious on the ground, while Jasper's zoo of exotic pets scrambled around what was left of their home. "Oh, jolly . . ."

James pulled me up to my feet and spread my hands apart as far as they would go. "Not to Stelmorir, love."

Rosana stepped in and split the shackles with her dagger. "You still have that crystal?"

I opened my fist, entranced by the fortune stone. I looked between the innocent little gem and the hulking ship beside me. "So that's what you do, little stone." Perhaps this explained some of the strange occurrences of my childhood, like when I swore my boots had shrunk three sizes or my tortoise had grown an extra foot overnight. I spread my arms and hugged Rosana. "Thank you."

I considered the ship, an idea forming in my mind.

I pocketed the crystal and took hold of the ladder on the *Burning Lotus*. Slowly, I pulled myself aboard, pausing about three steps up so Rosana could cut the shackle from my foot. On a magical adventure, it never hurt to have a Carver around. When I reached the deck, I put my hands on my hips and took a look around.

Strangely, Livingstone was nowhere to be seen. I supposed that was why he was called The Wraith. Even so, he was no longer my priority. We were back on course.

The *Burning Lotus* was an interesting legend. People claimed my grandmother's old vessel could sail anything—not just water, but land, fire . . .

Air.

I took the windlass and hoisted anchor, cringing as metal grinded against broken wood. The sails were already unfurled, depicting images of a fiery flower hovering against an iron sky.

And sure enough, the higher I lifted the anchor, the more I felt myself rising too—that the *Burning Lotus* was trying to leave the ground and break free from

Jasper's prison. I took the helm, the spokes humming with promise and energy.

I laughed to myself then looked over the port side and beckoned my crewmates to join me. "Come aboard, all, and hang on to your hats. We have a new vessel for questing," I said, feeling rich and infinite and free. "And tonight, we sail the skies."

Not just the skies.

The clouds.

Where Fortune awaited.

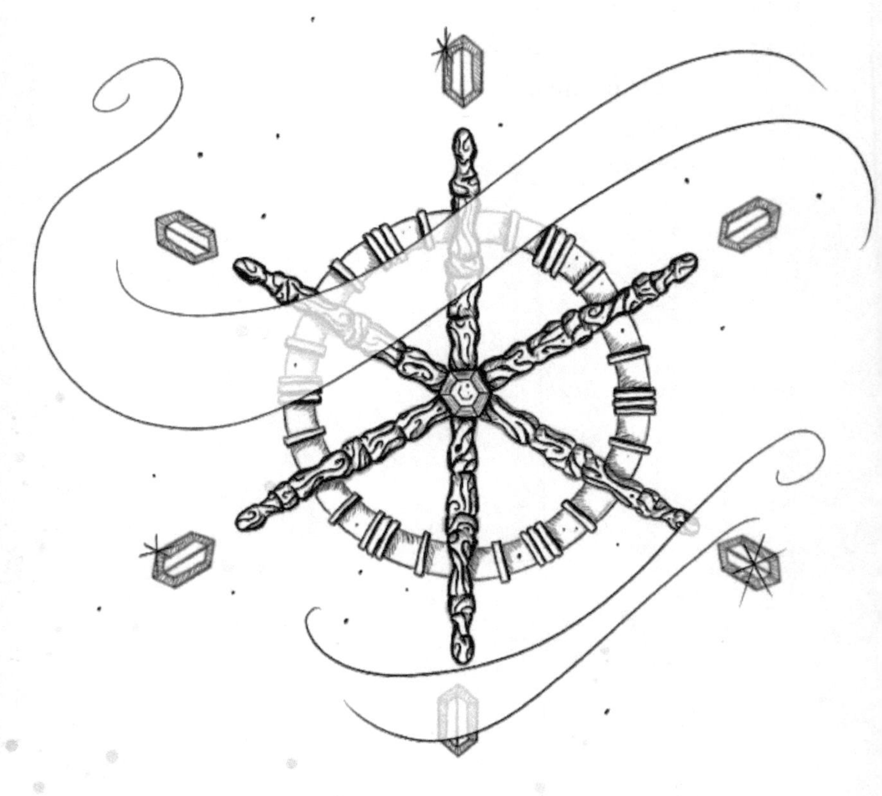

PART FOUR

FORTUNE'S WAR

KARINA

·:—•—:·

After my goodbye with Groff, Doris, and Boogie, the wish factory vacuumed me out of the control center. The first few seconds were the scariest as gravity let me go, and then the big metal tube over my head grabbed me with a loud sucking sound. For the next few minutes, I fell in reverse, laughing and screaming with my heart in my stomach. I imagined myself on a wild amusement park ride, a megaslide that zipped people up instead of whooshing them down. I shut my eyes most of the way until a faint, orange glow warmed my eyelids. The ceiling had opened up above me, where the tube shipped me right back to where I started: the wheel-shaped intersection where I first met the genie. I hit the ground, the floor snapped shut, and I dusted off my knees.

I turned in a full circle, bewildered that I still hadn't even seen half of the massive network of tunnels and canals. In fact, I wasn't even sure which path I had taken.

But the hub had changed in one major, mesmerizing way since I first arrived.

Thorns snaked and crisscrossed through every tunnel, converging over my head in a black, tangled knot of brambles. The network had grown so thick and raveled that I couldn't have chosen another pathway even if I wanted to. The vines had become as thick as my torso, each thorn about as tall as I was. Even if I still had Groff's sword, I doubted I could hack my way through all the tangles. I was bound to run out of stamina.

I also had to wonder if cutting through the brambles would hurt Thorne. Were vines part of his body, like fingers, or did they function more like hair? I remembered when Falk appeared to me as a kraken and I severed part of a tentacle. When Falk shifted back, he was missing a finger. The memory still made me cringe.

While I may have been standing in a hub of six possible paths, I had reached a dead end. Nowhere left to go. I wondered if I would've been better off climbing down the long way in the wishing factory, riding the conveyor belts and sliding down the ropes and ladders. But even the floor of the wishing factory had been corrupted by the weeds. I thought of Groff and the group, wondering how they were going to navigate the tangles.

Because where I stood, at the rate the vines were growing, I'd be smothered within the hour. How had our twenty-four hours really passed by so quickly?

Twenty-four hours, and Falk was closer to his goal than ever.

Twenty-four hours, and I had never been farther away.

Twenty-four hours, and Charlie still hadn't returned.

I pulled out the leather pouch Boogie gave to me. Perhaps the past twenty-four hours wouldn't truly be a waste after all. Then again, I had no idea what was about to happen. I only knew I had made a promise, and I only had one option left. If it was the last thing I'd ever do, I could keep one promise.

I opened the drawstring and emptied the pouch's contents into my hand.

I climbed up on one of the vines, took a deep breath, and cleared my throat.

"Thorne." My voice echoed in the chamber. "I have something that belongs to you."

I considered the red coin in my hand, small, light, and tarnished. The Bramble King had bet his entire existence on this object and whatever it stood for. Once upon a time, Thorne made a wish with all his heart, and he believed it would come true. He trusted me to help him make it happen.

I shouldn't have been surprised when *nothing* happened. The vines fattened, the thorns blackening and curling through the tunnels. They grew in a way that lifted me off the ground and toward the ceiling, dangerously close to intersection with the giant knot suspended

in the center of the hub. So this was my fate—to suffo-
cate in a thorny shrub, clutching a red coin that meant
nothing after all. Groff had even said so himself, now
that I thought about it. Whatever Thorne had wished
for, the genies wouldn't have been able to grant it anyway. They only gave "foolish mortals" what they needed
to grant their own wishes. How could I have been so
naive?

I rested my head in the curls of the branch I was
sitting on, letting tears come.

I'd tried so hard. I'd cared so much. I jumped into
a wishing well to save Lady Fortune, befriending ogres
and training genies on a job I had no idea how to do.
Shouldn't that have counted for something?

Through the blur of my tears, I didn't notice the coin
leave my hand until a gravelly voice spoke to me.

"Could it be?" Thorne asked, his voice coming from
everywhere.

I wiped my tears with my sleeve. The coin moved
away from me in a flash of red, sitting in a tendril of
vines that curled around its edges. The tendrils carried
the coin all the way up to the giant knot of brambles in
the center of the well, where I watched the coin spin and
tilt as if someone were inspecting it.

"It's been so long that I can hardly be sure," Thorne
continued. "Come to think of it, my memories have
become tangled with thorns over the years. This token
looks somewhat different from what I remember about
that fateful day."

My heart sank.

I moved my gaze all around, looking for the true source of the voice. A mouth. A pair of eyes. Anything that would indicate that Thorne was still vaguely humanoid. But all I saw were vines, thorns, and knots.

"But this crimson hue?" Thorne said, the vines carrying the coin all around the hub. "Lady Mirabelle used to wear a shade of red just like this. A particular dress. She wove it herself. I believe it was the first she ever made. I told her she looked nice in it and . . . and she made me a shirt in the same color, with shiny black buttons. Come to think of it, she made me a hat in the same color, too . . . pointed, tipped with jingle bells that shined so bright."

I cleared my throat again. "That's a nice memory." I sniffled. "She sounds very kind."

"Yes." The coin stopped moving. "The way this coin shines? It reminds me of Mirabelle's smile. Some days I had to work much harder than others, but I knew how to make her laugh. And everyone always said her smile lit up the castle. They were right. I always loved to see people happy. Especially Lady Fortune."

The coin reversed direction, traveling around the hub in a counter-clockwise direction. "Hmmm," Thorne said. "It's all starting to come back to me."

I smiled, my spirits beginning to lift. "What else?"

"The tree. The great weeping duskwood." Thorne spoke faster now, and his voice became clearer . . . younger, somehow. I kept my gaze on the coin, curious about its movement. It took me a while to realize the brambles were retreating, curling in on themselves and the thorns shrinking. The knot in the center of the well was slowly untangling, lowering me to the ground. The six paths that branched out from the hub were blooming again.

"It was our favorite tree." The excitement in Thorne's voice made my heart smile. "She thought the weeping duskwood was so strange—such an important reminder of the balance in the world. The red, such a lively color. The tears, always there to remind us that we needed a little bit of pain to appreciate the joy sometimes. Lady Fortune, my Mirabelle, insisted that the Wheel of Fortune be made from the wood of this tree."

Thorne took a deep breath, one that I could hear all throughout the chamber. The vines all trembled with his breath, rising ever so slightly, then falling. "And it was under such a tree that I made my wish to save her."

As my feet touched the ground, the remaining vines and thorns burst, disintegrating into dust. Every wall that had once been covered, every corner of the ceiling, and every inch of the ground that had been riddled with thorns now presented a clear path, bramble free.

And in the center of the room stood the creature— the man—who invited us into the well. I stood back as the thorns on his body broke apart, along with the wood that encased him. The bark split apart, revealing a bright ray of light slicing through the well. I shielded my eyes, turned away, and crouched on my knees, listening to the wood crackling, peeling, and falling to the ground, until all the sounds stopped and the well was silent.

If I listened, I might've heard my own heart beating.

Do I dare look? I thought.

"Karina," a clear male voice spoke. "Open your eyes."

I did what I was told, my mouth falling open as I stood in awe of The Bramble King. If he could even be called that anymore.

Splinters, broken thorns, and fragments of tree bark littered the ground, creating a little road between me and Thorne.

But Thorne looked nothing like himself. The man standing before me was a full, actual person without a hint of tree in his appearance. He was probably a little younger than Tio, not quite as tall, and very pale, though I imagine centuries without sunlight didn't help his complexion. His hair fell past his shoulders, along with his beard. Behind it was a face I felt I had seen before, which was a stupid and impossible feeling given that this man had been imprisoned in a plant since way before I was born. Still, I had this odd sense of déjà vu, like I had dreamed about him or something.

The man blinked, opened his mouth, and worked his jaw a bit. He massaged his cheeks then studied his hands as if he were seeing them for the first time. Every movement he made was slow and clumsy. He reminded me of the rusted Tin Man from *The Wizard of Oz*, trying to relearn the mechanics of his body one joint at a time. Elbows. Knees. Fingers. Toes.

Thorne studied me. "You . . . you broke my curse," he said. "You freed me."

I swallowed, my mouth dry and tight. "I didn't do it alone, Thorne. I had lots of help."

Thorne smiled. "About that," he said. "My name isn't Thorne. I finally remember now. You can call me Gavin."

Gavin. The name built the bridge for me, connecting all the dots he had laid out when he told his story. The love he had for Lady Fortune, down to the shade of red she wore, the brightness of her smile, and her love for great weeping duskwoods. I knew exactly where I had seen this man before. I saw him when the ghosts of Kesterfall showed me what happened to the Wheel of Fortune. Gavin had been a court jester long ago, serving the same family that fed and cared for Verdoro.

And in that family, there was a woman named Mirabelle, the woman everyone came to know as Lady Fortune.

The woman who never left her wheel unattended.

The woman who once loved a man named Gavin. The man before me stepped forward and extended his arm. "It's nice to formally meet you."

I shook his hand, still bewildered by the transformation. "I know all about you," I breathed. "And it's nice to meet you, too, Gavin."

Gavin ran a hand through his beard, his mouth agape. "You know of me?"

I nodded. "People have been telling your story for ages. It's like a fable. They say you loved Lady Mirabelle. They say you tried to protect her when Lord Falk arrived and destroyed the Wheel of Fortune. You're kind of a hero."

At the mention of Falk's name, Gavin's expression darkened. He turned away. "Falk was the one who cursed me to become The Bramble King. It was the cruelest affliction he could give me. Mirabelle, chained to the clouds, the highest part of the sky. And me, doomed to plant roots in the deepest wells of the earth. Falk put as much distance between us as he could . . . so much that I've forgotten the kiss of the sun, and Mirabelle surely can't remember the support of the earth under her feet."

I pointed to the red coin, which he held in his hand. "But all this time," I said, "your greatest wish was always within reach."

Gavin rolled the coin between his knuckles, a trick I wished I could do. "Always within reach, but never attainable. Not without help. You saved me. I remember now. I remember what I wished for."

My cheeks felt warm. I wasn't sure how to respond, but I knew I was happy. Whatever happened from here, I could know that I played an important part in history, and I didn't care if anyone ever knew it.

"I bet I know what you wished for, too," I said.

Gavin clutched the coin in his palm and then got on his knees. He looked up at me and held up the medallion. "May I share my wish with you, Karina? I have this belief that a wish is more powerful when you share it with somebody who wants the same thing. And you coming all this way tells me that you and I are allies. I think that if we make this wish together, Mirabelle might even hear us all the way from the clouds. I don't know if she has any luck left to give, but we can try."

I wasn't going to tell Gavin the secret of the wishing factory. After all, I'd made a pinky promise. But Gavin didn't need to know the secret of the well. He needed hope. We both did. What harm could we do in sharing it?

I got on my knees and took the other half of the coin, feeling just a little bit ridiculous. All methods of making a wish felt a little bit ridiculous the first time. Birthday candles. Blowing on eyelashes. I didn't have the patience to make a thousand paper cranes, but I tried once, and after I folded about thirty-four of them, I decided that felt ridiculous, too.

"Close your eyes," Gavin said. "We don't have to say it out loud. We just have to focus. And if we focus really hard on the same thing, I think it will work. It must."

We closed our eyes.

I knew exactly what Gavin was thinking. He was wishing Lady Fortune would be free. He wanted to see her again. He wanted to know she was okay. He'd been cradling this wish in his heart of thorns for years. I could almost feel it pulsing through his fingers.

Me? Sadly, I couldn't say the same thing. I tried to wish for Mirabelle to be okay . . . for the Wheel's protection . . . for the stones to fall out of Clova's hands and back into my own. I'd come all this way. Together, Gavin and I both wanted to save Mirabelle more than anything.

But my own heart belonged to my family. To *familia*. And whenever I felt lost, like I was in the well, *familia* was where my heart would always return.

Charlie, I thought. *You can come back now.* I never should've made us split up. Was he still searching for the coin?

I wish I could know if he was okay.

Gavin and I stayed on the ground like that until my knees were numb, each holding half the coin, our heads bowed. And again, I shouldn't have been surprised that nothing happened. Wishes didn't come true on their own, no matter how many people made the same one or how badly they wanted it.

When my knees couldn't take it anymore, Gavin sighed, let go of the coin, and stood, a sad smile on his face.

I looked up at him, holding the medallion all by myself now. "I'm sorry, Gavin," I said.

Gavin ran a hand through his hair and stared at the ceiling. "It was worth a try," he said sadly. "If nothing else, now we know our wishes meant nothing. We don't have to waste our time with it anymore."

"I'm sorry," I repeated. I was sorry for myself, too. I thought maybe Gavin would know a way out of the well, but I was starting to get the feeling he was just as trapped as I was.

"Well, then." Gavin sat down and wrapped his arms around his knees, pulling them to his chest and burying his head between them. "Glad to know I have a friend down here."

I put a hand on Gavin's shoulder. After centuries of waiting for escape from the wishing well, hoping for a way to see someone he cared about again, what words would've made a difference? I said nothing.

Gavin rocked from side to side. "Back in the day, before all of this mess, I also used to have a best friend. Besides Mirabelle, I mean. Someone I could tell all my troubles and know he was listening."

I nodded. "Maybe it'll help if you talk about him. What was he like?"

Gavin laughed. "Well, you're not going to believe this, but he was a dragon."

Verdoro. My heart leaped into my chest. Just think-ing about the dragon made me imagine I could hear him again. The beats of his wings. The way he called into the night when he flew free. The echoes of his mighty roar. The memories felt hazy and distant, yet also so vivid, clean, and so *real* that I allowed myself to look up and imagine I was hearing them all in real time.

Except that Gavin also looked up, a spark of recog-nition in his eyes.

"He sounded a lot like *that*," Gavin said.

I scrambled to my feet and turned in a circle, staring up at the dark. "Wait. You heard it, too?"

Gavin cupped a hand to his ears, stretching his neck and gazing high over our heads. Our shared memories were definitely growing louder. Crisper. He stood up so fast he nearly fell over again. "Is it . . . ?"

"It couldn't be," I said. *But why not?*

The roars multiplied, and before I could convince myself they weren't real, a familiar voice cut through them, and an orange glow crackled in the darkness. "Hang on, Rina!" Charlie said. "And please clear the runway. Golden Dragon Airlines, preparing for arrival!"

CHARLIE

This was how I knew Verdoro and I were best friends: After all my uncertainty, the doubts that I could fly him, and the realization that I had no idea where to go, the dragon led me straight back to the wishing well. I was mad at him for most of the flight, pleading with him to slow down and stop to let me think about where we were going. I was sure he understood, but I wasn't sure he cared. Verdoro had some real attitude.

When we arrived at Enzo's place again, thorns were everywhere, gradually unwinding and retreating into the well until Verdoro and I could dive in with style.

We landed, I dismounted, and my sister ran in for a hug. "Oh my god. Charlie, you're okay. I'm so glad. I'm sor—"

"Don't say it." I held up a hand.

Karina narrowed her eyes. "Excuse you. Did you just interrupt me when I was trying to apologize?"

I closed the gap between us and returned the hug. "It's just that you don't have to say you're sorry. I was the jerk, and you didn't deserve that. I still feel like mud. I didn't get the coin, Rina. I was following a fake. That elf guy tricked me into going back to Jericho Harbor. I don't even know how Verdoro knew to fly me back here."

"Oh, I believe that might have been partially my fault." The man in the center of the room raised his hand. I realized in horror that he was petting Verdoro, and Verdoro was letting him.

That was *my* best friend, thank you very much.

I squinted, looking the man up and down. "Umm. I hate to be rude, but uh, who the heck are you?"

The man bowed. "I am Gavin."

"The Bramble King," Karina added. "Charlie, he's *the* Gavin. Mirabelle's Gavin."

My jaw dropped. "Oh, no way. *The* Gavin? Like, Lady Fortune's boyfriend Gavin?"

The Gavin's face turned tomato-red. "Well, uh, yes, I suppose."

"How are you here?" I threw my hands up, fanboying a little. We were in the presence of Fortune's boyfriend! Such a step up from being chased through a jungle by Fortune's worst enemy.

"He was The Bramble King, Charlie," Rina said.

I studied all the broken wood on the ground, the dry vines, then looked back at the man in front of us. "*You were Thorne?*"

"Yes." Gavin rubbed the back of his neck. "And your sister broke the curse. She brought me the red coin I was about to wish on when Falk pushed me into the well and cursed me for all eternity. Well, until today."

I high-fived my sister. "Well, at least one of us found the coin." Except that I officially felt useless. "I'm sorry I didn't contribute more."

"Are you kidding?" Karina ran her hand along Verdoro's scaly back. "You found help. And you're here now. I had just been thinking how much I wanted to make sure you were okay. I had this terrible feeling something went wrong, and I hated myself for making us split up. After all that happened, I got my brother back, and I got to see my favorite dragon, too."

Gavin was having a blast playing with the dragon. He was so animated, so playful, that it wasn't hard to see how he became a court jester. He would make faces, drop to the ground, roll around, and Verdoro would bounce around making joyful dragon noises. They reminded me of our old family dog, Scrappy, the way we used to play together. And honestly, I was jealous.

Friend stealer, I thought. Technically, I was the friend stealer. Gavin was Verdoro's first best friend. I was just the guy who happened to come along next.

"I think we brought them here, Karina," Gavin said. "I was wishing to save Mirabelle tonight. I wished with all my heart that I could sprout wings and be reunited with my lady. You wished to see your brother again. It seems our wishes didn't match, but they wove together rather harmoniously."

Karina looked really confused by this, rubbing her chin and wrinkling her forehead as she thought about Gavin's words. To me, the idea made perfect sense.

Out of the corner of my eye, I thought I saw that big red genie in one of the six tunnels. We made brief eye contact, and he put a finger to his lips and faded away like mist in the wind. But I might've just imagined him. After all, the day had been never-ending. Exhausting.

"Charlie," Karina said. "I didn't get the crystals back."

My heart turned to ice. The crystals were the reason we'd jumped into the well in the first place.

"It wasn't the genie," Rina continued. "He was on our side after all. Remember all that talk about the Fortune Guard? They're supposed to be the good guys. Well, I guess they are. They made the Wheel of Fortune a long time ago, and recently, they were betrayed from within."

My mind flashed back to the mysterious conversation between Ryvendor and Lady Constance in the forest. Pieces fell into place. That's why Lady Constance said she'd been betrayed. "They were good?"

Karina nodded. "It was Groff . . . Ryvendor . . . Clova . . ."

"Lady Constance," I said.

"Me," Gavin said softly. "The Wheel was meant to be a collaboration of all life. Goblins. Elves. Ogres. Fairies. Etcetera. I was the human."

I needed to sit down. We were learning so much, and I felt like we'd accomplished so little. Karina and I had both failed our quests. I failed to retrieve the coin. She failed to protect the fortune stones. "We're bad at this," I said. "It's a good thing *we're* not part of the Fortune

Guard. Neither of us accomplished what we set out to do today. At least you found the red coin and freed Gavin."

"At least you found your death lizard," Karina said. "And we learned what Ryvendor and Clova were up to."

"We still don't know where Niraya and the queen are," I said. "What about Tio? Verdoro flew straight past the castle and somehow I just knew he wasn't there. You know Tio. He's going to get himself lost or something."

"Really, Charlie?" Karina put her hands on her hips. "Diego Rosas doesn't get lost. Not getting lost is like, his whole thing."

"He does, too, get lost. He just does it on purpose and people are okay with it. We both know it's different here. He can get *lost* lost here. Plus, do you know that there's a breach at Florindale Prison? If Lord Falk hasn't escaped already, he's about to. Ryvendor had this whole thing planned, and he told me in the forest that they were going to let him out. Even Lady Constance told me it was inevitable. I kept hoping Verdoro would fly me to the prison so we could stop it, but he flew me back here instead. Not that I didn't want to come back for you or anything," I said quickly.

Gavin ran his hands through his hair. "Lord Falk," he breathed, his eyes wide and panicked. "He's going to head straight back to Mirabelle. It's not safe. *She's* not safe. Nobody's safe. Oh, stars, Mirabelle."

Karina put a reassuring hand on Gavin's back, surprisingly calm. Something told me she knew all this already. Gavin, on the other hand, was a mess. Understandably.

"I'm sorry, man. I didn't mean to upset you," I said. "This is terrible all around. We have nothing. After all we've been through, we have absolutely nothing."

My sister didn't follow my lead. Had she even heard me venting? Instead, she just kept looking at Verdoro, and back at Gavin. *Hello?* I thought. *Come on, be stressed with me.*

Karina cleared her throat, the Rosas concentration stare cemented on her face. "How do we get to her?"

Gavin shook his head. "What do you mean?"

"Mirabelle," Karina said. "She's on a cloud, right? How do we find that cloud?"

My stomach churned. I knew exactly where Karina was going with this, and she was dead serious about it. I blew a raspberry. "Karina," I said. "Are we really thinking of doing this now? With no support? No Zid, no Niraya, no James or Tio. No magic. Not to mention, zero stones? Didn't you hear me say we have nothing?"

"Oh, I heard you," Karina said. "But we don't have nothing. I have you and you have me. We have Gavin. And in case you forgot, you brought us a dragon. We have everything we've ever needed. Charlie, we can rescue Lady Fortune tonight. We can do our part after all this time."

Gavin kneaded at his temples, like he was massaging Karina's words into his brain. I wasn't sure all this talk was good for him. Love made people do some pretty stupid things sometimes. Did he really think we could perform a sky rescue tonight?

"You two are brave," Gavin said. "You're the allies I always wanted."

Me? Brave? I smiled. Even Verdoro probably found that a little funny. Maybe Gavin really *was* a jester.

I waited for the *but*.

But I don't know how to find her.

But I can't bring you into this danger.

But we're not ready for this.

Gavin ran his hands along Verdoro's scales again. The dragon seemed thrilled, standing tall and majestic over our heads. He must've loved the belly rub.

My heart galloped when Gavin climbed up on Verdoro's back, grinning like the jester he used to be. "So," he said. "Let's go save Mirabelle. Verdoro will know the way."

KARINA

SKY RESCUE

◆

We rode for hours—Charlie, me, and Gavin, a trio of misfits on the back of a dragon. I wondered how in the world Verdoro could know how to find Lady Fortune with so many clouds in the sky tonight. I had a lot of questions about Lady Fortune's situation. What happened to her on cloudless days? How could anybody find her on a night like this, thick with an infinite horizon of dark, angry clouds?

And wasn't it scientifically impossible for someone to walk on a cloud? Clouds weren't solids, like cotton or popcorn. So even if we did find Lady Fortune, how would we know we could stand on the cloud with her?

Our safety was not guaranteed. In fact, this was almost certain to go wrong. But after everything Charlie and I had been through, we were survivors. We had the Rosas blood in our veins, the mark of the wild in our hearts, and I had learned a lot in the wish factory. That's not to say I wasn't glad to leave the well behind. I was ecstatic. When Verdoro flew us out of there, I literally screamed with joy.

We said little during the flight. My stomach was dancing. Charlie's knees were bouncing. Gavin would occasionally hum a little tune. I could only imagine the mix of emotions he had to be feeling after all these years. Fear, determination, excitement, doubt, all piled up and melting together like an ice cream sundae.

None of us were really guiding Verdoro. He had full control, a thought that would've given me goose bumps once upon a time. For the most part, he flew just below the clouds for the duration of the ride. That way, we were able to see the world below us. We flew over crystal waterfalls and rustic cottages, over the Woodlands of Florindale, and even over a steaming volcano, where we got so close to the mouth that the molten fires within warmed right through my boots. After that, I was cold. We flew through some drizzle. We saw some lightning in the distance, which made my palms sweat with nerves.

Right around the time we saw the first crack of lightning, Verdoro started to act strange.

He slowed his speed and soared up over the clouds, which I thought was probably for the best. When we went through, the humidity choked my pores, and my hair was wet when we came out on top. But almost as soon as we pulled above the cloud, Verdoro dipped back down.

And then back up again.

And then back down.

I tapped Charlie's shoulder. "What is he doing?"

Charlie shrugged. "I don't know. Why would I know?"

I held my stomach as Verdoro rose above the clouds again. "Because you're like, the dragon whisperer."

"Gavin, what is Verdoro doing?"

We veered back down. Gavin shut his eyes. "He's found something."

Charlie puffed his cheeks and massaged his belly. "I think I'm about to *lose* something."

"Don't you dare," I said.

Up.

Down.

"Is he okay?" I asked. "Does he want to land? Maybe we should give him a break."

"Maybe he's doing a trick?" Charlie said. "Hey buddy, don't get cute. You can show us your tricks later, okay?"

Up.

This time, the scene changed.

We weren't looking at the topside of a cloud anymore.

We were looking at a whole city on top of the clouds.

A pointed, white spire reached higher than anything I'd ever seen. I definitely would've seen it if it was there before. A series of red-and-gold pagodas circled the tower, and surrounding all of this, a black wall stood, blending into the foundation beneath us. I couldn't tell where the cloud ended and the wall began. My breath stuck in my throat.

"Aha!" Gavin threw a fist in the air.

"This is phenomenal," Charlie said, the understatement of the year.

Verdoro descended, and this time, his feet touched something solid. The landing rattled our bones before he broke into a run toward the wall, bouncing us with every step. I looked down. Verdoro was running on the clouds, and they were supporting his weight. The clouds were supporting us. I rubbed the goose bumps on my arms.

"It's real," I said. "The legends were all real."

Charlie gave the dragon a pat on the back. "Good job, buddy," he said. "We're here. And Lady Fortune is somewhere just beyond that wall. I feel it."

Gavin's voice turned grave. Deep and rough. "I feel it, too."

"What do we do?" Charlie asked. "Do we have an actual plan?"

"We shouldn't linger," Gavin said. "We set her free and we go. Lord Falk is bound to be on his way. Right this minute, I'd imagine. We cannot hope to defeat him. Only to outrun him."

And there was the flaw in the plan, the dark, glaring hole only growing bigger the more I thought about it. We didn't really know how to free Lady Fortune. Was there a key of some sort? Where would she be chained? And even scarier: What would we do when she was free? Where could we possibly hide her that would be better for her than this city of clouds? I couldn't exactly bring her home to Mom and ask if she could stay with us in Tucson. Lady Fortune couldn't keep running forever. Not when Falk could run, too.

What if Falk was already here?

While I silently debated myself on whether I felt ready to try standing, something popped out of the cloud between us and the gate. At first, I only saw a big pole, followed by something that looked like a bucket attached to a stick. Verdoro stopped running, springing into full defense mode. I could feel him growling beneath us.

"Security system?" Charlie asked. "Do we need, like, a password or something?"

Gavin rubbed Verdoro's neck. "Be still, my friend."

The back of my neck prickled. "What if that's Falk?"

Two large, colored sheets appeared below the bucket, gunmetal gray with fiery lotuses on them. As the stick rose higher, the wind caught the sheets and puffed them out like sails.

"It's a ship." My heart leaped against my ribs. Watching a ship rise from the clouds was a strange experience. When Charlie and I were with Niraya, we saw her old ship *Red Hood* sink into the ocean. This was like watching that happen in reverse. A glimmer of hope swelled within me, making me sit a little taller. "Do you think it's—"

"Hostiles," Gavin said. "A flying ship is no common sorcery." He dug his heels into Verdoro's neck. "Verdoro. Attack!"

"No." Charlie threw his arms up just as Verdoro leaped off the ground, soaring toward the rising ship. "Verdoro, don't attack. Abort."

Verdoro bucked in midair, beat his wings a few times, then flopped back down to the cloud, writhing with excited and nervous energy.

Gavin turned around. "Charlie, why would you do that? You're confusing him."

"Because." Charlie pointed straight ahead, where the full ship had risen in all its majestic glory and glided along the cloud as if on smooth waters. At the back of the ship, a hook-handed man, a woman in red, and a bearded dwarf waved their arms at us. "Those are our friends."

I clapped my hands and let out a loud whistle. "Queen Rosana! Zid! James!"

"Ho, wildlings," Zid called. "'Tis about time we reunited."

Gavin's jaw dropped. "They're allies?"

"Every last one of them," I said.

Gavin patted the dragon's back. "I'm sorry we confused you, chum. Catch up to that ship."

Verdoro lifted off the clouds again and swooped in toward the ship, closing the gap with just a few flaps of his wings. He pulled up so we had a bird's eye view—or dragon's eye view—of the deck, where Niraya stood at the helm in her red-feathered cap.

"One way or another, we're getting through that gate," I heard her say.

"Niraya!" I gave her a fierce wave, a giant grin on my face.

Captain Niraya Storm looked up, hands still firmly locked on the spokes of her wheel. When she saw us, her gaze could have burned me. Her eyebrows arched up into pointed angles, her eyes cold and fierce. "No. What in Fortune's name are you doing here? This is dangerous!"

"Glad to see you, too, Niraya," Charlie said.

Gavin's lips curled to the side of his face. "Allies, huh?"

I smiled. "Yeah. Her especially."

Niraya shook her head, returning her attention to the gate in front of her, which she was approaching with breakneck speed. She meant to hit it. "*Lotus* Crew," she said. "Brace!"

The ship rammed into the gate, twisting and bending an iron lock in the shape of a sun. Or perhaps a wheel. There was a sickening screech of metal, a grinding of wood, and quite a bit of grumbling from James and Zid. But when all was said and done, the ship was unharmed, and the gate opened to the city of pagodas.

As for Gavin, Charlie, and me, we simply went over the gate and landed Verdoro on the other side. Our dragon was pleased with himself.

I studied Niraya's new vessel. The figurehead was a large iron trident, and most of the front of the ship was coated in metal. I guessed that explained how it won a fight against a massive gate, even if the destruction wasn't entirely necessary. Niraya always did have a theatrical streak to her.

One by one, we all dismounted, Gavin taking the first risky step off the dragon and onto the cloud. He stepped with one toe first as if testing the temperature of a swimming pool, and then stepped a bit more boldly. When the cloud supported his weight, Niraya grabbed a rope, jumped off the front of her ship, and slid down with a stylish landing. I heard the *thud* when she landed, and yet I still tiptoed when I took my first step.

"Wow," I said, pawing at the cloud with my big toe. "Spongey."

Niraya closed the distance between us. "Come here, lass." She pulled me into a tight, almost maternal hug, smelling of leather, salt water, and just a hint of smoke. "We ran into some trouble out there. Fire, arrest, sorcery, the usual."

I grabbed my hugs from Zid, Rosana, and even James, who wasn't exactly the warm and fuzzy type.

"Dare we ask about your latest voyage, lass?" James asked.

I rubbed the back of my neck. "It's been an adventure. We have a lot to fill you in on."

Charlie nodded. "Yup. For starters, you all have to meet Gavin. *The* Gavin. Fortune's boyfriend Gavin."

"Verdoro's best friend Gavin," I added.

Charlie narrowed his eyes at me. "Yeah, no."

Gavin stepped forward and bowed. "Pleasure to meet you all."

I'd been expecting a bigger reaction. A *no way* or even a *harrumph* from Zid. But nobody said anything. They just stared. They didn't even stare at Gavin. They seemed to be staring *through* him.

James was the one to break the silence. "And who is the woman?" he said. "She wasn't on the dragon with you."

Gavin came back up from his bow. "Woman?"

James tipped his chin up. "Over yonder."

Our footsteps were quiet on the cloud, which was a double-edged sword. If Falk were around here, he could've snuck up on us with embarrassing ease. But if

Falk *were* here, it wouldn't have mattered after I turned around. Somebody else was here.

My heart just about danced out of my chest when the young woman approached, walking calmly from the spire with her hands clasped behind her back. She carried a soft smile and wore a green dress, the color of luck. I thought I knew who she was until I saw her bare feet. *No chains,* I thought. *Could this really be her? Is it . . . ?*

The doughy look of love on Gavin's face confirmed it all.

The woman walked right up to me and Charlie, stopped, and smiled. She smelled like fruit and cinnamon. Like Mom's raspados.

My pulse tightened. *What do I do?*

"Hello," the woman said. "I'm Mirabelle. I'm glad to finally meet you."

CHARLIE

THE WHEEL OF FORTUNE

A pop quiz for Uncle Diego's show: What does one say when they come face to face with the woman who controls all the luck in the world?

A: Nothing.

B: Hi.

C: It's nice to meet you, too.

D: Make a joke.

I decided to kneel, the cloud spongey against my knee. "We're, uh, *lucky* to meet you, Lady Fortune."

Karina gave me the side eye.

"Please don't kneel," the woman said. "And please, call me Mirabelle. You must be Karina and Carlos, the Rosas twins."

Karina cleared her throat. "We're glad to meet you . . . Mirabelle."

I couldn't believe we were on a first name basis with her already.

Mirabelle curtseyed then studied each of us in turn. "I've seen you before. The Wheel is rather fond of you, you know. But I never quite understood why it showed you to me. If I may ask, why have you come all this way?" She asked it so casually and easily, as if we'd traveled from Tucson to Phoenix instead of, well, from the center of the earth to the heavens themselves. "Please forgive me. It's been ages since I've seen another human. I've been quite lonely. It seems strange that suddenly I should have so many visitors."

"Well, we're all here to rescue you," Karina said. "We've heard the stories about how Falk chained you to a cloud, and he's after the Wheel of Fortune. It's time to get you down and back to Kesterfall. We can keep you safe there."

Mirabelle rubbed the back of her neck and turned away, averting her gaze. "Oh."

Oh? After all this, all Lady Luck had to say was *oh?*

After an awkward pause, I raised both hands in the air, jazz hands style. "Yay for rescue." I gave Verdoro a pat on the leg. "A free dragon ride home. Aren't you excited?"

Mirabelle clasped her hands at her waist. "My sweet boy."

Wow. She called me a sweet boy! My cheeks turned hot, only for all the heat to drain from my face when Mirabelle approached the dragon.

Mirabelle touched her fingers to a long, thin scar on Verdoro's belly. "How I've longed to see you again after the incident at home." She frowned. "Time has been kind to you, precious guardian, but somebody in the cruel world below has not matched that kindness. My heart is sore at the sight of your scars, but it also reminds me you are strong."

Verdoro cooed at Mirabelle's touch, lowering his head and brushing it against her shoulder. She looked tiny standing beside him, and yet he was clearly the baby. The high-pitched sounds of pure joy. The bright, beautiful eyes. Love like that didn't bloom overnight.

"And you, handsome," Mirabelle said, stepping away from the dragon.

I waved a hand over my face. "Aww, shucks, ma'am. Come on."

Karina nudged me. "She wasn't talking to you."

Mirabelle walked past me and clasped hands with Gavin. The clouds lit up with a shade of bright-electric blue under their feet. At the same time, thunder crackled all around us, and I felt it in every inch of my bones, a gentle warmth that buzzed from my toes to my nose.

"Well, she could've been," I whispered. "I'm way handsome."

Gavin twirled Mirabelle in a circle, her dress fanning out like a bright-green flower. He caught her, dipped her, and said, "I've missed you."

Karina bounced on her toes and tugged on my sleeve. I could practically see all the sparks leaping from her fangirl heart. "Awww! Look at them!"

"I never left you," Mirabelle said. "I've been up here watching you all these years."

Karina sighed. "Wow."

I rolled my eyes. "Like OMG, stop. It's totes adorbs."

"Isn't it, though?" Karina asked.

Secretly, my heart *was* melting a little.

The lightning faded away, restoring the clouds to their smoky color. Mirabelle broke away from Gavin's hold and approached us. "I . . . I'm afraid you will be disappointed in what I have to tell you," she said. "I cannot express how much it means that you came all this way to rescue me. I've been up here following your adventures, and I've seen the things you've done. I saw your arrival in Florindale and Kesterfall. I've seen your sacrifices. Your pains. Your every move. And what you've done to get to me is incredibly selfless and brave. For your trouble, I owe you more than I can give."

I jammed my hands in my pockets, blushing a little. "Nahhh, though. It was nothing."

Karina shook her head. "We did what we thought was the right thing. We did what we thought a good person should do, just like our uncle taught us. Like our mom taught us."

"And you've been taught well," Mirabelle said. "I struggle to believe in good people and bad. The world I lived in was never that simple. It's why I had my Wheel created. I could never decide who was worthy of luck and misfortune. But I know that there are selfless, kind, wonderful people in the world. For you to come to rescue me, I believe that was good."

Zid tugged on his beard. "And so?"

"Alas, my friends, I cannot return to Florindale with you."

Zid gasped.

Karina and I exchanged glances, and I wondered if we'd misheard Mirabelle. An anchor sank in my chest.

"*What?*" Niraya stepped forward. "I beg your pardon, ma'am. I'm Captain Niraya Storm of the *Burning Lotus*. You tell us we came all this way for nothing? Because I did *not* come all this way for nothing. You will get on that dragon's back right now, and you'll let us take you home."

I cringed. Niraya always had some bite to her, but to order around Lady Fortune herself? The pirate must've been really mad. Truthfully, I was pretty mad, too.

Mirabelle turned away, wringing her hands and looking at the ground. She looked so ashamed, so sad. And yet the next thing out of her mouth was a firm, "No. I will not."

James leaned back against the front of the ship, looking bored and unsurprised. "She was never going to make this easy, mates. You come to expect these things after a while."

Zid stamped his foot. "Harrumph." He elbowed Rosana. "Make her change her mind."

Rosana shrugged. "I don't know what you want me to do."

I cleared my throat. "I don't understand. Why don't you want to leave? You've been stuck here for years. Don't you want to go home?"

Mirabelle looked up, her gaze much harder now. "I'm not sure what you've been told, but I am not being held here against my will. This cloud is not my prison. It is my fortress. I must defend it. After Falk declared war on me and vowed to assemble the Wheel of Fortune, I chose to live here. Up here, only those with the strongest wills can find me. Up here, the Wheel is safe."

I gasped. "The Wheel of Fortune?"

Karina's jaw dropped. "You mean it's *here*? With you?"

"That is correct. Of course, it is rendered powerless without the seven crystals of fate. But it is better for the Wheel to be powerless than in the hands of Lord Falk. Still, I must not leave my post. I appreciate that you've come all this way, but I'm afraid you've wasted your time. I cannot leave." Mirabelle gave Gavin a hurt, knowing look. "Not even for love."

Gavin lowered his head. "After all this time . . ."

Mirabelle stroked Gavin's chin. "I know what you've been through. The Wheel showed me many things. A cursed forest. A wishing well. A king and an explorer. All of you. Had I known you were going through all of these trials for me, I would've tried to intervene."

"You mean we're not the chosen ones after all?" I asked. "You didn't pick us to do any of this?"

Mirabelle shook her head. "I surely did not."

"What do you mean about the Wheel showing you things?" Karina asked.

Mirabelle looked toward the spire. "Follow me to the tower. After all the trouble you've been through, perhaps I can show you."

She might as well have told me we were going to meet my favorite soccer player. I jumped in the air. "Really? No way."

"Are we really allowed?" Karina asked.

Zid, Rosana, and James exchanged excited whispers. Niraya was more stoic, her jaw working as if she were processing what we just heard.

Mirabelle nodded. "Yes. Please, follow me."

I turned to Verdoro and ran a hand along his tail. "Stay here, buddy," Gavin and I said in unison.

I laughed with Gavin then scowled when he wasn't looking.

Verdoro let out a low whine, steam curling from his nostrils.

We followed without a word, Karina and I gawking at the pagodas. Birds soared through the clouds beneath our feet, and I wondered how we didn't fall through. Zid never stopped tiptoeing. Every step he took was tiny and careful, a hilarious sight for such a stocky man. He caught me snickering about it and scrunched up his face, fuming and *harrumph*-ing his way through the clouds.

What would the Wheel be like? We'd seen a vision of it in the Kesterfall mountains, but we also knew the things we saw hadn't been a thousand percent accurate. After all, the mountains also showed us a vision of our deceased tio, who was not actually dead. Struggling, yes, and not at his healthiest after days in the dragon's jungle, but still very much alive.

"Wish he could see this," I told Karina. I couldn't take my eyes off the spire. The closer we got, I made out all the figures that had been carved into the facade. People. Places. Flowers. Weather. Tio would've loved every inch of it, or at least wanted to know more.

Karina sighed. "I know. We'll just have to remember enough to tell him all about it. We'll write everything down and make sure he knows. He's here in spirit."

Niraya flashed us a sly little half-smile. "Now that I've met him, I can see how much you're like him."

"Aye," James added. "If the lad wasn't a magnet for trouble, you two scoundrels decided to ride a dragon into Hell itself."

"Hell?" I asked. "We're standing on a beautiful cloud right now. If anything, this is the good place."

James laughed, revealing a mouthful of gold as he scratched his neck with the dull curve of his hook. "So, you still think this will end well. That's rather endearing, mates."

"Why wouldn't it?" I asked.

Rosana elbowed the pirate, a warning in her eyes. "James, don't be horrible."

"*Don't be horrible*, she says. Pah." Zid shook his head. "Also don't breathe. Don't be a man. Don't even be a person. James's bones are made of horrible. Cologne, cheese, and things that are horrible."

James shook his head. "My days of arguing with petty men are over. Save your energy, mate."

Zid glowered. "Sea dog."

When we reached the spire, I was holding my breath, barely able to contain myself. I wished I had a camera with me.

Mirabelle put her hand on the door, but before she opened it, she looked at us all. "When you see the Wheel, I would request that you do not touch it. It is . . . quite temperamental. Even the slightest tap can set fate off course."

She pushed the door open, the hinges squealing as we entered a bright, ethereal sort of room, like walking inside of a diamond. Light refracted from mirrored walls along every side, creating an illusion of infinity.

And at the center of it all, a wheel moved back and forth on its own accord. The Wheel stood about my height, and it looked a lot like the helm on Niraya's old ship, with a few major differences. This one was about as wide as my arm span. On each of the six spokes, I noticed a little round socket that reminded me of Uncle Diego's old necklace. The spherical pendant he wore would fit cleanly and perfectly into any one of those holes.

I wasn't sure if there'd ever been a socket at the center. If so, it had already been filled by a big clear bubble about the size of my head. If I squinted, I could sort of see things inside it. Shadows. Flashes of color. Mostly a lot of weird blurs.

I wanted to touch the Wheel so badly. Our group circled it, marveling and oohing and aahing.

"It's true," Niraya whispered. "The stories I read as a little girl are all true."

"Now I understand why you can't leave," Karina said. "How would we ever get this thing back down to earth? Even Verdoro can't carry something that huge. We were made to believe it was a spindle."

"The Wheel of Fortune has taken many forms. A spindle, yes. A ship's helm. A globe. Whatever suits it best. At least up here, it is safe in whatever form it chooses." She peered into the center. "It is in this room that I watched your adventures. The orb in the center shows me things."

"So you had one of the orbs all along," I said. "One of the seven, right?"

Mirabelle nodded. "This one remained with me. What do you know of the others?"

Niraya reached into her pocket and pulled out a brass locket shaped like a clamshell. She removed one of her gloves and pried open the locket. A pearl fell into her hand. "I have one."

Karina gasped. "You had one all along?"

"Not all along," Niraya said. "It was given to me long ago, and I went through a lot of trouble to get it back."

I shook my head. "You and your secrets, Niraya."

"I'm a pirate, what can I say?"

"She was *wanted*, too," Zid growled. "She didn't bother to tell us until we reached Malumbra."

Karina looked at her feet. "Falk has the others," she said. "All but one. As far as we know."

Mirabelle went white. "Oh."

Gavin took Mirabelle's hand. "My lady, Falk is coming for you. Wheel or no Wheel, we need to get you off this cloud. That man has been after this for centuries, and he's strong. He's going to try to take it from you."

Mirabelle straightened her back, curled her hand into a fist, and spoke as calmly and softly as the wind. "Very well. Let him come."

Niraya threw her hands up in the air. "Did you hear him? Lord Falk is coming. He's going to fight."

"Are you sure this is what you want?" Gavin asked. "I'll stay with you if you wish, but we can also run. There are worlds for us to see. We can take the dragon and explore. We'll make our own luck."

"Dearest ones, I know exactly what's coming," Mirabelle said. "Falk thinks he knows the same. But I have no intention of making this easy for him. He is unwise to bring a fight to me again. If he wants my Wheel, he'll have to go through me and my dragon."

I looked at Karina and mouthed, *Dang, she's fierce.*

Gavin sighed. "Then I suppose he'll have to take it from me, too. I may have been a simple court jester, but I'm ready to defend you, my lady. I always have been."

Niraya crossed her arms, her lips a thin, flat line on her face. "For the record, this plan is madness. But I told you I didn't come all this way for nothing." She rolled up her sleeves. "If I stay and fight for you, I need to know you're all in. That man is not coming to tango."

Mirabelle raised a brow. "I assure you I'm no flower to be stepped on."

My shoulders sagged. I didn't want to fight Falk again. I thought we could do all of this without another battle—that we could just land on this cloud and persuade Lady Fortune to leave—and yet here she was insisting on a fight.

"You know Falk isn't coming alone, right?" I asked. "He has, like, these elves and dwarves that want to help him. He has dragons. He has the orbs and whatever they actually do. What do we have?"

"Foresight." Mirabelle peered into the crystal. "I already know he's on his way. This shows me that he will arrive by dark. You may return home if you wish, or you may stand with me. I shall remain here."

I looked at Mirabelle's Wheel. I always thought a crystal ball would glow and light up with crisp, clear images like a movie screen, but as far as I could tell, it was just a big, meaningless glass ball. I took a hesitant step closer, and Karina followed. "Can you really see Falk in there?"

Mirabelle clasped her hands behind her back, a sad smile spreading across her face. "Look with care, my dear."

I squinted, my eyes straining from the effort. I saw my own inverted reflection in the center, tiny but bloated, almost a chipmunk version of myself. "I give up."

But before I could step away, the overlord appeared.

He didn't appear as a clear, solid movie image, but as a quick flash of darkness. Like black lightning in the corner of my eye. At first, I didn't even realize it was him, but when I softened my focus, the darkness thickened, filling the ball like smoke. He was gone in a few seconds, but Karina continued to stare, her focus only growing deeper.

"Did you see him?" I asked.

"The more I try to see anything, the more the ball hurts my eyes. It's like one of those 3D posters. If I just relax, like I'm trying to look *through* the ball . . ." She blinked. "I see a big, black chariot. He has these, like, demon horses, and his sidekicks are beside him, and he's . . . Oh. Oh, no. It can't be." She stepped away, her eyes filling with tears. She pressed her hands to her temples.

I put a hand on her shoulder. "What's going on, Rina? Tell me."

"He has him, Charlie." Karina's lip quivered, and finally, the tears burst free. "Falk has Uncle Diego."

If there was one thing I knew about my sister, it was that she hardly ever cried. Karina was a rock. So when she cried, it broke me. Whatever she saw had truly bothered her. "No," I said. "That can't be. Falk can't have our tio. Let me see."

I peered into the crystal again. *Man, I'm going to have a headache soon.* The eye strain was something else. How did Lady Fortune not need glasses after centuries of peering through this thing?

When Tio appeared, my stomach twisted.

He sat behind Lord Falk in the chariot, expression calm and serene, like he was watching a nature documentary rather than sitting next to an evil overlord. And Tio's eyes looked *wrong*—a little more gray than brown, robbed of the adventurous, youthful gleam he was known for. He didn't blink. He didn't turn his head. He simply stared ahead, his lips a thin, flat line. Even his hair looked wrong, and Tio's hair was a *thing*. People posted memes about it—the way he'd spend all day running through a desert, crawling through bushes and caves, even swimming through dark waters, and still have shiny, perfect hair at the end of an adventure. That was no longer the case today. The shine was gone, and so was the texture.

It took me a few seconds to realize King Enzo, Ryvendor, Clova, and Neoma were there, too, the king and the Jericho guard in strange trances of their own. If Ryvendor and Clova weren't sitting in the chariot with them, I would've sworn that Tio and Enzo were shifters, the way Falk posed as a man named Evan when we'd first met. The men in that chariot were definitely shaped like Enzo and Tio, but they most certainly couldn't have been Enzo and Tio. I refused to believe it.

I turned away, my stomach lurching.

"Mate," James said. "Are you all right?"

"No," I said. "We're not. He has my uncle and a woman from Jericho Harbor and . . . he has the king."

Rosana shoved past James and rushed to the Wheel, her eyes fraught with panic.

"I can't do this," I said to no one in particular. "I'm done. I'm done with all of this."

I sat down next to my sister and buried my head in my hands, too distraught to share my thoughts. She rested her head on my shoulder.

One by one, Niraya, Rosana, and Zid took turns peering into the crystal. One by one, they came away with the same pained expression on their face. Rosana's was the worst. She didn't even have the energy to cry.

Zid scowled, his hands balled into fists at his sides. "That's not my king," he grumbled. He tightened his fists, his jaw muscles trembling, and then he turned and punched the Wheel of Fortune. "That is not my king."

Rina wiped a tear from her eye. "That's not our uncle."

James took a seat between me and Rina, his legs curled under him. He hadn't even looked in the crystal. "I was in the wild with your uncle for a number of days," he said. "Never have I sailed with a man who has more fight in him than Diego Rosas. You know I would've perished in the den if he hadn't convinced me to leave the cave with him? I had all but given up—hoisted anchor and put up the sails, never to venture out again."

Niraya sat on Karina's other side, saying nothing. I thought of my latest conversation with Io. Sometimes the best listeners were the ones who said nothing at all.

"Your uncle reminded me what would've been missing in the world. He wouldn't let me forget the special things. Niraya. Love. Nature. Light. Children." James gestured to me and Rina. "I never really liked children."

"Gee, thanks," I muttered.

James waved my comment away then took my face between his hand and his hook, meeting my gaze. "You listen to me, mate," he whispered. "Whatever's coming in that chariot, you *must* fight it. Your uncle expects you to. He needs you to, and we owe it to him."

Karina scoffed. "Why would you tell us we have to fight our uncle? We're not going to do that."

"No," James said. "Never fight your family. Fight that thing that means to destroy it. You know that's not Diego, just the same way I know the other man isn't Enzo. I don't even need to look to know that. I've fought battles with my king. I've won wars with my king. And the man who helped me take down the Ivory Queen would never ride with Lord Falk."

"Then who is it?" I asked. "Huh?"

James let go of my face and stared at the Wheel. "You and I know better than anyone that there are other powers out there. You've seen them in action. You know there are powers that corrupt wolves . . . corrupt dragons."

Rina threw her hands up, a spark of recognition in her eyes. "It's the nature stone. They're controlling him with the same power that corrupted Verdoro, Charlie.

If Falk's coming to complete the Wheel, of course he'll have that stone with him."

"And of course he'll use it," I said.

James nodded. "Aye." He made a fist. "Unless we take it from him, like pirates do."

Rosana rubbed her elbows as if she were cold. "If Falk is controlling them, then this will be incredibly difficult. My husband has become one of the most powerful Carvers Florindale has ever seen. Remember his knife?"

I thought of Enzo and Rosana and the first time we met them, when they stood against Falk and dueled him in Florindale Square. Their knives held a particular magic I didn't fully understand, and to be honest, it scared me. I didn't feel afraid of it before, but if Enzo was possessed by Falk and we were going to have to face the magic of both men, then I didn't like our odds.

"We'll need to be careful," Niraya said. "If we're all staying, then I suggest we prepare."

Mirabelle peered into her crystal again. "At the rate they're flying, I estimate we have until sundown. We will want to be ready before they arrive. If only your loved ones weren't in that chariot, I could have made it hail tonight. Falk is not fond of hail, you know."

James scratched his neck with the blunt end of his hook. "What else should we know, fair lady? Surely you must have some other tricks up your sleeves."

"Hmm. Maybe." Mirabelle studied her toes, twisting her expression and rocking on the balls of her feet. "I have some ideas, but we do not have much time. Come closer, and listen carefully."

KARINA

THE WAR FOR THE WHEEL

———•———

The sun had melted away, and all we had were stars, the light of the Wheel, and a little bit of torchlight. The pagodas in the city were built in such a way that the tops could be lit on fire, which Verdoro took care of for us. Charlie and I spent some good time with the dragon, playing and exercising and flying in little circles to keep our minds busy. This was especially difficult given our uncle's situation and the overwhelming guilt that sat in my gut. I was convinced all of this was my fault. *I* wanted the adventure. *I* wanted to chase the Fortune Stones when Charlie and Uncle Diego just wanted to enjoy our vacation. *I* pretended we were the chosen ones.

When Mirabelle told us we weren't, I realized how foolish I'd been to think otherwise.

What if this was our last night together? All I'd done was put us all in danger.

"I know what you're thinking," Rosana said to me. "Don't."

I fidgeted with a loose tuff of cloud that had broken free and floated toward me, like cotton candy. "What do you mean?"

Rosana gave me a sly smile. "I was a lot like you when I was your age. Me and Enzo. To be fair, he went looking for *me*, but when he did, I was always pulling him into something wild. Fighting evil queens, tumbling into mirrors, even being entered in a jousting tournament when neither of us knew a thing about jousting." She laughed. "After a while, I started to wonder if I was bad for him, but then I realized I was just the believer. I believed in our cause, and I believed in us. The world needs that, you know. The believers, and those who keep them going." She tapped my forehead with her finger. "Just think about that tonight. Keep your head in the game, girl."

I really, really didn't know if I could.

Over the next few hours, we moved Niraya's new ship into the center of the city, just outside the spire. We relocked the gate. We gave Verdoro some much needed rest. We swapped stories with Niraya and her crew. Gavin entertained us with some of his old jokes, which didn't come as naturally after so much time in the well. Still, he had heart. I really wanted to see him be happy, along with Mirabelle. I wanted to see everyone be happy, but I didn't see a scenario where happiness would come for all of us.

And this brief moment of happiness we made in the clouds would not last forever.

The chariot approached when the night was at its darkest. We heard the wheels rumbling, the crisp beat of wings against the air, and the rattling of cargo underneath us. Our feet rumbled from the commotion. My teeth chattered from all the nerves.

"Here we go," Mirabelle said. "Be ready."

We walked outside the tower and formed a line of six: Me, Charlie, James, Zid, Rosana, and Gavin. Everyone except for Niraya, who was positioned at the helm of her ship. Having one of the fortune stones, we all agreed that we needed to keep her there. Behind the rest of us, Mirabelle sat perched on Verdoro's neck. Standing with them, I didn't feel so small.

Not until the gate opened.

I waited for the black chariot to enter, but instead, Falk's army entered the city on foot, loosely veiled by a thin fog.

"Do not engage," James said. "We wait for Fortune's orders."

Falk walked in the middle of his own line, Ryvendor and Clova at either side, followed by Enzo, a woman I didn't know, and Uncle Diego. Seeing him in person was somehow even more heartbreaking than seeing him in that crystal. He was looking at me, but he wasn't really seeing me. He was walking right in front of me, but he wasn't really there.

Skeletal horses flanked the six of them at either side, each at least seven feet tall. Neither was quite as tall as Verdoro, but each was equally intimidating based on girth and muscle and the demonic, hollow glow in their eyes. I hated them.

When they stopped walking, our two lines faced each other, silent for a long time. I didn't like my odds against any one in their line. Everyone except for the woman wore a stone. Enzo's was embedded in his knife, which sat sheathed in his belt.

Oh, god, I thought. That was five stones. We had two up here.

All seven were accounted for.

Wind danced through the clouds, rushing through my hair, rustling the neckline of Falk's tunic, and whistling all around. For a few minutes, it was the only sound I could hear.

Mirabelle spoke the first word. "Falk." Her voice was crisp and commanding coming from above us. "You were unwise to come here tonight."

The overlord grinned, held up his hands as if to show he wasn't holding anything, and took a step forward, his boots kicking up black puffs of cloud around him. "But Mirabelle," he said. "I've been planning this trip for ages. Nothing could stand in my way after all this time."

"I would argue that a *lot* has stood in the way," Mirabelle said. "Time and money. Weather and terrain. Monsters and men. Do you feel that Fortune favored you?"

Falk chuckled. "I don't mean to say this was easy, only that it was fated. Tonight, I will finally claim the

Wheel of Fortune I was destined to have." He turned his gaze toward me and extended two fingers, each one pointing at me or Charlie. "And I owe it all to you."

Charlie made a fist. "We'd never help you, buzzard face, and neither would my tio. Not even Neoma."

The woman in Falk's line growled. So this was Neoma, the woman Charlie told me about.

"You let them go or—"

"Your precious uncle has been instrumental in locating the final orb for me. His funny intuition as an adventurer delivered us right into its hands. How fortunate I was to have the combined powers of your uncle, your king, and this moon dweller light the way for me."

Rosana's hand hovered over her dagger. "Let them go. You'll release all three of them at once, or you'll have us to answer to."

Clova brandished a staff that stood almost as tall as she did. "Lord Falk answers to nobody, twerps. We offer you one warning. Stand aside and concede the Wheel to His Lordship, or perish at the hands of the new Fortune Guard. Think carefully, maggots. In the clouds, nobody can hear you scream."

Mirabelle grabbed Verdoro's reins. "It is you who will suffer, Falk. This is *my* cloud." She raised a fist in the air, the light of her Wheel casting her shadow over me. "Everyone, be ready."

My heart pounded in my ears. Charlie and I were supposed to stay with Mirabelle and the dragon to guard the Wheel itself, but Clova was looking at the dragon like a meal, her eyes wild and glowing. I had a feeling

Falk's little army would go for the dragon first. Verdoro was the most dangerous creature on the field besides Falk. If I was too busy protecting the Wheel, I wouldn't have much space to protect the dragon who had come to mean so much to me. Not to mention, somebody had to knock some sense into my uncle, and to do that, we had to steal Falk's orb.

Don't break from the plan, I told myself, watching the shadow over me. We were to spring to formation whenever Mirabelle brought her hand down.

But before Mirabelle could do anything, Enzo plunged his knife into the cloud, and the tufts beneath our feet transformed. They swirled and cycloned, forming a large, dark mound that sprouted wings, a tail, and a pointed face with a red, glowing mouth.

The king had created his own dragon, and when it was done transforming, he was sitting on top of it. In a voice that wasn't his own, he said, "Begin."

The cloud dragon lunged, and so did Verdoro. Mirabelle and Enzo were locked in battle, their dragons clawing at each other and spewing fire.

Rosana grasped Zid's shoulders. "Do you think you can break the horses? Make them listen?"

Zid scoffed. "Those aren't horses. Those are Nightmares."

"So you're telling me you can't?"

"I'm just saying they're called Nightmares. Of *course* I can break them. Who do you think I am?"

"A dead man!" Clova raced in from the side, a fiery look in her eyes as she raised a sword over her head. "Say goodnight, twerp."

Zid pivoted, his sword clashing against Clova's in a ringing of metal on metal. "Perhaps later, Rosana. I have a kick in the pants to arrange."

As Rosana prepared to help Zid, one of the Nightmares thundered toward her, charging like a train. James shoved her out of the way, grabbed the reins as the Nightmare passed by, and allowed himself to be dragged away. If I knew him, he was going to try to mount it while it was galloping.

In all the commotion, Gavin ran for Ryvendor, both men armed with staves.

Behind us, Niraya fired the first cannonball from the *Burning Lotus*: a fizzle, a boom, and a screech in succession as Enzo's cloud dragon took a hit to the stomach. The dragon writhed and Enzo clung to its neck, digging his magic dagger deeper into the cloud form to restore the hole Niraya's cannon formed.

"I need to get that knife away from him." Rosana took her own dagger and constructed some cloud illusions of her own. Shark fins razored up from beneath our feet and zipped about the battlefield, creating waves and ripples wherever they lurked. She made a large bird that burst out of the cloud and circled Enzo's dragon, taunting it and swooping for the king. The bird would open its talons with every dive, poised to grab Enzo's dagger, but every time, he brought his own knife over his head and cleaved the cloud bird from the sky. Never to be discouraged, Rosana only made more.

"Somebody stop him," Gavin yelled.

I felt like I'd swallowed bees as I saw Ryvendor and Neoma sprinting toward the spire, a shining orange orb dangling from his fingers. Gavin ran after him, his face red and drenched in sweat.

"The Wheel's unguarded," Charlie said. "We need to go protect the tower."

My attention shifted from this person to that, dragon to dragon, Nightmare to ship, and a question loomed in my mind. With everyone fighting like this, where was Uncle Diego?

When I saw him, my legs turned to lead. Uncle Diego was on the far side of the battlefield, standing tall in that cool-as-Superman pose. And he was shielding Lord Falk, who watched the battle with a wild gleam of amusement in his eyes. My stomach dropped as I realized Falk's plan. Knowing how much we cared for Uncle Diego, Falk wouldn't let us lay a finger on him until we'd gone through our uncle.

I have to get through to Uncle D, I thought, just before the second Nightmare came barreling toward me.

"Come to the tower," Charlie said. "We can't let Ryvendor get in there."

"I need to talk to Uncle Diego," I said.

Charlie grabbed my sleeve. "We'll worry about him later."

The second cannon boomed behind us. What if Niraya hit Uncle Diego?

When Ryvendor entered the building, my legs sprang into action, and I ran with my brother.

"This is a nightmare," I told him.

"Go get the pirate witch," Clova said to one of the actual Nightmares. "She has an orb."

The skeletal horse beast raced for the ship.

"Charlie," I said, "do you think you can slow that thing down if I go after Ryvendor?"

And to my great horror, Charlie spun around with his teeth gritted, giving me a forceful shove in both my shoulders. I lost my balance and toppled onto my back, tears springing to my eyes when my head hit a hard bump in the cloud. In all our years of growing up together, Charlie had never done anything to hurt me on purpose.

My ears rang and my vision swam as Charlie morphed into a short, ugly dwarf. When the transformation was complete, Clova stood over me, cackling and hissing at my gullibility.

"You stupid little twerp," she said.

She ran away and made a dash for the spire as I pulled myself back to my feet.

"Oooh, I really hate her," I mumbled. Heat flooded my cheeks, and my shoulders were tight.

Before I could get back on my feet, Enzo's cloud dragon took flight above me, heading straight for Niraya's ship. Verdoro followed. A dizzy spell took over me, the stars blurring and swirling together. We were already losing. A burst of bright-orange light flashed from the spire, followed by a burst of blue.

"Lass, are you all right?" I was relieved to see James standing over me, hair matted and sweaty. He extended his hand, but I didn't take it right away. "They just put two of the little treasures in that Wheel. We need to keep fighting."

I scooted back and shook my head. "How do I know you're you?"

James looked hurt for a second, his eyebrows knitting together. Then he shook his head. "Fair lady, I don't even know if I'm me right now. This is one scuffle I didn't ask for."

Sounds like him, I thought. Somewhat reluctantly, I extended my hand. He pulled me to my feet.

"Where's my brother?" I asked.

"Up here!"

I didn't know whether to laugh or scream when I saw Charlie on top of the Nightmare that approached me. James raised his sword and rushed to shield me, but the Nightmare trotted up to him with a soft gait, like a show pony in a parade. Charlie was beaming from ear to ear. "Sup, you two?"

I shook my head. "Uncle D would kill you if he saw you up there." A chill passed down my spine. Technically, Uncle Diego *could* see Charlie. Our uncle was here. He just wasn't *here here.*

Charlie shrugged. "As long as no one tells Mom. Hey, wanna ride to that pirate ship over there? We should help Niraya."

James scowled. "You think I'm getting on that heathen?" He shook his head and took off running for the ship, calling out behind him. "You are one sail short of a full mast, mate."

I grinned and approached the Nightmare. "Remember how Mom called us The Nightmare Twins when we were in kindergarten?"

Charlie helped me up onto the beast, and I found my balance behind my brother. The horse was big enough for the two of us, but it was probably better that we left James behind. "If she only knew," he said. "You ready?"

I raised a fist in the air. "After that ship."

But things were not looking great on that ship. Smoke curled from the sails of the *Burning Lotus*. Verdoro and Enzo's dragon circled, spiraling high overhead and spitting arrows of flame at each other. Niraya hadn't fired a cannon in minutes, probably out of fear of hitting Verdoro instead of the monster. She and Gavin were aboard locked in a dual with Ryvendor and Clova.

Zid was trying unsuccessfully to tame the other Nightmare.

Rosana was up in the crow's nest using her dagger to summon more cloud forms, each more fantastical than the last. A sea serpent rumbled around in every direction, gushing water from its mouth and putting out the flames the dragons were creating. While this was a great defense for the ship, the water had the unfortunate side effect of spilling onto the deck and drenching Niraya and Gavin.

When another dragon appeared over the spire, I thought maybe it was one of Rosana's cloud forms. It wasn't as big as Verdoro or even Enzo's form, but it was a crystal bluish white, richer than any of the iron forms Rosana or Enzo had made from the clouds.

And this one had both a rider and a man soaring beside it.

Charlie slowed the Nightmare down and I squinted, trying to identify the man on top of the beast as it joined the spiraling circle over the *Burning Lotus*.

"Where did that third dragon come from?" I asked.

And whose side was it on?

Blue flames intermixed with Verdoro's red ones and Enzo's dark ones, and the three dragons' paths braided together as they spiraled around the city like a demon roller coaster. They'd leave the ship alone for a while and zip around the pagodas, only for Enzo's dragon to return and launch another assault on the ship minutes later.

"It's Io and Snowmunch!" Charlie finally exclaimed. "The man on the dragon is Io!"

"And Pietro's with them," I said. The Flying Man, armed with a crossbow.

The Wheel of Fortune moved back and forth and went round and round, and I supposed people did, too. Before tonight, I never thought I'd be glad to see Io again. I was still trying to reconcile the man I'd met with the man Charlie told me about before the battle. My brain couldn't match the two.

The battle raged on for what felt like hours, and my dread only boiled as the night went on. Every time I thought the Wheel was turning in our favor, it would spin back the other way.

Zid finally tamed his Nightmare.

Clova seized Niraya's orb.

As they flew over the spire, Io, Rosana, and Mirabelle defeated Enzo's dragon, showering the city in an explosion of white mist.

But Enzo was on that dragon, and he plummeted from the height of the tower.

My pulse quickened and throbbed in my neck. "Enzo! He won't survive the fall."

"Oh god, I can't watch." Charlie closed his eyes.

The fall seemed to happen in slow motion, Rosana screaming and using her blade to conjure a hasty rescue. She must have been exhausted from battle, or unable to focus the way she usually did, because instead of summoning a powerful creature or something that could catch the king, all she could pull from the cloud were thin, wispy tendrils of fog that faded away as quickly as they appeared.

But just before impact, Verdoro dove and scooped Enzo up in his snake-like tail.

I brushed my forehead with my sleeve. The dragon saved the king. Fortune was in our favor.

"You can open your eyes, Charlie," I said. "He's okay."

A heavy breath escaped my brother's lungs. "Whew. I wasn't ready to see something like that."

The battlefield was silent for a while. Without the cloud dragon and without Niraya's stone, each side of the battle had lost a major asset. There were only three orbs of fortune left before the Wheel would be completed.

The silence fell away when Falk started laughing. Until Verdoro caught Enzo, Falk and Uncle Diego had stood far from the action, and now they were moving into the city. Uncle Diego continued to shield the overlord, who grinned like he'd just won the lottery.

"Oh no," Charlie said. "Look what Tio's holding."

We'd all been so afraid for Enzo that we forgot to watch for his greatest weapon: the dagger that fell into Uncle Diego's hands.

Falk put his mouth close to Uncle Diego's ear. I read the overlord's lips:

"This is your destiny. Your greatest discovery. Do what you were made for, Diego Rosas."

My uncle marched toward the spire.

"Yes, my liege."

CHARLIE

MY WORST NIGHTMARE

Karina and I stood at the entrance to the spire, and my stomach felt bubbly and tight as Falk and my tio paraded toward us. Somehow, we had to stop him. We had to get through to him.

James approached us, sword at his side with his eyes trained on Tio. "I think you two would be wise to go inside with everyone else."

I swallowed a lump in my throat. "Don't hurt him. Please."

"That is not my intention, mate."

Karina shook her head. "We're not going inside. We're not leaving him."

"Look," James said. "I don't want to see your hearts break."

"You told us to fight," Karina said firmly. "You told us to fight anything that's threatening our family. Now let us. *You* go inside."

The pirate rubbed his eyes. Then he held his sword out to Karina. "At least take this?"

Karina accepted the sword then tossed it on the ground. "We don't need it."

James gave us a sad look then picked up his sword and stood aside. "I won't leave you two."

Niraya and Zid walked out of the tower and stood beside us. Neither said a word.

When Tio started up the steps, I threw myself in front of him and spread my arms apart. "Tio, no."

Tio sidestepped, making a beeline for the door.

I mirrored him, my pulse pounding in my temples.

When I put my palm on his chest to block him, Tio stopped, and so did Falk. Tio stared through me, his eyes cold and gray, and spoke in a voice that wasn't his own. "Move, Charlie."

A tiny breath escaped from my lungs. *He still knows me.*

He took a step forward, and Karina rushed to my side and helped me block him. With my free hand, I reached for the pendant around his neck. "I'm not letting you do this."

"This is our destiny," Tio said. "You must not interfere."

I looked for a glint of the man I knew. The Skee-Ball warrior. The TV hero. The travel guru. The Oreo-loving friend of dragons. Any version of him would do. I just wanted him back. But I didn't see Diego Rosas at all in those eyes. I only saw something like a dark winter night. A zombie. An unfeeling shadow of a man.

"Uncle D," Karina pleaded. "Please listen to us."

Falk let out a terrible, thunderous laugh. "Don't waste your time, pathetic girl. Your uncle exists no more. He cannot hear you as long as he belongs to me."

"Then release him." Niraya raised her sword. "Are you so cowardly that you'd hide behind a man who never would've followed you on his own?"

"Fight us yourself, you lazy hound," Zid challenged. "I'll take you mano a mano."

Tio raised Enzo's dagger over his head, and a flash of green light burst from the tip of the blade. The cloud rumbled, and a wave beneath our feet rolled up the stairs. Everyone toppled to the ground except for James, who caught his balance on the door. As Tio and Falk made their way inside, James rushed in behind them.

"Mate," he said. "Think about what you're doing. Think about who you are and what you stand for. This isn't it."

Tio paused, his foot hovering over the ground mid-step.

James grasped Tio's shoulder. "Did you hear me?"

"I . . ." Tio revolved on one heel, a thread of recognition in his eye.

"Uncle D?" Karina said.

A flash of light burst from within the tower.

When we got back to our feet, everything was chaos.

The Wheel of Fortune had transformed. The golden helm was no more, replaced by a rotating water wheel with the crystal still at its center. Rosana was trying to wrestle the dagger from Tio's hands. Ryvendor and Clova entered and seized Rosana by her wrists. Falk took the dagger from Tio's hands, plucked the orb out of the handle with two fingers, and began to scale the moving water wheel, Gavin and Io at his heels.

Karina and I ran to Tio's side.

"Uncle Diego," Karina said. "I know you're in there. I know you can hear me. Remember when you first saved me and Charlie from a dragon? Not from Verdoro. The dragon in your backyard. The train. We were so terrified, but we knew you would always protect us. We didn't have to be afraid for long because we were with you. And we were family. We *are* familia. Do you remember that word?"

"Familia," Tio croaked, sounding as though his throat had been scoured with sandpaper.

I looked at Karina. "Did he just understand you?"

A ball of lightning webbed out from the Wheel of Fortune, shrouding it in such a powerful aura that I had to shield my eyes.

When the brightness faded away, I ventured a peek.

Mirabelle and Falk were both flat on their stomachs, breathing heavily, and inches in front of them, the Wheel of Fortune stood tall.

It had become a helm again, bright, majestic, and taller than any Ferris wheel I'd ever seen. I counted the orbs at the spokes and the center.

Seven.

Falk rolled over on his back and flashed an impish grin. "It's so beautiful."

Beautiful as it was, I'd never seen anything more terrifying. My heart slammed against my chest.

The Wheel of Fortune was complete.

KARINA

THE MASTER OF FORTUNE

◆—◆

Nobody said a word as Falk climbed to his feet and studied the golden wheel.

All our hard work had been for nothing. Charlie and I had been eaten by sea monsters, lost underground, attacked by wolves, and endured so many other misfortunes to prevent this moment from happening. Falk was never supposed to win, and here he stood in front of the complete Wheel of Fortune, looking smug and satisfied as he walked a full circle around the helm.

We failed, I thought.

Charlie buried his head in his knees.

"We really weren't the chosen ones," he said.

Uncle Diego stirred on the ground. "What just happened?" he wheezed.

"You helped me claim my prize," Lord Falk said. "After all this time, I've finally won. The Wheel of Fortune is mine at last."

The crystal in the center flickered and swirled.

Mirabelle sat up, her eyes filled with tears. "All these years," she said. "I tried so hard to prevent this from happening. This world will never be the same."

Charlie buried his hands in his hair. "But I don't understand. Isn't it still yours?"

"The Wheel no longer answers to me," Mirabelle said. "Falk has completed the Wheel. He's made it whole, and the betrayals of the Fortune Guard have changed the loyalty of the crystals. The Wheel will only hear Falk's requests now. I can merely interpret its temperament."

Falk's thunderous laugh echoed across the clouds as he took a bow. "But of course. I'm the master of all fortune now." He made a show out of scratching his chin, pretending to be lost in thought. "What shall I use it for first? How about all the luck in the world? Or maybe all the wealth? Ahh, yes, wealth and riches. Immeasurable riches and wealth. A mountain of gold sitting on an island I'll have to myself."

With that, Lord Falk stepped up to the Wheel and gripped one of the massive spokes. He rocked it back and forth, building up some momentum, and gave the helm a whirl.

I watched in horror as the spokes went round and round, end over end a dozen times while the crystal in the center flashed and whirred.

After what seemed like an eternity, the Wheel dragged to a stop.

Gold lights spiraled within the crystal, followed by a thick, black fog.

Within a blink, Lord Falk stood draped in riches that appeared out of nowhere. An outfit made for a prince, all silk that shimmered in silver and gold. Black velvet shoes. A crown of emeralds and sapphires. A thin gold chain dangled from his neck. He looked down and studied his outfit, a huge grin spreading across his face.

"It works," he said. "The Wheel of Fortune is really mine. I can have anything I'd like. *More* riches. Power. Unbridled magic."

Mirabelle wiped a tear from her eye. "Fortune is not to be used this way."

"But it is. I can be anything, have anything, do anything I wish now. Control nature. Alter reality. The Wheel favors me."

He seized the spokes again, but this time, they didn't budge. Falk applied pressure, leaning back on his heels and pulling the Wheel in his direction. "Come here, woman. Make it move again."

Mirabelle dragged her feet, approaching the crystal to study the image inside. "Your last request is still being fulfilled," she said. "That's why it won't move."

Lord Falk wrinkled his brow. "Come again? There's more?"

Mirabelle sniffled and cleared her throat. "A wish of that magnitude takes time to fulfill. You wouldn't expect a rose to bloom so quickly? Or a match to consume a forest?"

"I am no matchstick, you fool. I'm the blaze," Falk said. "Make the Wheel hurry. I want to ask it to destroy the Rosas family."

I grabbed Charlie's hand. "Maybe it'll be quick."

"Don't worry. He'll never get the chance." Pietro hovered into the air and rocketed toward Falk, fingers outstretched in front of him.

Ryvendor spun on his heel, raised his staff, and swatted Pietro aside. "Go down!"

The Flying Man landed on his back, arms sprawled at his sides and all the wind knocked out of his lungs. Just a few feet away, Neoma stood over Io, teeth bared and eyes wide with fury.

Mirabelle pounded on Falk's chest. "I won't let you hurt these people. Their hearts are pure. And I don't control the Wheel anymore. I cannot tell it what to do."

She paused and took a breath. "And if I did control the Wheel, I would've designed a thousand possible fates for you . . . to roam the mountains of Kesterfall as a ghost, feeling and speaking only when the next snow falls. Or perhaps you would be better off in Jericho Harbor, thirsting for the moon but never able to drink from it, chained to its light. Perhaps you shall be a plankton in the belly of a kraken, forever doomed to dwell in the dark depths of the ocean. All these fates and more might have been yours, but none of those fates shall come to pass." Mirabelle dropped to her knees and buried her head in her hands. "You got exactly what you asked for."

I looked at Charlie. All those things Mirabelle described would've been true karma, too. Falk would've finally known everything he put us through. So then what would it be? Was he really going to have something better? A "get out of jail free" card? A lifetime supply of chocolate? Would he really just get to walk away happy and free because the Wheel of Fortune ordained it?

Mirabelle lifted her head, the orb inside the Wheel throbbing with black smoke. "With your victory in mind, know this."

Falk scowled. "Aren't you done talking?"

"No," Mirabelle said. "Because I need to tell you where your mountain of gold is. In fact, if you please, I believe Verdoro can take you."

The overlord stroked his chin. "Verdoro belongs to me again, doesn't he?"

Charlie bristled next to me. "He never did, Buzzard Face."

"Silence, boy!" Falk took Mirabelle's chin in his hands and spoke with the icy tone of a snake. "Continue."

Mirabelle gestured to the crystal in the center of the Wheel. "The Wheel of Fortune has determined that you will find your mountain of gold on Stelmorir. You will go there tonight, and there, you will cling to the beach as a cluster of thorns." She smiled. "I see now after all these years: Wheel or no Wheel, balance will always be protected."

Falk stiffened, dread painting his face a pale shade of white. "You wouldn't tell me a lie."

"Of course not." Mirabelle smiled sweetly. "And neither would the Wheel. Would you like a ride to your destination?"

Lord Falk grasped the Wheel by one of its spokes again. "I shall undo my last wish and make a proper one." He gave the Wheel a tug, but it stood firmly in place. He yanked on it a few times, sweat beading on his forehead. "Move, you stupid thing. Make it move!"

"I already told you I can't."

"I know you've done something. And I promise you I will not be going to Stelmorir." He pointed Enzo's dagger at Mirabelle. "Make. It. Move."

I stood and rushed in front of Mirabelle, arms at my sides. Charlie dashed in front of me, doing the same, and then Uncle Diego shielded Charlie. Falk and our uncle stood eye to eye, the tension in the room thick enough to chew on.

"*Move*," Falk said coldly.

Mirabelle gently moved me aside. "It's okay, dear." She parted Charlie and Uncle Diego then marched right up to Falk. "You don't want your dragon ride to Stelmorir?"

"I have no intention of going to Stelmorir. I know you've done something, woman. You've been a thorn in my side for far too long. Well, this ends tonight, Mirabelle. You and these wretched Rosas kids can all say good night!" Falk raised the dagger, prepared to strike . . .

A crack of lightning flashed from the center of the Wheel, illuminating the floor at Falk's feet.

And he dropped through the cloud with Ryvendor and Clova, a clap of thunder drowning out their screams.

When the thunder died down, the world around us was silent.

Falk. Gone. Vanished.

Could it really be over?

Mirabelle sighed. "I did not know this would happen today, but as I told you, the Wheel is temperamental. It only takes the slightest tap to set one's fate off course. I did not determine Falk's fate. He wove his own. The Wheel simply acted as interpreter. The sum of all his actions was a lifetime on Stelmorir. There is a balance to be maintained after all. Fortune is designed to rise and fall like the tides, and we are designed to sail those tides as bravely as possible. We will never control the winds. Only the sails."

With that, she grasped two of the Wheel's spokes, applied her foot to its base, and tugged. The Wheel popped off its hub with hardly a sound, and Lady Fortune crushed the Wheel over her knee, cracking it into several pieces. Splinters trickled at her feet until all she held were two individual spokes.

Charlie and I exchanged a look, wrapped in everything we were feeling. Awe. Horror. Disbelief. After all the time people had spent hunting for her Wheel, Lady Fortune just destroyed it with her bare hands? She took a knee and plucked the seven stones out of their sockets, each falling into her palm and rattling like simple marbles.

"Umm," Charlie said.

Mirabelle rubbed her chin. "I do seem to be forgetting something. Hmm." She snapped her fingers. "Ah. That's right. Verdoro, would you come here please?"

Verdoro ambled into the tower, tilting his head like a curious dog. He looked at me and Charlie as if waiting for our permission.

I gave him an encouraging nod. "Go on, boy."

The dragon trotted to Mirabelle. She closed the gap between them and gave his belly a loving pat. "I've missed you, my friend." She tossed the seven stones carelessly into a pile on the ground—or the cloud—mixed with all the splinters from the Wheel. I still couldn't believe I was watching her put the whole thing in ruins. "Now, my dearest dragon, would you please show our friends your favorite trick? I trust they've seen it by now."

Trick? Charlie and I exchanged a glance.

"You might want to stand back," Mirabelle said. "Way back."

Verdoro sniffed the remains of the Wheel, reared back his head, and within seconds, a thick beam of fire poured from the dragon's mouth and showered the space in front of him.

We watched in disbelief as the Wheel of Fortune made its final transformation: a pile of ashes.

"Okay, I'll be the one to say it," Niraya said. "Ma'am, with all due respect and all, I don't understand why you just did that."

While she had only said what we were all thinking, I had an idea. My time with Groff and the genies made me realize something. "You don't need it anymore."

Mirabelle nodded. "I've been here for ages, and the Wheel did not turn. I did not distribute luck or misfortune in any way. And still, the universe guided you here to set me free. All of your trials set you down this path. You encountered both bad luck and good, and you navigated it all with admirable bravery. Falk is proof that this artifact has caused more pain than prosperity. It has corrupted the hearts of men, and needlessly so. With such greed in the world, it is far better that the Wheel ceases to exist. One way or another, the winds blow a little luck to people every day. The question is, do they feel it when it arrives? And when it changes direction, will they venture to ride the winds?"

If Mirabelle was right, then destroying the Wheel of Fortune was the best thing to do. We could do without it. I thought of the wish factory underground. Groff chose not to grant wishes because he wanted to give people the ability to grant their own. *Teach a girl to fish . . .*

"We went through a lot of bad stuff to get here," Charlie said.

"That is to be acknowledged," Mirabelle said. "And commended. There are many ways in which the universe has not been kind to you. There were circumstances you couldn't control, but your virtue overpowered them all to get to me. Can you think of some ways that Fortune favored you anyway?"

"We're together," I said. "No matter what, the Rosas will always be familia. Even when Uncle Diego went missing, I knew in my heart that he was still out there."

"When you decided we had to split up," Charlie said to me, "I knew we were still family."

"And we're stronger for it, too." Uncle Diego spread his arms and welcomed us in. I recognized those famous hugs.

This was the Diego Rosas I knew.

CHARLIE

❖

We took three dragons back to Florindale: Snowmunch, a cloud dragon, and Verdoro. Falk may not have wanted his free dragon ride, but Karina and I welcomed ours with open arms. What kind of *loco* denies a ride on Verdoro's back?

Mirabelle offered to fly us over Stelmorir on the way back, but Karina and I turned her down. We figured it was smarter not to tempt fate.

"What do you think will happen to him there?" I asked. "Falk, I mean?"

"I heard most people don't survive Stelmorir," Karina said.

Mirabelle smiled. "You've heard correctly. *Most* people don't. Some do."

I thought for a minute. "Are you saying that because you think Falk will?"

"No. I mean we're currently in the presence of someone who has."

"Did you?" Karina asked.

Gavin turned around and aimed a finger at Uncle Diego. "No. He did."

"What?!" Karina and I said in unison.

"Tio," I said. "What is he talking about? That's not possible."

"But it is," Mirabelle said. "One of the seven pieces of the Wheel of Fortune was buried on Stelmorir. I suspect Falk knew this, but he was not brave enough to seek it on his own. But your uncle has a certain reputation for braving the elements. Now I see why."

Tio smirked. "Minor details."

The sun was shining when we arrived in Florindale. Thankfully, we were allowed a smooth landing this time, free of burning javelins or evil overlords.

While we took our time to rest and clean up, news spread through Florindale Square like wildfire. Despite Enzo's and Rosana's efforts to slip in quietly and peacefully, the townspeople were overjoyed to learn that the king and queen had returned home. In fact, they prepared a feast to celebrate the victories: that Enzo and Rosana were safe, that my family had been found, and that Lord Falk had been sent to a much stronger prison than the last one he was in.

They also whispered tales that the king had temporarily gone mad, that Lady Fortune had abandoned her post, that Florindale Prison was in ruins, and that there were werewolves in their midst.

We discussed it all at Enzo's palace during dinner, and man, I would've hated being a king. Enzo's world was safe from Lord Falk, and yet there was still some damage control to do. How exhausting.

"Ahh," Enzo said. "It's so nice to deal with non-magical, non-world-threatening problems like gossip and a restless town."

I wrinkled my nose. "Really? Why?"

"Because that means things are finally calming down," Rosana said. "And that there are non-magical good things happening as well. Kids are playing outside again. People are becoming interested in dragon rights again. And I can sit down and have a hot meal with my loved ones again."

As strange as it was to admit, Rosana's words made me sad. The thought of things "calming down" was wonderful, but it also meant we'd have to say goodbye.

Goodbyes weren't all terrible, though. The only proof we needed was that when Enzo hosted us all for dinner, he surprised us with a reunion with beautiful wolves that protected us once. Nella and Oliver. They were alive, and they remembered us. As I played with them and gave them some puppy love, I understood something. When hearts were bonded—human, beast, or magical—goodbyes were never final.

"What will you all do now?" Karina asked.

Mirabelle and Gavin held hands. "I suppose we make our own fortune now. We see the world."

Niraya smirked. "I sail on and try to stay off the wanted posters."

"With your luck?" James asked.

Pietro rubbed his chin. "I kinda want a dragon of my own now. Flying myself everywhere gets exhausting."

Zid nudged Io in the arm. "I need to show these guys proper dragon riding techniques."

"And I need to thank you," Io said. "You gave my people the chance to start anew. I can see the world again. I'll do it in honor of my brother and sister, and of you all, the best adventurers I know."

Neoma stood up. "I guess we should raise our goblets to the Rosas family."

Niraya raised her goblet. "To our little . . . *familia*."

I swallowed a lump in my throat. *Familia*. It wasn't just about blood; it was about bonds. Friendship. Love. And all that mushy goo. These people had all become a part of *my* familia. We were a circle now. A wheel, with all its spokes and parts centered around one hub. And nobody could ever destroy that.

My last word was to Verdoro, and yes, I cried a little. Zid always said dragons can understand us. Verdoro didn't just understand me—he really knew me. I recognized this in my heart as he lowered his head and let me wrap both arms around his neck, his warmth radiating all the way into my bones.

I closed my eyes and rested my head on the dragon's neck for a while. "I know Mirabelle and Gavin will take good care of you now. But this isn't goodbye. You know that, right? I'll see you again?"

Verdoro's head went up and down, a low moan sounding from his throat.

There was a quote I heard Niraya say once: something about how huge the ocean was, and yet sometimes, two ships meet.

We had to go back to our own oceans now, but as long as there were rain clouds and stars to wish on, I could look up. The sky was my interstellar ocean now. Any shooting star could be my dragon—my flying death lizard—not there to bring me wishes, but to remind me that the Rosas are strong and we've been making our dreams come true all along.

KARINA

LA FAMILIA ROSAS

⸱◆━━━◆⸱

The door swung open before I could touch the knob. The scent of smoked meat poured from my home, quickly overpowered by the smell of fresh laundry. Before I could process it, my stepfather, Jorge, had wrapped me and Charlie both in a tight, powerful hug. "*Hola, mis queridos.*"

"Jorge!" I mumbled into his t-shirt, barely able to move my jaws in his embrace. "Hi. Can you let go? I want to put my stuff down."

My stepdad loosened his grip then held my shoulder at arm's length. "Welcome home, you two." Jorge moved on to Tio and met him in a bro-hug. "*Que onda, Diego?* Come make yourself a plate. We've got crickets *con queso* and grilled worms and tortillas and all your favorites you missed in Switzerland."

Thankfully, Jorge actually meant *carne asada*.

"It's good to see you again, Jorge." Uncle Diego followed up the hug with a long, complicated high five. It ended in a rocket ship where his thumb was the head and Jorge's writhing fingers were supposed to be the body and the fire. When the rocket went over their heads, it exploded with no shortage of sound effects. I rolled my eyes.

I set my suitcase on the ground and took in the familiarity of home. The photos on the entertainment center, which followed me and Charlie through the grade levels as far back as kindergarten. The magazines on the coffee table, crisp and unread in a neat pile under the remote. The smell of warm apple empanadas that led me right into the arms of my mom.

She hugged me and rocked me from side to side, followed by Charlie. "You're home."

Charlie closed his eyes, resting his head on our mom's shoulder. "We're home," he repeated.

Mom kissed each of us on the cheek. "You've grown like two feet taller since you left," she said. "What did you even eat out there? Oats? Tell me everything."

Charlie and I exchanged glances. "It was good."

"Mhm. All that time away and it was good." Mom raised a brow. "Where's your uncle?"

I grinned. "He's in the living room with Jorge."

A smirk crept across her face, and she grabbed a wooden spoon coated in steaming apple empanada filling. "Oh, he's not gonna hide from me that easily. Diego Jose!"

Uncle Diego peeked around the corner. "Ha, uh, hey there, Lexi! Long time no see."

Mom crooked a finger at him. "C'mere."

Uncle Diego took one step forward, still far from arm's length. "Hi."

Mom beckoned him closer with the spoon. "Closer. I wanna show you something."

I would never get over Uncle Diego's approach to survival, the way he prioritized danger.

Terrifying dragon capable of breathing fire? Approach with caution and offer it cookies.

Five foot seven Alexia Rosas, our mother and the woman who once used to make Uncle Diego play Barbies with her? Do not engage.

Uncle Diego made a face at me that looked like, *Oh brother, here it comes.*

"You can't avoid her, Tio," Charlie said.

"No, you can't." Mom raised her spoon before tossing it on the counter. "I missed you." She hugged him, a big sisterly smile on her face. I recognized that smile on my *own* face.

Uncle Diego's eyes were wide. "Oh." He winked at me and pretended to mop sweat off his forehead. *Whew.* "Well, this is nice. I missed you too, Lexi."

Charlie and I exchanged a smile. Mom wasn't going to beat up her brother after all. The trick was that we all had to be cool and steer her away from specific questions. We rehearsed a lot of the predictable ones and planned our answers on the plane ride home. Only one nosy kid raised a brow.

"So," Mom said, "what did you bring me from Switzerland?"

I looked at my feet, racking my brain for something I could give her from the limited collection I brought home. Maybe a dragon egg from Zid, which he swore would never hatch? Still, I broke a major sweat bringing it through customs, and it didn't exactly say, *We thought of you in Switzerland.*

Uncle Diego pulled two keychains out of his pocket, each adorned with a red-and-white plus sign. *Whew.* I had forgotten he grabbed those at the Swiss airport. Mom and Jorge accepted them with hugs and smiles.

"You know I was joking, right?" Mom said. "You didn't have to bring me anything."

"I know it's not much," Uncle Diego said. "But I do have something a little better in mind. Some important news. A decision I made in Switzerland."

Charlie and I exchanged hasty glances. News? Now Uncle Diego was way off script.

Uncle Diego cleared his throat. "I am not renewing my contract with the network. After this season, I'm officially done with *Off the Beaten Path*, and I'm moving back to Tucson. Full time."

His words set off fireworks in the room—big, bright, and loud.

Charlie pumped a fist in the air. "Yes!"

Mom clapped her hands and threw her arms around Uncle Diego. "Oh, I always knew this day would come," she said. "I'm so proud of you and your show, but the kids are crazy about you. You have family here."

Jorge put Uncle Diego in a headlock and gave him a noogie. "Welcome home, bro."

"Are you serious?" I dried my tears and went in for a hug. "Not that I'm not happy for you, but you love what you do. Why would you stop?"

"*Because* I love what I do," Uncle Diego said. "I love traveling with you two. Traveling on our terms. Traveling for me and not for an audience. I want to go looking for the hidden gems of the world—the *real* places off the beaten path. Not the crowded monuments and tourist attractions, the half-staged survival encounters. And I think I want to write some books about them."

"Books?" Charlie asked. "What kind of books?"

"Oh, I have all kinds of ideas." Uncle Diego's voice rose with excitement. "What about a guide to survival in the fairy-tale wild? How to approach a dragon, why you shouldn't try to give it an Oreo, what to do if a sea monster swallows you whole, how to deal with pirates, all that stuff."

I laughed. "Uncle D, you're known for writing about bears and quicksand and poisonous plant life. What will people say if all of a sudden you start writing about werewolves and ogres? You know nobody's gonna take it seriously, right?"

Sure enough, Mom raised an eyebrow. "Dragons and pirates?"

Uncle Diego winked. "And sea monsters. They'll call it a fun, fictional tale. We'll call it a memoir. A survival guide. In fact, you could help me write it. We can come up with a nom de plume and call it like *Roses in the Dragon's Den* or something."

"*Roses in the Dragon's Den?*" I raised a brow, although truthfully, my heart was skipping. Uncle D was gonna let me write an actual book with him? This is what I always wanted. I never told him I'd already started one in Switzerland. "Why *Roses in the Dragon's Den* exactly?"

"Ah, I get it. Rosas. Roses," Charlie said. "God, that's so dorky, Tio."

Uncle Diego reddened. "It was just an idea. But I'm serious, you two. When I do get out and travel again, I thought maybe once in a while you'd come with me. I might need you two out there."

"What do you mean?" I asked.

"Well, you're the experts. I need someone to help keep me alive out there. Save me from the dragons, brave the elements, all that stuff."

I gave Uncle Diego a look like, *Are we really gonna talk about this stuff in front of other people like this? In front of Mom?*

But Mom just looked lost, raising a brow at Jorge. "Are they speaking in code?"

And Jorge laughed. "It's a tio thing. You wouldn't understand."

Oh Jorge, you poor man, I thought. But then I wondered: What if Jorge *did* understand?

Charlie gave Uncle Diego a playful slug on the arm. "Good for you, Tio. You do need us. You're obviously hopeless without us."

Deep down, I would always be the six-year-old who was convinced that Diego Rosas was Superman, because in the best bedtime stories, sometimes the heroes needed saving, too. Lucky for Uncle Diego, and for us, our family would cross oceans to stay together, and I don't just mean our ancestors from Spain. We'd fend off werewolves, journey to the center of the earth, and fly to the clouds for each other. The proof was written in our bones.

"You'll always be my heroes, you two," Uncle Diego said.

Mom leaned against the kitchen counter, arms crossed and a look of love on her face.

I rubbed my eyes. Suddenly they were feeling a little watery. "Well"—I punched Uncle Diego's shoulder—"you've always been mine."

Charlie was always too cool to be sappy, but within a second, he went from playful punches to gracious hugs, and I couldn't help but join in. Uncle Diego was probably in shock, because he didn't say anything for a few seconds. Instead, he sniffled and pulled us both in. I committed the moment to memory.

"So what did you have in mind?" Charlie asked. "Where are we going next summer?"

"Next summer?" Uncle Diego shook his head. "I have some ideas, but I don't know about next summer, *locos*. That's way too late."

Charlie raised a brow. "Too late? We have school, dude. You can't just pull us out whenever you want."

"Since when do you like school?" I asked.

"C'mon, I wanna learn. Duh."

Uncle Diego chuckled. "You're right. You need to fill your heads. I was thinking more like winter break. We'll go see the Archive of Mysterious Beasts, or just close our eyes, spin a globe, and go wherever our finger lands.

We'll really venture off the beaten path, just the three of us. Lexi, Jorge, you're more than welcome to come, too . . . if you can keep up with us."

"Oh, that's how it is now?" Jorge cracked his knuckles.

"That's exactly how it is."

Mom rolled her eyes. "As a Rosas, you're supposed to know: We may all look pretty—"

"But we'll still prick you," I finished.

"Yeah, true." Uncle Diego dipped a finger in the empanada filling and then crammed it in his mouth. He closed his eyes. "Mmm. Tastes like adventure."

I thought of Enzo's wishing well and the quarter I threw in. Later I learned that Charlie and I had been thinking the same thing: *Whatever adventures I have in life, I wish to share them with family.*

And here we were. Some wishes did come true.

How did we ever get so lucky?

THE END

EPILOGUE

STELMORIR

Legend whispers that I am a fallen star, but I have no memory of my origin. Dead or alive, I feel things, and I have wants and needs. When the sun passes overhead, the light never greets my sands—my skin. I do not want the light. Hermit crabs burrow in shells of shadow. The dark waters surround me, throbbing with movement, and I feel every tread of my doomed visitors. Sunlight would be too much for my senses.

My latest guests don't understand that I can taste every word spoken in my presence.

Tonight the words are bitter.

"This is all the master's fault! We never should have trusted him."

"You absolute potato of an elf! This is your fault, and in case you haven't noticed, we live. How about we start to plan our escape? The Rosas twerp did it, and we have magic on our side. Magic will always protect us."

Potato. Magic. *Escape?* I think not.

My vines slither out of the jungles, starved for bones.

I only protect those who respect me. They need not fear me.

My sands still taste the final words of the last man they consumed:

I will always find you, Diego Rosas.

Long after the words fade away, a phoenix sings, simply existing in the protection of my shadows. And at the heart of my existence, three red rosebuds sprout, grasping for living, beautiful starlight.

Perhaps they'll even drink in the moon, and they'll bloom like fire.

Perhaps they'll reach far beyond and ignite the worlds in all their warmth and beauty.

Perhaps they'll soar.

For here, there be dragons.

ACKNOWLEDGMENTS

I completed the first draft of this book in late 2019, and the world changed in about forty different ways between then and now. It occurs to me that there were several times when I didn't think this book would see the light of day, and now that I sit down to write the acknowledgments, it's like exhaling. This was "the little sequel that could"—one that people asked me about often—and I hope it brings people just a little bit more joy as we heal from COVID-19.

Krystal: Thank you for five years, five brilliant projects, and an unknowable quantity of tough love comments as my editor! This may be our last book together, but you have filled my creative well and given me so much to carry forward as I continue writing. I will always credit you as one of the first to believe in me, a great friend, and a creative partner.

Silvia, Janelle, Maira, and Katie, my beta team! You each saw this in a different phase in its journey, and every single one of you provided such important feedback to make it better over two years! Thank you all for your eagle eyes and your candor and your shouty caps and for caring enough to help me fill the cracks.

I changed day jobs since Roses was published, and I was terrified that I'd lose my balance. But my work familia didn't just tolerate me and my "5 to 9 life." They embraced me with open hearts and made me feel like this matters. That is you, Thrive Crew: Michelle, Alex, Karla, Patrick, and too many folx to name. You know who you are, and I am forever your fan.

I've had a few young readers reach out to me in the past year to tell me their favorite parts of ROSES, ask about the sequel and suggest some things they wanted to see, and I hope you all know how much you influenced the outcome! That includes you, Khi and Madison! Thank you!

Karina and Camila: One day you're both going to be old enough to read this and you'll probably want to know more. When that happens, come find me. I hope you like Oreos.

To the rest of my familia: Thank you for believing and for always keeping my wishes safe. Mom, Grandma, Fred, Carmen, John, Adriana, and Patricia. Much love to you all!

Thank you Melissa Stevens and Amalia Chitulescu for another BEAUTIFUL collaboration. I make the words happen, and you package them up. You are the real life genies in publishing!

And last but never least: another thanks to you for joining me on another journey. Make a wish. There will always be more stories in Florindale and I don't think I'll ever quite leave it for good. But I did discover some new worlds in quarantine… care to go exploring with me?

ABOUT THE AUTHOR

Jacob Devlin grew up in southern Arizona, where he loves to write, draw, and fall in love with stories. His 2019 novel, ROSES IN THE DRAGON'S DEN, won three recognitions, including the Silver Medal for the Children's Fantasy category in the Reader's Favorite Awards. He loves fantasy stories that center the ideas of family, adventure, and inner strength, and his greatest joy is to create characters, words, and worlds for people to escape to!

You can learn more about him by visiting www.authorjakedevlin.com.

OTHER BOOKS

THE CARVER
THE UNSEEN
THE HUMMINGBIRD
ROSES IN THE DRAGON'S DEN
BRAMBLES IN THE WISHING WELL
A THOUSAND DREADFUL CURSES (coming
Fall 2021)

www.ingramcontent.com/pod-product-compliance
Lightning Source LLC
Chambersburg PA
CBHW021242190726
48289CB00005B/1452